WHAT PEOPLE ARE SAYING

WITHOUT

"I love this story & the writing lyrical, romantic & spiritual. The reader is taken on a journey that is savored long after the book is put down. You can't help but continue to think about the truths & possibilities explored."
Elise Ballard, author of *Epiphany: True Stories of Sudden Insight to Inspire, Encourage and Transform*

"Danielle Boonstra is a raconteur for love and miracles. She shares her truth through her stories and empowers others to do the same."
Gabrielle Bernstein, author of *Spirit Junkie*

"The late 18th century springs to life in this heartfelt novel about healing past hurts through a present willingness to open to higher truth and enduring love. Danielle Boonstra creates passionate, memorable characters, seamlessly weaving contemporary and historical for a deftly rendered, compelling, and inspiring read!"
Susan Dugan, author of the essay collection *Extraordinary Ordinary Forgiveness* and the linked short story collection *Safe Haven*.

Without Fear of Falling

A Novel

Without Fear of Falling

A Novel

Danielle Boonstra

Winchester, UK
Washington, USA

First published by Soul Rocks Books, 2013
Soul Rocks Books is an imprint of John Hunt Publishing Ltd., Laurel House, Station Approach,
Alresford, Hants, SO24 9JH, UK
office1@jhpbooks.net
www.johnhuntpublishing.com
www.soulrocks-books.com

For distributor details and how to order please visit the 'Ordering' section on our website.

Text copyright: Danielle Boonstra 2012

ISBN: 978 1 78099 788 9

A CIP catalogue record for this book is available from the British Library.

Design: Stuart Davies

Printed and bound by CPI Group (UK) Ltd, Croydon, CR0 4YY

We operate a distinctive and ethical publishing philosophy in all
areas of our business, from our global network of authors to
production and worldwide distribution.

To my grandfather, J.W.L. Scruton.
This all began with you.

Acknowledgements

This is my very first novel and so there are a great many people to thank. First I want to thank my friend Meredith for mentioning NaNoWriMo (National Novel Writing Month) to me and to the NaNoWriMo team for doing your thing. This is where "Without Fear of Falling" was born.

Thanks to my hugely talented editor, Amanda Berlin. You saw so much potential in that messy first draft. I cannot thank you enough for your guidance, expertise and love.

Thanks to Susan Dugan for your incredible generosity and direction. I admire your writing and your approach to life. You are a wonderful teacher.

Thanks to Ola, our Tuesday Night ACIM facilitator. I love you for all that you do.

Thanks to EVERYONE at John Hunt Publishing, especially Alice Grist, for your kindness and willingness to help make my dream come true.

Thanks to all the people of the Bruce who I've met over the years, especially Kim, Karen and Rowan.

Thanks to my unbelievably loving friends. Cindy, you were this book's first big fan and your love for it and for me kept me going. Macha and Laurie, your endless love, wisdom and support mean the world to me. Corinne, thank God for you. Christy, your love sustains me indescribably. Gabby, I thank you for being you and for creating Her Future. Elise, who was such a supporter of this book and had so many ideas on how to improve it, and she was right. Tanya & Amy, my former roommates who supported my writing from the very beginning and who support all I do. Alex, for all your love and enthusiasm. Tina, my friend forever... Thank you. Kimmy, who read this book in a day and demanded more sex scenes. And to Livy, there are no words. I love you all from a place I can't even name.

Thanks to my family. My parents, for everything... again there are no words. My brother, I know I can always count on you. My mother-in-law, who adored this book and told all her friends they had to wait to buy their own copies and to my father-in-law, I love you both. My sister-in-law Melissa, who was a fan right from the beginning... you may know a published writer now, but I've always known an incredibly loyal and loving person in you. My sister-in-law, Laura who gave me wonderful feedback and who I just love for always being herself. To my Aunts Sharon and Linda, I feel your love and support all the way here in Ontario. To my grandparents, all four of you, for your love, attention and laughter in childhood and beyond.

To my children, Noelle and Ivan, you are my greatest teachers. I love everything about you both.

And to Michael, my partner and best friend. I love you, always.

"There are no accidents in salvation. Those who are to meet will meet, because together they have the potential for a holy relationship. They are ready for each other."
A Course in Miracles (M7)

"Your heart and my heart are very, very old friends."
Hafiz

CHAPTER 1

There is a place in the world where the wind can cut you and lift you at the same time. I have lived there forever it seems. You feel harmed and inspired all at once…vulnerable and yet safe. It exists at the tip of a peninsula bordering two bodies of water that merge into the most serene and crystal blue. One side is harsh, the other calm. Love and fear collide here and yet only one can be true.

I like love.

Tobermory is a Canadian town, small and thin, that beckons divers of the deep and roamers worldwide. And yet those who live here year-round are few. It takes a strong soul to suffer the silence of the North. Silence beats of truth. It conveys all the things we'd rather not hear. And that is why we like the noise.

Tobermory bears the bruises of its history. Shipwrecks are easily spied and tales are readily told to anyone willing to listen. Its people bear bruises too. Those of us, whose families have lived here for generations, have seen many harsh winters and an equal number of hard times. Those who are newcomers are here for escape, for peace. Peace is expected among the quiet, but rarely found.

I like it best here in November when the shops close down, and it's too soon for ice fishing. I like the uncompromising chill in the air. During this time my town bears little resemblance to the sunny, tourist-ridden destination of summertime. There is an empty trill, as if the symphonies of voices that collect here in the warmer months have faded, albeit reluctantly, into the background…haunting us. We walk among it, barely aware, going headlong into the long, dark cold ahead. We exist there.

I have lived in Tobermory my entire life. My name is Suellen Scarlett Stewart, but everyone calls me "Ellie". My mother was seventeen when she gave birth to me and at the time she had been more than a little obsessed with the movie Gone with the

Wind. I once asked her why she had named me after the whiny, bitchy sister and not the beautiful heroine. Her response: "Don't kid yourself, Ellie. Scarlett was a real bitch too." Neither of us have ever been south of Owen Sound. I've never left the Peninsula. While Frances had always lamented her sheltered life, I've always kind of brushed it off. In my mind I've been every-where.

I have struggled with a few things in my twenty-two years, but the quiet was always there, waiting in the backstage of my mind with a serene smile and peaceful brow. I have had visions since I was small. These visions have comforted me and overwhelmed me depending on what I see. I've seen flashes of columns with crowds of people, a horse-drawn sleigh scaling a snow-covered hill; a dense jungle filled with men armed with spears...the list goes on. I see them bright and quick and then it's gone.

When I was a child, I would tell my mom in excited detail what I saw and thankfully, she always believed me. The first vision I remember describing to my mom took place at a river bank with reeds that towered over me, thick as bone and just as strong. I saw myself as a teenager, sending a doll on a raft down the river.

"What did the doll look like, Ellie?" she asked patiently.

"It almost looked like a real baby, but it didn't move so it must've been a doll. I'm crying though. I don't want to send my doll away," I told her, recalling the sadness of that moment as if it were happening again right then.

Frances' amusement shifted into anxious concern right before my eyes. The next day she broke down and took me to see Mrs. Dawes, a local psychic who also happens to be the owner of the health food store, The Natural Touch. I was eight years old.

The residents of Tobermory call Mrs. Dawes many things: gypsy, psychic, fortune teller, but she accepts none of these. She claims that everyone can "see" and that she has merely done more "seeing" than most. She would work at the store during the day, and in the evenings she would take people into the back room and offer her insight, healing hands or just a friendly ear.

I remember the day we went to the health food store and instead of buying bulgur or kale or carob chip cookies, we continued on to the rear of the shop. I resisted the urge to grab a licorice as we walked past the bulk bins. To me, The Natural Touch would always smell like patchouli, honey and wheatgrass, but that day it was different. There was something lighter and yet heavier in the air. The atmosphere felt dense with possibility, as if I was walking into something that had already been carefully laid out for me. I felt protected, though I had no notion of what I needed protection from.

It seemed more like a visit to a doctor than anything. I was eight; I had no context, no comparison.

Mrs. Dawes was kind and she smiled wide. Her eyes were calm, expectant. She never showed any sign of surprise or even boredom, just pure patience. When my mother told Mrs. Dawes about the visions, she simply nodded her head and smiled. She was slightly shorter than my mother and rounder too. Her curves were comforting, almost as much as her soothing voice and the way she called me "Love". With Mrs. Dawes there was something to cling to. She would never let you drop.

Turning to me she crouched down a bit so as not to look down on me. And with her big blue eyes bright against her long, fuzzy red hair she stared straight into me. "Are you finding it frightening, dear?"

"No not really. It's not too bad. Sometimes I see people crying and stuff, but I don't know why. That's when I turn it off," I answered shyly.

"Oh? You can turn it off, can you? Interesting," she remarked quietly. Her bangle bracelets jingled as she brought her index finger to her mouth in contemplation. I was a puzzle and yet it seemed that, in mere moments, she figured me out and has understood me ever since.

"What's interesting? What? What is it?!" asked my mother in agitation, her wavy blond hair flitting about her heart-shaped face.

"Calm down, Frances. You'll scare the girl. I can't say for sure, but it seems as though your daughter is having visions and if I were to venture a guess, I would say they are visions of past lives." Mrs. Dawes' voice was gentle. I remember my mom just staring at me for a moment, her mouth open with a look on her face halfway between impressed and horrified and all I could think was, 'What the heck are past lives?'

"Past lives? I just thought they were like daydreams or something. How can we be sure?" she asked.

"I would say it's not really a matter of being sure, Frances. These visions are coming up for Ellie for a reason. Something needs to be healed. She is meant to learn something from this and she is also meant to teach."

My mother considered that for a moment. Biting her lip and glancing at me she asked, "Who is she meant to teach?"

"That will just have to be shown to her now won't it?" said Mrs. Dawes giving me a wink. "In the meantime, I'm giving you a flower remedy to administer any time she feels anxious. It's perfectly safe."

Frances seemed relieved, if only a little. She combed my hair with her fingers as if reaffirming I was her child, thanked Mrs. Dawes without looking her in the eye and asked if there was anything else she should be doing.

"Just pay attention. And Ellie, there's nothing to worry about. What happened back then cannot harm you now. Now is when the healing is done. Now is where the miracle happens."

She patted my blonde head and swept a freckled hand across my cheek. I appreciated her kindness, but I still don't understand what's going on. Did these visions make me special or weird somehow?

"Am I weird?" I mumbled.

"What's that, love?"

"She asked if she was weird," Frances clarified.

Mrs. Dawes threw her head back with a laugh as if to communicate that she should have told me this sooner. "No, Ellie, not at all! We all receive different gifts in different lifetimes. This is just one of yours. It makes you no better or weirder than anyone else. It is merely a tool, something to help you through life, and if you choose, to help others. Do you understand?"

I nodded and in that moment, decided to trust her.

"You know, my dear, I could use some assistance around here. How would you like to help me out on Fridays after school? You could sweep the floors and help me unpack my deliveries, if it's okay with your mother of course."

I looked up at my mom with hopeful eyes. She smiled at me and told me I could as long as I went there straight off the bus and then came right home when I was done. Hugging her hips, I thanked her. The thought of a grown-up lady like Mrs. Dawes needing me made me feel so good. Mrs. Dawes helped me believe I was normal. I felt safe with her, at home somehow. I remember thinking to myself: Why couldn't she be my mother?

As we left the store my mother said to me, "You're going to have to be patient with me, baby girl. I don't know what the hell I'm doing at the best of times, never mind this stuff. You just...you're just growing so fast. I feel like I'm losing you again."

"Again?" I asked.

"Hm?"

I looked up at her. "You said 'again', mommy. You said you feel like you're losing me again."

She screwed up her nose at this and dismissed my comment with a wave of her hand, "I didn't mean that. I don't know why I said that."

A flash of an older woman, my mother's mother, swept

through my mind's eye. "You look like grandma when you do that."

Frances looked at me with mock severity. "For the love of God, Ellie, please don't ever say that again."

I don't remember my grandparents too much because they moved to Florida before my second birthday. My Uncle Hamish went to university and medical school in Toronto and did his residency in Sarasota. It eventually set in that he was unlikely to move back so Frances' parents up and moved to be close to him. When my mother asked why, my grandmother replied "He's a doctor, Frances. He can take care of us. Besides, what's for us here in Tobermory but wind and winter?"

My mother said she wanted to offer herself and I as reasons to stay, but didn't. After all, anyone could have a baby. Becoming a doctor took brains and talent. Hamish held more promise than Frances ever could.

John and Judy Stewart became images to me...people who would send and request pictures of me through the years. I would listen to their thick Scottish accents on monthly phone calls and feign interest in people who never saw fit to visit me or my mother. I never really felt their absence, but Frances did and for that, I felt badly.

My grandmother's sister, Deborah, left the Bruce a few years after. She moved to Sauble Beach with her boyfriend and never looked back. Frances wasted no time in buying Deborah's home, gladly leaving her parents' bat-infested farmhouse behind. My only memory of that place was the high-pitched squeals of the bats between the walls and floors and how it drove Frances insane.

Our new home was a lovely old house with a grey board and batten exterior and a garnet-coloured door. The stairs squeak, but light streams in effortlessly through every window throughout the day, as if the sun decided each should have its turn. It overlooks the bay, and one can watch the boats come and go.

I have always loved looking out across the lake to the lighthouse and have, since I was a little girl, imagined a kindly old man there, keeping watch, keeping us safe. He doesn't exist, mind you. There hasn't been a lighthouse keeper there since the 1950s, but I like the idea that someone kind watches over me all the same.

CHAPTER 2

After that first meeting, I helped her every Friday after school for six years. It was my time spent with Mrs. Dawes at her store that I attribute to my sanity. As long as I had Mrs. Dawes to speak with, I didn't need anyone else. In her I had a friend, sympathetic and unwilling to judge. The kids at school were like background noise, ever-present and begging to be ignored.

I showed up to work the very next Friday and the first words out of my mouth were the ones I had been holding all week long: "What the heck are past lives?"

"Oh Ellie!" she exclaimed with a laugh. "You do like to get right to the point don't you?!" It sounded to me like a question that didn't really need to be answered so I kept quiet, waited. "You, my dear, have not always been Suellen Stewart. You have been born and have died many times. You have been men and you have been women. Each time you come back, you are given what seems to be a different situation and yet it is always the same. You are always on a fruitless search for what is yours already. We all are and we all will be until we remember. In the meantime, we die and we get born, over and over again."

I remember blinking at her several times and then seeing her laugh at me good-naturedly. It was clear she was saying something important, and I remembered the gist of it I think, but I had no idea what it meant. I wondered if I ever would.

The visions kept coming in what seemed to be a random fashion. I was young, I was old. I was a handsome man, a haggard woman. The pictures shifted and changed; the settings and times never the same. One time when I was riding in the car with my mother, I looked over at her and saw a man in a turban praying silently. Instantly I knew this was my mother somehow, in some distant time and place. I kept it to myself though, not because I thought she'd be upset, but because I didn't like talking about it too much. I didn't like feeling different.

I would, however, confide in Mrs. Dawes about what I saw. Mostly she would just smile and say: "That's nice, dear." Or at times she would ask for more detail with pursed lips and a knitted brow.

Her questions helped me to softly work past the fear around my visions. Though they remained brief, over time I was able to interpret what I saw more easily. Instead of trying to figure them out, I let them wash over me and comprehension came effortlessly. I remember seeing a quick flash of a woman making bread in a stone fire oven. In an instant I knew the year was approximately 1600 and the woman was me. There was a little boy playing at my feet and I had a strong sense he was my mother, Frances.

Another time I saw myself in a tent sitting around a fire with a group of men. I was a young man and I saw myself passing a pipe to an elderly man. I knew that he was Mrs. Dawes. I told her about this memory and I could tell that she was intrigued.

"Was I dressed in feathers?" she asked immediately.

I squinted tightly, trying to recall. "Yes. You were. The feathers were all around your head, like the chief in Peter Pan. I thought you were really smart. I was wishing you were my father because you were so much wiser and kinder than he was."

She smiled and quietly replied, "I know, love."

I remember wondering how she knew, but then deciding not to ask. Somehow I figured that one day I would know what she meant.

During this time, my mother shopped at the health food store less and less. She would drive all the way into Owen Sound and stock up on all the grains, vitamins and incense she needed. Frances never had an unkind word to say about Mrs. Dawes, but I could feel that something wasn't quite right. Not having a father around, I revelled in having both my mother and my "boss" to look up to. I innately knew that Frances would never begrudge me that.

The more time I spent with Mrs. Dawes the more relaxed I

became about everything I saw. It wasn't long before I started having glimpses of the present and future.

Once when I was nine I remember dreaming soundly. I dreamt I lost my breath. My left arm went numb and the right clutched my chest. Gasping for air I tried to scream, but no sound escaped my lips. I remember feeling terrified and then suddenly calm. The last thing I saw was the cuckoo clock in front of me striking three, mocking me.

When I awoke the following morning, Mrs. Fisher, our next-door neighbour, was sobbing with my mother in our kitchen. Mr. Fisher had died during the night. He had gone downstairs for a glass of water at three in the morning and never made it back to bed.

For a few moments I was awash with guilt, as if I had killed him with my mind. I felt tears forming in my eyes and a sudden sense of panic. I was just about to run to Mrs. Fisher and confess what I had seen the night before when I heard a voice: *You know better than this Ellie. You saw it; you didn't do it.* I shook my head as if to force the voice flying out of my ears. I thought to myself that I had spent so much time with Mrs. Dawes that she now lived inside my head.

I took a deep breath, wiped my eyes with my sleeve and ran to feel the comforting embrace of my mother.

"It's ok, baby. I know it's sad, but mommy's here," she said in a whisper, tucking my hair behind my ear.

I would see Mrs. Dawes later that day and she would tell me everything was ok, but for now I only wanted my mother. I wanted her scent, her feel and her soft, reassuring voice. With my mother, words were not necessary. I could just cry. That was enough.

Mrs. Dawes was the one who introduced me to meditation. Even though my mom had been meditating for as long as I could remember, there was something cooler about Mrs. Dawes doing it. She taught me to sit up straight and to focus on my breath. It took me a lot of tries before I could do it with ease. I kept hearing distracting noises, or thoughts about what I had done at school would pop into my head. Mrs. Dawes told me to gently brush them aside and again focus on each inhale and exhale. At first I thought it was boring, but then I began to feel so calm and loved. It felt like arms were hugging me tight and mouths were whispering that I was ok. I had never felt so safe in my life. Mrs. Dawes said that is how we are meant to feel all the time. She would often say that the feeling of love and security is who we really are.

When I was twelve I had a vision as I was filling up the herb bins. I caught the smell of kelp and suddenly, I experienced a flash. I was floating above everything. Below me was a cloak strewn about the rocks. There was a great big dog pawing at it and then I heard a loud bang. At that, the vision was gone. It shook me for a moment and I had to take more than one deep breath to recover.

I had been caught off guard by a vision before, but this was different somehow. I was more a part of that scene than the others, as if I was closer to it in time or in being. I was able to communicate none of this, but the feeling was there all the same. That vision lingered, as though something about it could no longer be ignored.

Mrs. Dawes happened upon me and my confusion was written all over my face.

"What's the matter, Ellie?" she asked pulling up another milk crate to sit beside me.

At first I hesitated, but eventually explained to her what I saw. For a moment I thought I saw tears in her eyes, but they were never shed. She simply nodded, gave me a hug and reminded me to record it in my journal. I did as she instructed later that night and I often thought about that scene. It looked so much like Tobermory and yet I knew somehow that it wasn't.

CHAPTER 3

When I was fourteen, I gave up working at the store. I never told Mrs. Dawes that I was quitting. There was a silent understanding between us that once I started high school, I wouldn't come around anymore. After getting off the bus that first Friday, I walked past her store and stared straight ahead. I could feel her watching me walk by, could sense her silent resignation. She was letting me go. She understood.

I was almost angry with her for not asking me to come back and work for her. I wanted the opportunity to tell her that I no longer needed her. It bothered me that she would not give me the satisfaction. I hated that she "just knew".

Reaching high school in Tobermory was anti-climatic. I had to transfer to the school in Lion's Head, a town fifty kilometres south, starting in the fourth grade because there weren't enough students to continue locally. Lion's Head Public School wasn't even a proper high school since kids as young as four go there too. I suppose I didn't know any different, but TV and movies showed me that I was missing out somehow.

My teenage years were awkward to say the least. While most of my classmates drank beer and got high, I tried desperately to hide the visions and attempted to block them out. I was successful for the most part. The tender understanding I had felt with Mrs. Dawes suddenly became silly.

All these doubts I had about past lives and the relevance of what I was seeing began to surface. I started to think I was crazy. I even asked my mom to put me on medication so I wouldn't have to deal with it.

She refused.

It made me try to wish away my time in high school. Nothing seemed right. My mother began dating a local painter named Jack Bailey and all she wanted to do was paint. Who did she think she was? As if just anyone can paint. It was ridiculous. Jack was undeniably himself; flamboyant, honest, unapologetic and talented as hell. I had to hold back tears when I glimpsed a portrait he had done of a local fisherman, pensive and pained. The yellow rain hat, the lines in his face, the cigarette in his mouth: each brushstroke spoke of compassion, respect.

Jack mostly left me alone. Though he once quipped "If you had something intelligent to say, I imagine you would have said it by now. We'll talk once you've had your heart broken...once you're interesting." I had an inkling of what he meant, but I resented him nonetheless. He was taking my mother from me. I felt rejected and even though I was pushing her away, I didn't like to feel pushed back.

"What's so amazing about Jack anyway?" I asked her as we were putting groceries away.

"Amazing? I suppose there's nothing so amazing about him. I just like him...a lot. He challenges me."

"Whatever that means..." I said, rolling my eyes.

Frances grabbed the almond milk from the bag and bent down to put it in the fridge. "It means he helps me learn more about myself, about what I'm capable of. You'll have that one day, Ellie. Someday, someone will show you who you are and all that you're meant to give to the world."

She stopped to look up at me and gauge my reaction, but I wouldn't give her the satisfaction. I was too annoyed. Really, there was nothing she could have done to change my teenage attitude. It was unfair to her and I knew it, but I didn't care.

I turned on my heel and walked away muttering, "Whatever."

I was lonely. I resisted all the visions my mind attempted to show me. As soon as one would pop up, I would force myself to black it out. High school was no time to be strange. I wanted to fade out and float along. Then soon I would be an adult. Then I could deal.

Everyone at high school was nice enough. I didn't get picked on, but I also barely spoke unless spoken to. It's possible that drugs and alcohol would have helped me fit in, but no one ever offered me any. Frances is a vegan health-freak and so stealing anything mind-altering from home was out of the question too. Unlike my peers it very seldom occurred to me to get drunk or high. There was a part of me that feared it would only make the visions worse and that was the last thing I wanted.

My saving grace during this time was Tynan. Tall, white-blonde hair and perpetually clad in denim, he had an aura that drew you in. Kind, witty and unafraid, I watched him tease without insulting and convince people to do things that, only two minutes earlier, they had no intention of doing. You know you're getting swindled, but you endure it just to see him smile and to know that for a moment, his attention is for you and you alone.

I admired Tynan from afar for a month during ninth grade before I worked up the courage to talk to him. Flashes came every time I looked in his direction, flashes of bodies he'd been. I tried, unsuccessfully, to wish them away. The one that was relentless was of him as a hunter in Mongolia. His jaw square, determined; riding his horse proudly over the plains as a rainbow chased his form. He owned each moment, even then.

One day during lunch, I spotted my chance to talk to him. He was standing against a tree, smoking a cigarette and I felt that he was awaiting my arrival. My eyes must have spoken my wonder and admiration, because the second thing he said to me after 'hello' was, "I think I should tell you up front that I'm gay. It's nothing personal, of course. Men are just beautiful, you know?"

Yes, I knew.

"That's ok," I said, nervously tugging on the straps of my backpack. "I just wanted to say hi."

He smiled at me widely, came to my side and put his arm around my shoulders, "Well hi, Ellie Stewart, I'm Tynan Malpass." Offering me his cigarette casually he asked: "Do you smoke?"

I shook my head.

"Gotcha. You're smart not to start, you know." He took a long, sweet drag. "Tell me, Ellie, why haven't you talked to me before? I mean, I moved here two years ago. It's not a big school. Why now?"

I considered how to respond to that for a moment but decided to be honest. "I'm lonely," I said simply. It turned out to be the right tactic. Tynan is big on sincerity.

"Uh-huh, well, not anymore you're not. Ok?" He bent his head towards mine and willed me to look at him. His blue eyes full of sympathy beneath feathery white lashes, I nodded lightly. I tried not to betray how happy I was to hear those words. He would be my protector.

If there is one thing that Tynan is good at, it is accepting people for who they are. He once said to me: "It's not like you're ugly or even plain. It's more like you exist simply to fade into the background. Is that your aim? There's nothing extraordinary about your looks, but you're clearly pretty. I don't know how you do that. You must work hard at appearing to disappear."

He was right. I wanted to skate through life unnoticed, unquestioned.

Another time a teacher had described me as shy and Tynan piped up right away in my defence: "She's quiet, not shy. There's a difference."

There is a difference, subtle though it may be. Shy implies I have something to say but I keep it to myself out of fear. I am quiet, waiting for the words. Whatever it is that needs to be said by me is lying dormant somewhere, holding still until it is stirred.

I feel a stirring coming on.

CHAPTER 4

Ellie

I walk past Stokes' Fish 'n' Chips up the hill along Little Tub Harbour. It's the first week of November, two weeks after my twenty-second birthday. The chill in the air is biting and yet reassuring; reminding us all that winter will once again invade and dominate.

My blonde hair is flying in the wind so I reach a gloved hand up to sweep it over my left shoulder. Clad in my autumn uniform of a Nordic sweater, black tights and hiking boots, I hug myself tightly. I am safe.

I work at the local dive shop. I've been here two months and am amazed at the breadth of knowledge I'm expected to have regarding diving and diving equipment. I was hired as a favour to my mom. The owner of the shop, Dave, is in her drumming circle and after hearing my mother complain for months about my unemployment, he finally broke down and offered me a position. I have a sinking suspicion that Frances described me as a "quick learner". The thing is, learning how to properly bag groceries is a far cry from gleaning the seemingly impossible intricacies involved with diving in Northern Ontario.

Living in Tobermory all my life however, I do know that divers are an interesting bunch. Misfit daredevils, bored mommies, overconfident tourists, Tobermory sees them all and they come from all over the world. This is another reason I tell myself that I have no need to travel. The world truly does come to me.

On any given day there are travellers from places like Germany, Japan and Joplin, Mississippi. For the past two months I've been pretending to know what I'm talking about to all of them. Thankfully, there is usually an instructor around for questions that could result in life or death.

Today a group of men in their fifties are in the shop looking around and laughing with each other. Dave is explaining something about oxygen tanks to them and every so often I feel him look in my direction, waiting for me to come over and learn something, or hoping I'll take on the knowledge through osmosis.

A couple of the men wander from the tank discussion and begin to look at the dive suits. Over and over in my mind I tell them not to approach me and not to ask any questions. Unbelievably though, one of them dares to ignore my silent plea.

"What's the temperature rating of this dive suit?" he asks from behind a rack of suits. He has a bit of what sounds like an Irish accent, muddled over time by years in Canada perhaps.

"Uh, I'm pretty sure it indicates the rating on the tag there," I say. I'm not sure at all, but I pretend otherwise hoping my guess is correct. Thankfully it is.

"Oh yes! Thank you, of course," he says with a laugh as though it's impossible I could have offended him.

It never ceases to amaze me how happy people are to be here. I mean, I like it here, but I have to. They like it because of its beauty, its promise. There is something so untarnished and real about this place. We adapt to the land. We don't expect it to adapt to us. It wouldn't in any case.

The man takes a step towards me and then turns to look me in the face. For a second, he looks surprised. I can only surmise that he didn't expect me to be so young, but he remains quiet for another thirty seconds, just staring at me. "Is everything ok?" I ask, finally.

"Yes, of course," he laughs self-deprecatingly. "I didn't mean to stare."

"Are you Irish?"

Again, he laughs. He puts his hands in the pockets of his down-filled vest and shifts closer to me. "I am. You've got a good ear. I lived in Limerick until I was twenty and then moved to

London. Ontario, not England. I've lived there ever since."

"Ah I see, that would explain the muddle," I reply, hoping to sound more confident than I feel.

He appears charmed by my cheekiness. "Do you dive, my dear?"

"Oh God, no!" I shout in spite of myself. "I mean, I've never been able to muster the courage."

Now he laughs loudly. "You live in the diving capital of Canada and you've never gone diving?" He's doubtful and yet amused.

I wave a hand in front of my face, "Don't get me wrong, I love the lake. I love water! There's just something about diving into the unknown that frightens me. And all those shipwrecks? They freak me out. I'm sure you'll hear all about our town's history during your stay here. People love to talk about it."

"I see," is all he replies with a gentle smile. He steps closer to me and I think I notice what looks like a flicker of sadness in his clear blue eyes. It's there for a millisecond and then it's gone. I wonder for a moment if I've said something wrong.

"So you must be part of that private charter group, eh?"

"Yes, exactly. We're here for one week of diving and then next week, we'll just hang out...maybe do some hiking. Our plans aren't too firm."

"Are you going to the Fathom Five?" I ask him. It's a National Park and a favourite dive site for tourists because of all the islands and shipwrecks it holds.

"I'm ashamed to say that I haven't really looked at the schedule. I'm actually afraid of chickening out. My son thinks I'm crazy for doing this in the first place. I suppose I figure the less I know ahead of time, the better."

Laughing, I nod. I can totally understand that logic.

He pauses for a moment and then says, "Could I ask a favour of you?"

Older men have asked me this question before and the favour

in question has left me nauseous so I'm cautious, "Um, sure."

"I'm here in Tobermory with the son I just mentioned. His name is Declan. He accompanied my friends and me here because…well, he needed a change of scenery. He doesn't know anyone here obviously, but he's about your age. Would it be okay if I told him to come by here one time to meet you? Maybe you could show him around?"

I am momentarily relieved and then realize that this will mean hanging out with a complete stranger. This man seems genuine though and I cannot bury the feeling of wanting to please him. "I'd like that," I say with a smile and then reach my hand out to him. "I'm Ellie by the way."

"Alistair O'Shea," he says bringing a hand to his heart and offering me the other. "It's nice to meet you, Ellie." In that moment I realize how handsome he is. He has salt and pepper hair cut short and the loveliest creases that appear around his eyes when he smiles. He is also nearly a foot taller than me. As he steps closer, I notice that he looks familiar and if he had reached out in that moment to hug me to him, I would not have been taken aback at all.

I'm nervous thinking that he can tell I'm analyzing his appearance. Fumbling for words I offer: "The store closes at five. He can meet me outside if that works."

"I think that will be perfect, Ellie. Thank you." He studies me for a moment and sighs, "Hmmm," and then turns to leave.

Was there something about me he didn't like? But then why would he want me to meet his son? I had questions, but I just let them all go. Maybe everything would be answered when I met Declan. One could hope.

CHAPTER 5

For the rest of my shift I can't think straight. Why did I agree to this? I don't do things like this. I don't agree to show strangers around a town as wide as my toe. It's ridiculous! We could run out of things to talk about in ten minutes flat. Could I make a break for it? Could I just leave a sign in the window saying I had to leave early because of a family emergency? Damn this living in a small town! He'd just ask around and in a heartbeat he'd know I was lying. I bite my lip and look up at the ceiling...I'd have to go through with it.

In a flash, a movie starts in my mind's eye. I don't block it out. I let it play.

A man walks toward me and I can tell he is angry. It is dark, the sky is clouded over and the rain is pouring down in buckets. His clothes, now soaked through, consist of an overcoat, gloves and a top hat...as if returning from a long journey. He is tall, with dark hair and he is carrying a letter. I can see that he is scowling, and yet I am overcome with desire for him. Even though I know he is angry with me, my head spins with anticipation.

"Louisa! How could you?"

And then it's gone.

"Oh!" I inhale sharply. That was the most vivid vision I have had in a long while. It shakes me up and reminds me of why I had repressed these for so long. I could see someone clearly; there was fluid movement and emotion. I had almost forgotten how overwhelming my visions could be.

I reach for the phone to call my mom and knock over a cup of pens in the process. My hands are shaking. Before I can begin to dial the numbers, the door to the shop opens. I look over and time stops for a moment.

It's him.

I know him. By sight and by soul, I know him.

"Uh, hi...are you Ellie?" he stammers.

I recognize him as the same man in my vision and yet different. He is tall with a strong and yet apprehensive presence. His hair is light brown and messy in a way that makes me want to run my fingers through it. But it's his eyes that draw me in. They are a crystal clear blue. I could be reborn in his eyes.

He's waiting for me to answer.

"Yeah, that's me. You must be Declan," I say shakily. He's so goddamned familiar. It's leaving me light-headed and breathless. What's more is that I can tell in an instant that I am having a similar effect on him.

He walks toward me and sets down the backpack he's carrying.

"Sorry I'm so early. I wasn't sure how long it would take me to walk here. This place sure is small. I mean...you know...not that that's a bad thing of course." He is definitely nervous. Placing his hands in his pockets he sways slightly back and forth and stares at the floor.

"Oh yeah, it's really small. We like it that way though," I say trying to reassure him. Something about his anxiety puts me at ease. I am thankful to be the calmer one for once. "I just have to balance the till and then we can go. Five minutes tops."

I see him pull his phone out of his pocket to check the time and let my gaze linger on him a moment. I feel like I would have recognized him even without the vision. It's as if there is a rope from my chest to his. We are unknown and yet bound. There is something safe and lovely about him. My head is light with pockets of air where reason and critical thinking should be.

I take a step and just like that, I see another scene in my mind's eye.

It's an assembly room and it seems to be around the year 1800, maybe a few years earlier. That is how it feels. There are candles above and beside me. I am surrounded by light and heat. The people are dressed in the most beautiful clothes, formal and elegant. It's a party...no, it's a ball. I am here with my father. The music is divine and so is the wine...

"Ellie? Ellie! Are you ok?"

I open my eyes to see that somehow I am now on the floor and that Declan is holding me, worry plain on his face.

"Oh, I'm sorry. Did I fall?" I ask bringing a hand to the back of my neck and pushing myself up with the other.

"Yeah, well it was more like you passed out. You slapped your forehead and then you just dropped. I didn't think people actually did that." His laugh is nervous as he helps me to my feet. His hands are warm.

"I didn't either. Do you always have that effect on women?" I cannot believe I am teasing him.

"I didn't mean...no, I'm sorry. I shouldn't have said that. You looked so helpless. I should be trying to make you feel better," he says shyly, looking away.

"Let's try this again, ok? I'm Ellie," I say giving him my hand.

"And I'm Declan. And again, it's nice to meet you, Ellie." He takes my hand and just holds it for a moment while studying my face. Eventually, he has to let go and I can still feel the effect of his touch, warm and strong.

I start to close up the shop. Declan pretends to look at the merchandise, but I catch him stealing glances at me. There's something about his presence that gives me confidence. I sense this man standing six feet away from me is the same man I envisioned from so long ago.

It's bewildering. I have no idea why any of this is happening and yet I feel safe in the discovery. By showing him around Tobermory I feel I'm at the beginning of a story that began long ago. As silly as it sounds, I begin to feel as if I am meant to be his guide.

This is not what I do though; this is not how I work. Normally I hide; I seek out the comfortable and familiar. Meeting this man, and taking the lead is about as far away from my regular mode of operation as I could possibly allow myself to get.

There is a comfort in the belief that this is somehow divinely written, but then another part of me dislikes giving up that kind of control. I want to know that I could turn around and run home if I wanted to right this second.

Perhaps I could, but I don't.

Declan and I head into town and I breathe in the cold, misty air. The lake is so near it permeates every molecule of this place. We wear it wherever we go and it cannot be shed. It seems impossible to imagine not living near the water. I think I would suffocate somehow, as though the sight and sensation of water were necessary to my survival.

Wrapping my scarf around my neck I look over at Declan who is clearly not dressed for November on the Bruce. He flips up the collar of his black jacket and shoves his hands in his pockets. He has sideburns. I hadn't noticed that before.

His profile is striking. Looking at him head-on you see his youth, a sadness in his eyes and a plea for understanding. From the side however, he appears almost severe, pensive yet incredibly handsome. The sight startles me for a moment.

Searching for distraction and calm, I ask Declan where he lives and if it's near the water.

"I live in London -Ontario not England- in a loft apartment, so no. To tell you the truth, I don't really like water that much. Pools are ok I guess, but lakes and oceans…I don't know. I don't like anything where I can't see the bottom," he tells me.

I give him a sympathetic look. "Well, that all depends how shallow the water is usually, I suppose, but our water is pretty clear here." Declan stares straight ahead. I continue, apparently undaunted by his silence. "So why did you come to Tobermory then?"

His expression is unreadable as he stares down at the ground. "I guess I was looking to escape. Sometimes people…I don't know. Sometimes I just can't handle people," he replies.

I watch him dig his hands deeper into his pockets looking uncomfortable. The wind picks up and rushes loud in my ears. It fills a void between us. Declan shakes his head as if to rid the noise from his ears. It's an odd thing to do, but I pretend not to notice.

We walk in silence. The thought crosses my mind to reach out and take his hand, but I let it pass. I have to remember that we just met. My heart sinks a little at the reminder that I have so much to learn about him. He's a stranger to my experience if not to my heart.

Beginning to feel a little ridiculous, I decide to break the quiet by pointing out some landmarks and giving him a little history of Tobermory. This seems to put him at ease, and finally the mood is lightened. I tell him about "The Tugs", a wreckage of four small tug boats not far from where we are in Little Tub Harbour and explain that Big Tub is on the other side of the peninsula.

"Let's go up the hill and I can show you the inn. It's very pretty." I turn to move up the incline.

"Oh, I know. That's where Dad and I are staying."

"Right...of course." Well, if he doesn't like water, our tour will be limited to a grocery store, pubs and fish 'n' chip joints. "Hey listen, why don't we go grab a coffee and I can tell you about some things in the area. Though I have to say that if you're not willing to venture out onto the water, you may become bored pretty quick. Do you like biking or hiking?"

He's not listening to me. I can tell he wants to say something. I feel my face go red as it dawns on me that I have been babbling. Normally I pride myself on being the observer, the listener in a conversation. It's an unwanted novelty to be the leader. It makes me want to run.

"Look, it's totally cool if you're not up for coffee," I mumble. He still says nothing. I reach into my purse to check my phone and hope he'll be the next one to speak. Softly I tell him I have to be somewhere anyway and turn to go.

"Ellie, wait! I'm sorry. I'm acting like a real weirdo here. It's just..."

"Just what?" I ask looking for an explanation, any explanation that doesn't end with me being a total nag. "I know we've only just met. I'm sorry for talking so much."

I'm lying of course. We haven't "just met", but I'm not ready to discuss that yet. I surprise myself with how hurt my voice sounds. What will I do if this man doesn't ever want to see me again? That can't be how this all unfolds. There has to be more to this.

"It's just...well, I can't shake the feeling..."

"Yes?"

"I know you, Ellie. It's not that I 'know' you, but I know you... like I remember you. You seem so familiar...your face, the sound of your voice. I can't explain it, but I just have to tell you and clear the air or I'll be staring at you all night wanting to tell you." He looks almost relieved to get this off his chest. I can't believe what I'm hearing. He felt it too! I'm so excited I want to scream! I feel as though everything has become clear. I feel a message whispering to me in the far reaches of my mind: Help this man, Ellie. Let the visions carry you through this and then you will know what they are for...

"I know you too," I say with a smile. Grabbing his elbow I yell, "Come on!" and lead him to the Vista Restaurant.

CHAPTER 6

The Vista is where wood panelling and dust-ridden plastic plants go to die, but thankfully, the food is good. Declan and I settle into a booth and order two waters. We're both buzzing and I am almost giddy. We're the only patrons here and yet it feels as if we fill the room to overflowing.

I start thinking about what all of this could mean. My whole life has been like a teeter-totter, a series of tiny ups and downs. I was a C student, never athletic, not very artistic. The only things that set me apart from being depressingly average were my visions. Maybe a part of me would have loved to brag to people about them, but I never did.

Here now, sitting before me so innocently was the reason for everything I have seen. And if I can help him, room can be made in my mind for something else. With the visions gone, I can hold space for my own happiness, my own joy.

I text Tynan and ask him to meet us. I want him to meet Declan and to like him. Is that too much to ask? I wonder.

"I've never been in this position with a stranger before. It's a little strange, eh?" My voice is small and excited, like a little girl.

He looks slightly confused. "Um yeah, I'm not sure what you mean exactly, but I am hoping you can tell me how we know each other. Have you been to London? Where did you go to University? It's driving me nuts!"

I feel sick to my stomach and have to look away from him. He thinks we've met before...in this lifetime. He has no idea.

"I didn't go to University," I mutter, struggling to think of what to say next. I can't tell him about the visions. He'll think I'm crazy and then he won't ever want to see me again. In that waking dream I felt the love and the longing for the man in the cloak so viscerally. It is clear to me he is here sitting before me once more in different skin, different clothes.

My attraction for him sits in my chest, heavy and ridiculous.

He doesn't know who I am.

"Oh, I see." Declan looks away for a moment, confused. "Did I say something wrong? You said you knew me too, right? I just wondered where it was we met. It's ok if you don't remember." Declan reaches across the table and squeezes my hand. I want to pull away because I'm so mad at myself for being so stupid. His hand is so warm in spite of his questionable choice to not wear gloves.

I let myself relax.

"Sorry, no. I don't remember either. We'll figure it out I'm sure," I say and silently tell him: Don't let go.

He flashes me a wide grin that somehow causes his eyes to look bluer and opens his menu. It's a dangerous feeling, but I am overcome at once by the notion that I would say anything to see him smile like that again. I shiver at the thought and instinctively bring my scarf back up to my neck and wrap it snugly.

Lifting my gaze briefly to his face, I inhale quickly and wonder how I will be able to keep from staring at this man...this ancient love.

Tiny bells ring as the front door opens. It's Tynan.

He arrives in his usual fashion, messenger bag across his shoulder and head held high in genuine confidence. As he approaches our table, I notice a flicker of recognition between the two men and see Declan blush, clearly uncomfortable.

"Do you two know each other already?" I ask looking at one and then the other.

Tynan ducks under the strap of his bag, removing it and addresses Declan directly. "In a way we do, right, man?"

Declan shifts in his seat and doesn't quite make eye contact with anyone. "We bumped into each other the other night over by Big Tub Harbour. It's no big deal."

Tynan opens his mouth to say something, but then he seems to reconsider. After a moment he says slowly "It's good to see you again." His expression is unreadable as he sits down beside me.

Declan grabs his menu without making eye contact and mutters: "Likewise, man."

I want to ask what the hell is going on, but I don't. Neither seems to want to talk about the circumstances of their meeting and to be honest, I'm a bit afraid of what went on between them. The thought that Declan might be gay occurs to me, but if that was it, Tynan would have made it crystal clear to me. He's always acted like a big brother. He must see Declan as some kind of threat to me, but why? I make a note to myself to talk to him about that later.

"What's everyone getting? How about a big basket of sweet potato fries; how does that sound?" My voice is way too loud. If the guys didn't know how uncomfortable I was, they do now.

"Sure Ell, sounds good." Tynan flashes a smile, but it doesn't reach his eyes.

"And I think I might order a Cosmopolitan!" I beam. The static between these two is making me say things I would not normally say.

Tynan rolls his eyes. "How can you drink that syrupy shit? They have a decent Merlot here, you know."

I roll my eyes right back at him. "I know. I just feel like a Cosmo tonight."

"I'll go to the bar and get that for you, Ellie," offers Declan, obviously relieved to have an excuse to leave the table.

As he gets up to leave, I narrow my eyes at Tynan and cross my arms. He looks innocently at me and shrugs.

"What's going on?" I whisper.

"I think I could ask you the same thing, Suellen." Tynan's tone is now that of a father's. I'm not amused.

"None of your business, Mr. Malpass."

"Oh really? Then why am I here? Admit it, Ellie, you wanted my approval." His voice smacks of so much self-assurance that I want to grab his ear and twist it. Tynan brings out the child in me sometimes.

"No, we just met..."

He chuckles and nods his head in wide-eyed sarcasm. "Right..."

I pout and I know it's not attractive, but I hate it when he's such an adult and when he's so goddamned right. I hate not having comebacks, but I never do. Words fly so fast out of Tynan's mouth and I can't keep up. He knows it and he almost always takes pity on me.

Declan brings drinks: my Cosmo, Tynan's wine and a light beer for himself. I can't get excited about my little pink drink. My disappointment is heavy and I feel a vision trying to peek through of an older man with his head hanging in despair. The man seems familiar and his grief is thick.

I push it away.

The rest of the evening is spent in strained conversation and concern that my best friend loathes this man who I am more than a little afraid of falling for.

CHAPTER 7

Ellie It's only seven in the morning, but I know Mrs. Dawes will be at the store already. Her routine was always to arrive at the store around six, meditate and then take a nap. My hope is that this hasn't changed. And if I'm honest with myself I am hoping she hasn't changed. These new visions and the arrival of Declan are rocking my world a little. I need an anchor.

Walking up to the store, I see a sign on the door: "Come on in" it says with a crudely drawn smiley face at the bottom. I open the door thinking how odd that is when I hear Mrs. Dawes calling my name.

"I'm in the back, Ellie! Come on through."

I weave my way through the vitamin displays and bins full of tea wondering if she bought herself a security camera for the storefront. Breathing in the familiar smells, I smile to myself with anxious anticipation. I haven't spoken to this woman in eight years. Part of me feels like an intruder. I breathe deeply and keep walking.

I can see that I am walking backwards and forwards at the same time. My past is serving my future somehow. It's all coming together...that is the feeling that hangs lightly in the back of my mind, but I don't know how to verify its truth.

"Oh there you are! It took you long enough," she says as soon as I find her in the back room. She's on the floor going through a box of old books, reading glasses perched on the tip of her nose and her red hair tied back in a messy bun. She's wearing a bright orange silk vest that is much too big for her over an old white t-shirt and faded black yoga pants.

So far, so good; she looks the same. My chest warms at the thought.

"What do you mean? Did you see me at the front door? And what are you doing down there? What's all this?" I ask, pointing at the slew of boxes.

"My, my we have a lot of questions this morning! I would have thought you'd start with 'It's so good to see you, Mrs. Dawes...after all this time."

I swallow hard. "It is. It is good to see you. I mean, I know that we wave to each other at Foodland, but it's not the same."

"No, love, it's not." She stands up, opens her arms wide and I run to her. She feels and smells exactly as I remember: soft and musky. I let myself bask in her motherly embrace and suddenly Frances pops into my head. I'll have to tell her all about this. I can't keep any of this from her.

Mrs. Dawes gives me a big squeeze, bringing me back to the task at hand. "I have to know; how did you know I was coming?"

"Ah-ha! Excellent question, but I don't think I'll answer it. Now come and sit down, Ellie. Just move those papers and you can even lie down on the couch if you want." She motions to the brown and yellow striped sofa that is clearly older than I am. "Don't argue! Lay down and I'll explain. I know why you're here."

I do as I'm told and then squint my eyes at her doubtfully, "You do?"

"Yes, I do. I've been waiting for this day for a long time. You're here about the visions, right? My guess is that they have been a little clearer lately? Don't look so surprised, my dear. I am a seer, you know. Plus, I saw you with that young man last night walking along the harbour. There was no doubt in my mind that you had a connection with him. I felt immediately that you recognized each other and knowing, as I do, that you've never ventured too far, I figured the memory of him was from a previous life." She smiles at me in an attempt to quell my shock. "So just lay back. We're going to relax you and you're going to tell me what you see."

I open my mouth to protest and then think the better of it. I did come here for answers. Settling myself back onto the couch, I look up at the ceiling. Posted to it is a picture of what looks like a part of the milky way…swarms of stars pooled together to make the most vibrant blue. I breathe deeply and close my eyes instinctively. I focus on this image in my mind's eye and hear Mrs. Dawes' voice vaguely in the background. It happens almost effortlessly. She mutters something about being calm and serene and then I hear numbers. She seems to be counting backwards…

"Tell me where you are." I hear her voice say.

"I'm at a ball. He's here!" I exclaim.

"Ok, Ellie. Here's what I want you to do: Remove yourself gently from the picture. You're going to describe what you see as if you are floating above the scene, ok? Can you do that?"

I take a deep breath and I nod, or at least I think I do…

CHAPTER 8

Louisa London, England – 1790

The room was warm and lit by a hundred candles that shone once at the wick and again as shimmering orbs that danced about the room. Soon forgotten are the rain and the mud, the foul smells and the sickness. London society was all astir as Mr. Henry Madison was having a ball. Eligible bachelors drank wine and shook hands as they surveyed the room for money and beauty. Everyone was herded into the ballroom and announced with name, land and title all in the same breath. Here high society mingled with high society.

Miss Louisa De vale was here with her father, Sir Thomas De vale, a very wealthy gentleman and a baronet. Her beloved mother had passed away ten years ago. Many of Sir Thomas' friends had advised sending her away to school, but he simply could not. Louisa's presence had soothed and comforted him. She had cried, of course, when her mother passed, but it did not seem to haunt her as it did him. Her father had been beside himself with grief and was overcome with a kind of helplessness previously unknown. Perhaps it was uncommon for a father to be so close with his daughter, but Louisa understood that she reminded him so much of her mother and her lively, innocent spirit eased his heartache just enough to get through each day.

A ball was not at the bottom of a list of places she wished to be at this moment, nor was it at the top. She comprehended that it was part of her role as the daughter of a baronet to make appearances in society. Her mind drifted to the stack of books at her bedside, but she calmly brought it back to the splendour of her present moment. She would make the best of it.

The music floated seamlessly throughout the ballroom and seemed to cast a spell. Louisa had never wanted for a dance partner before and tonight was no different. Her auburn hair, bright green eyes, easy manner and, of course, her fortune, made her a favourite with many men, young and old. She was kind, pretty and intelligent: three things that seldom seemed to exist together among the *ton* in London. She would dance until her feet begged her to stop and then go out and dance some more.

Louisa felt her father's proud, admiring gaze and then turned to hear him declare, "My dear girl, have I told you how lovely you look this evening? You have your mother's eyes, yet you are the spitting image of my own dear mother." He paused and shook his head with a mixture of sadness and wonder. "I cannot believe you are two and twenty."

His face was full of kindness. He was a tall and stout man with big, expressive eyes and hair the colour of silver.

"I thank you, father. You are too generous." Louisa bowed her head. She was acutely aware of how blessed a life she led and her father was one of her many blessings. "Isn't this delightful? Are we not fortunate?" she asked with a wide smile looking about the room.

"We are indeed, my dear. Come now though, Louisa, not one of the fine gentlemen here are of any interest to you? You still maintain that you will not marry?" Sir Thomas shook his head in good-natured disbelief and did not wait for her to reply. Although he would never say it to her, Louisa knew he felt strongly that marriage and family brought happiness and stability. Perhaps he found it difficult to see how she could flourish without the love of a husband and children of her own. She was an only child with very few living family members. After his death, she would be quite alone.

For Louisa however, the prospect of marriage was a dismal one. The men she met were mostly kind and attentive, but they often had little to discuss. They had all been educated at some of the finest institutions in the country, but seemed loathe to share what they learned. The male sex in general appeared to be more interested in complimenting her beauty than discovering her opinion on politics and literature. As much as she enjoyed flirtation, the idea that she must bind herself to one of these men for life seemed unimaginable. She was indeed grateful for the fact that she did not need a husband. Louisa would inherit her father's estate upon his death and she was already worth thirty thousand pounds. She had decided to live as an old maid, albeit a very wealthy one.

Of course Louisa would never be idle. It was not in her nature. In truth she fancied herself a philosopher. She had read Thomas More's Utopia and some ancient Indian philosophy. Lately though, she had been most intrigued by Gnosticism and the notion that spirituality was meant to be more of a personal experience. The works had belonged to her mother, whose own father had met an Italian monk and purchased the books for her. Louisa's mother, Mary, had a father much like her own who encouraged her to read and to indulge her curiosity about life and the world.

She had never met her maternal grandparents, the Boyles, but from her mother's description of them she knew she would have loved them. They were both Scottish-born, as was her mother, and both came from noble families. According to Louisa's mother, her grandmother had been fair and kind, while her grandfather had been passionate, intelligent and a collector of fine Scotch. Mary Boyle was born on the Isle of Mull off the western coast of Scotland and lived there until she was nine years old before the family moved to London. Mary had always had fond memories of her time on Mull. Apparently at one time they had the finest home on the island, but it was now long-deserted.

"Excuse me, Sir Thomas?" asked Mr. Madison, the host of tonight's ball and an old friend of Louisa's father. He was a short, slight gentleman, nearly a head shorter than Sir Thomas. His voice was characteristically quiet and so he had to repeat himself three times before the baronet heard him.

"Ah yes, Mr. Madison! A lovely evening you have given us, sir. Louisa and I cannot thank you enough for your hospitality," said Sir Thomas slapping the smaller man on the back.

Mr. Madison managed to smile through the obvious pain, "You are most welcome, sir. And good evening Miss De vale. I am honoured to have you both here. There could be no ball without the De vales. It simply would not do." He inched slightly away in anticipation of another friendly blow. "Now, my reason for coming to see you is that there is a young man who would very much like to make your acquaintance, sir. His name is Mara and I believe he has done quite well for himself. From what I can gather, he has made his fortune by connecting wealthy investors with engineers constructing new towns and ports. Specifically he has been working with the British Fisheries Society. I know it is not customary to speak of such things at a ball, but his offer will be of interest to you, I believe, sir. May I introduce him to yourself and your daughter?"

Louisa looked about the ballroom to see if she could spot this Mr. Mara. As she scanned the room her gaze was drawn to a tall, handsome man with dark hair and a stiff, serious mien. He stared directly at her as if he had been waiting for her to notice him.

Their eyes were locked for a moment until he looked away embarrassed, apparently, at being caught by her. Louisa's own fixation was broken by the sound of her father's voice, "Yes of course, Mr. Madison. Bring the young man over!"

She watched as Mr. Madison walked over to the man she had been so struck by and led him in their direction. Her heart leapt in anticipation, but she would have to wait. At that moment, her intended dance partner came to collect her and brought her to the dance floor. Looking back to where her father stood, she observed introductions being made and Mr. Madison leaving with a bow. What was being said? She wondered.

Mr. Mara was dressed like a gentleman, in fine clothes and well-groomed, but he seemed uncomfortable as though he thought himself an imposter. Louisa smiled at the thought and mused about how refreshing it would be to know someone who was not born into society. He turned his head briefly to discover her looking at him. From this shorter distance she could see how dark his eyes were. They matched his hair, his coat and even, perhaps, his mood. She smiled at him and he quickly looked away.

Louisa's partner prattled on about his father's estate in Hampshire. Men were always telling her about the estates of their fathers. She nodded politely, but could pay only sparse attention to what was said. Moving her gaze back to the mysterious black-eyed man, it was clear that Mr. Mara was nervous speaking to Sir Thomas. He could not have been more than twenty-five years old, half her father's age. If only she knew what they were speaking of. Louisa knew it was ill-mannered to be so curious, but she could not help it. She wanted to be involved. She wanted the sound of Mr. Mara's voice to wash over her like a cool, symphonic wave and she longed to see those ebony eyes up close.

William

William Mara looked down at his hands, absent-mindedly massaging his knuckles. He had been waiting months for this introduction and now that it was here all he could do was fidget. *What is the matter with you, William? We have made proposals like this before. It's either a yes or a no and there's an end to it.*

He had worked hard to arrive at this point. Growing up in poverty meant he seldom dealt with the very rich, much less members of the upper spheres of society, except to see them pass on the streets of London from time to time in their fine carriages. How very different his life looked now. It was still difficult however, to reconcile this reversal of fortune in his thoughts. He was not rich, although he was successful to be sure. Owning a house of his own with two servants and finally being able to shop for finer clothes made him feel satisfied, yet there was a part of him that always felt like the poor, filthy boy from Newgate Street. Until he could rid his mind of that feeling he would keep striving, keep searching.

Raking his fingers through his dark, unruly hair, Mr. Mara began to look about the ballroom. He had never been to an event such as this and he had to admit to himself that he was quite uncomfortable. If only he could have approached Sir Thomas someplace else. He disliked the idea of doing business in a ballroom, but it could not be helped. Mr. Madison had been kind enough to offer the introduction and William was in no position to dictate the terms of it. In any case, he and Sir Thomas were not likely to cross each other's paths any other way in London.

He continued to shift his stance and looked nervously about the room as his gaze fell upon a vision in emerald. A young woman stood directly in front of him, but twenty feet away. He felt a jolt in his chest and a haze in his head. Her brilliant red hair was swept back with black feathers and with a likeness that was quite eerie, her eyes appeared to match her green dress. Embarrassingly, he could not look away and his boots seemed fixed to the floor as if he would next sink where he stood, pulled under by some invisible force.

She was taken to the dance floor by another man and William shook his head in an effort to remember himself. It was then that he noticed Mr. Madison standing in front of him offering to take him to meet Sir Thomas.

"Sir Thomas, allow me to introduce you to Mr. William Mara. Mr. Mara, this is Sir Thomas De vale of Overfield Manor in Gloucestershire." Mr. Madison was pleased. He appeared to rejoice in connecting two men who might otherwise never have met.

"Sir Thomas, it is an honour to make your acquaintance. I have been waiting for this day for many months now. Thank you for agreeing to speak with me," said William in a voice much louder than he had intended. He inwardly cursed his tenseness and with a deep breath, attempted to cool his head.

"Speak with you, lad? I thought we were meant to meet and exchange pleasantries! Your manner is so serious," exclaimed Sir Thomas with a kind-hearted wink.

William winced at his teasing. He had never been one to take well to jokes, but it was clear the baronet intended to have a little fun with him. Sir Thomas crossed his arms about his chest and leaned back to give Mr. Mara the floor, "Ok, then! Out with it lad! You have my attention."

William cleared his throat and attempted to look the gentleman in the eye. "Sir, I have an investment opportunity that may be of interest to you."

"Is that so? Alright, let's hear it."

"Yes, sir; I am to help oversee the construction of a fishing village in the northwest area of the Isle of Mull. Fish are plentiful there. The community is in need of organization and there are many opportunities for a man of your station to profit. I know, sir, that your late wife was born in Mull and so I thought it might be of particular interest to you," said William looking down slightly for a moment at the mention of Mrs. De vale.

"That is true, Mr. Mara. My darling Mary was indeed from Mull. I am curious how you knew that!" William felt himself go red. "Do not be uneasy. I am even more curious about your proposition. Call on me tomorrow at my home on Turks Row," said Sir Thomas, offering his hand to William.

"With pleasure, I look forward to it."

And with that, William finally relaxed for the first time in what felt like days. He turned to walk out of the ballroom, but not without first scanning for a sign of Miss De vale. She was easily found, for as it happened, she was looking straight at him.

She stood by the refreshments where a servant was pouring her a glass of punch. He wanted to approach her, but schooled himself to pause. He knew he would have to ask Sir Thomas or Mr. Madison for an introduction. It was against propriety to speak to her without one. There was no need to complicate things, he told himself. He had come here to accomplish the task of speaking with Sir Thomas and that was now completed. Instinctively he felt speaking with her would only confuse matters and he was unwilling to risk all that he had attained. He would walk away from her, but how he would undo the feeling that he was somehow bound to her he knew not.

Louisa

The baronet rejoined his daughter and she poured him a glass of punch. There was only one question on her mind.

"What did he want, father?" She had been disappointed to see that the gentleman had left before she could secure an introduction. She had been denied something she wanted and was unaccustomed to that. The feeling of frustration that followed felt filthy, unwelcome. A calm whisper in the back of her mind said: Later.

"Who, my dear? Mr. Mara?" She nodded, trying to stifle her interest like a gently-bred young lady would do. "Oh, it was business. He has an opportunity he would like to present to me. It involves Mull, where your mother was born which, I might add, was information that the young man was somehow privy to. I must say I find that I am very intrigued." Sir Thomas took a sip of his punch and swallowed it reluctantly, distaste plain on his face. "Louisa, please tell me there is tea somewhere about. I cannot have another drop of that vile concoction."

Louisa stifled a smirk. Her father could really only drink tea or wine, anything else caused him to become petulant. The punch had been a mischievous experiment on her part. "Of course father. I shall pour you some."

"Thank you, my dear. Now, what was I saying? Oh yes, I have

been thinking of involving myself in some kind of a project, though I confess Scotland was not really on my mind. Still, it would be a diversion. I am getting older! We do not want my mind going soft now do we?" Sir Thomas laughed at his own jest, but Louisa's mind was on a different point.

"How curious... He knew that my mother was from Mull specifically? Is this why he approached you, sir?" she asked, now unable to hide her genuine interest.

"I believe that was part of the reason, but let us not speak of this any further. We are at a ball after all! The gentleman is to call tomorrow at our home. I will know much more by then and will share every detail with you. I promise," he reassured her. Sir Thomas took her hand and patted it to reassure her. He then offered his arm to her and as she took it they walked to a part of the room that allowed them to better view the dancing.

Louisa knew he would keep his word. Since she had turned nineteen her father had kept her abreast of all the estate and business dealings because he knew she intended to remain single. Although most of the day-to-day issues would be handed over to a steward and solicitor, he seemed to feel it important she know as much as possible. They were both aware it was unconventional for a father to share this kind of knowledge with a daughter, but they trusted one another and it seemed needlessly unkind and unwise that Louisa be kept in the dark.

"Might I ask, father, could I be present during your meeting? I confess there is something about Mr. Mara's request that troubles me, though I cannot say what at present."

"If Mr. Mara is agreeable to it, I do not object. Now, I do believe your next partner has come to fetch you," he said motioning to a gentleman approaching behind her. "Enjoy yourself, Louisa. You read and study so much and are so often alone; go be merry. No more talk of business!"

She smiled mildly at her father as she let go of his arm to take that of her dance partner.

Louisa went through the motions of the dance, but her mind was engaged elsewhere. She felt haunted by Mr. Mara in a way that both startled and excited her. This attraction to a stranger was territory as yet uncharted. Did this sort of thing happen to everyone? Did all people, at one time or another, feel drawn to another person in a way that seemed beyond their control? Louisa laughed as she realized how seriously she was being and resolved to keep her focus on the ball and think of Mr. Mara no more. Surely she could keep this promise at least until tomorrow when he called.

CHAPTER 9

Ellie

"Three, Two, One and you're back" says a voice, softly. "I brought you out because this is your first regression. I don't want to keep you under too long."

I vaguely recognize the one who is speaking now as Mrs. Dawes.

I open my eyes too quickly and feel the light abrupt and all too bright. Sitting up, I peer through the slits of my fingers to re-orient myself. I'm disappointed to be done so quickly. I wanted to spend more time with this woman...this me of the past. "I was fine, Mrs. Dawes, really."

"I'm sure you were fine, but I'd rather give you a sense of what it's like first." She gets up and walking over to her desk, she pours a pitcher of water and fills two glasses. I sit up on the couch and accept mine gratefully. I hadn't realized how much I had been talking.

"Well, love, that was definitely interesting! You were Louisa! And so the enigmatic Mr. Mara from back then is the same soul as your new friend Declan, eh?"

I whip my head in her direction. "How did you...?"

She waves her hand at me dismissively. "Ellie, please. Let's just agree that I know a lot of things. If I feel the need to explain something to you, I will. If it's the loving thing to do, I will do it."

I nod at her. "I had a flashback -when I first met Declan- of a man walking toward me in the rain. I know now that William was that man and at the time I sensed that the man was Declan in this lifetime."

She reaches across from the chair where she was seated and pats my knee. "I've had past life memories of my own, you know. For instance, you were my father in a previous life."

"Your what? How come you never told me that before?"

She shrugs. "I never felt the need to. Plus I knew you needed some more experience with these visions. When you're willing to trust yourself, you realize that you just know. But of course, at some level you realize that already. We're so fixated on physical proof in this world."

She's right. It's not necessarily helpful for me to know everything right now. I sense that. I hadn't realized how much I had been missing her wisdom. "If I had not met you, I doubt that I ever would have come to believe in reincarnation."

She stares into the bottom of her water glass as if inspecting it for a tiny floating object. "Well, maybe you would and maybe you wouldn't have. Does it really matter? The strength of your visions is a testament to the fact that you need to heal some things that took place in your lifetime as Louisa. You need to deal with it now, Ellie, not later. That much is clear."

"Why that specific lifetime though? I've seen snippets of others."

"Exactly. You've seen snippets of others, but since you've met Declan they've become more vivid, right?" I nod, remembering my promise not to ask questions. "Well, he's back Ellie. William is back as Declan to heal the hurts the two of you experienced all those lifetimes ago. This is a gift. Whether he knows it or not, he's giving you a gift."

I shift uncomfortably at the mention of the word "hurts". "You think we harmed each other in some way? Do you think he's back for revenge or something?"

She laughs lightly. "No, love. That is not what I meant. We humans are always misunderstanding one another. We look for reasons to hate and also to feel guilty. You don't always need to go poking around a past life to unearth this stuff, but apparently this is what is most helpful for you at this point in your life. Just go with it."

"Should I tell him? About the visions, I mean."

Mrs. Dawes stands up and stretches her arms above her head

as she says, "Here's the thing: you don't really need his physical body to heal the wounds of the past. Healing is done on the level of the mind. You're healing as you're recalling these events. His physical presence did trigger the memories, but the rest you can do on your own. If he's got something to heal, I am sure it will come out. For now though, let's just focus on you. Ok?"

I get up and hug her, overcome with gratitude. I squeeze her tight and let my face rest in her fuzzy red hair. Surprised at first, she quickly yields to it, hugging me back with equal fervour.

This is what I've been waiting for! I have direction. And even though I don't know what to expect, I am so thankful to have her guidance. "Bless you, Mrs. Dawes!" I say into her hair not wanting to let her go. "What would I do without you?"

"Well, my dear, you don't have to find out. I'm here for you. We are in this together. In the meantime, go about your normal life. See your friends; go to work. Meet me here the day after tomorrow at the same time and we'll have another session. Sound good?" Her smile is warm, replete with quiet understanding.

"Yes absolutely. I cannot thank you enough," I say, finally releasing her.

How have I not seen the miraculous woman I now see? It's obvious I had taken her for granted for far too long. I wrote her off as an eccentric when I was in high school for no good reason. Clearly I had let my own fears about my visions blind me to a willing and able guide.

I leave the store feeling like a weight is finally being lifted. Maybe I'm not a freak after all. Maybe this has all been to help and not to make me feel so separate from everyone.

I think about my mother and how much I want to share this all with her. I think about Tynan and I wonder if he will understand.

Mostly though, I think about Declan and how hollow it feels to be missing the presence of a stranger.

CHAPTER 10

Declan

She is impossibly pretty and yet she has no earthly idea. How can that be?

I know where I recognized her from now. It was in my dreams, my nightmares even, but I won't tell her that. The last thing I want to do is scare her off.

Can I do this? Can I be normal? Sane? In love? People like me don't fall in love. We stalk, draw endless pictures; we write tortured poetry. We don't fall in love. So I think maybe I should leave, go back to London before I lose everything I've built and forgotten. But I can't stop thinking of her…

I had to blink twice when I saw her: A face of flawless joy and kindness, hair the colour of Prairie wheat and eyes like the bay of her birthplace.

Ellie matches this land, lays upon it accepting and yet denying it with that look in her eyes that says she knows something we don't. Will she tell me what she knows? How much of what she hides will she show me?

Anything is possible, Mom always says. I could be the one she lets in. It could be me.

And then I think how stupid that is. She doesn't need a crazy fuck-up in her life. Let her be, I tell myself. Let her be.

I stumble from my hotel bed to the mirror. I look so pathetically sad in comparison to her, as though serenity was her race and melancholy mine. Even when I smile, my blue eyes droop.

And I really need to shave my head. Who needs the responsibility of a comb? Not this man.

I hear the wind outside my window as it whistles and howls and I'm glad to be inside. I've always despised the wind in my ears. It's the fear that the noise of it is blocking out something important that I need to hear like the honking of an oncoming truck, or a lover calling my name.

Ellie flashes in my mind again and instantly I want to see her naked. I would be good to her. I would not just love her and leave her. No, I would give her all the parts of me that are rational and I would be gentle.

I want to see her naked, but I want her secrets too. I want her lightly-freckled arms, her morning breath, her crappy pop music (I imagine this is true) and her perfection. I have an image of her already formed in my mind. I've assumed a lot of things about her, but I'll surrender it all for her truth, whatever that is.

Is it normal to want another person to balance you out? She is everything sane, kind and lovely. I feel damaged at the core. At the very least, my mind is damaged. She could help me laugh at myself. She could help me.

God help me. I'm mad. I need some wine.

Ellie

Looking down at my phone I notice a missed call from my mother and six texts from Tynan. Not feeling up to questions from my mom quite yet, I send Tynan a message saying I will meet him at the Town Pump. But instead of heading there, I find myself walking up the hill to the inn. Taking a seat on the bench across the street from it, I pull my thick, black cotton dress down so that my tights don't catch on the wooden slats. I look up to the windows tucked behind the wrought iron railings and wonder which one is his.

Just then I can feel someone behind me. I turn around to see Declan carrying a brown paper bag, his face softened by a smile.

"Well, I guess it was only a matter of time before we bumped into each other again, eh?" he says casually. I notice that in the bag he's carrying is a bottle of wine. He must have just come out of the liquor store.

"Isn't it a little early for that?" I ask with a giggle and then blush at my awkward clichéd joke.

"Is it?" he asks, with a questioning look. "In any case, I wasn't planning on drinking it now."

I look away slightly and wring my hands together nervously. "I'm sorry. I'm being nosy."

"No, no! It's fine, really. You're not." He's shifting his gaze between me and the ground. I can tell I've made him anxious...again.

"I hope last night wasn't too uncomfortable for you. Tynan is charming, normally, but he was a little intense last night. He takes on the role of big brother when other guys come around."

Declan twists the top of the paper bag around the bottle neck and avoids my eyes, "I don't think Tynan likes me too much..."

"Really? He's protective of me for sure, but you and I just met so... And anyway, he just needs to get to know you," I say with confidence I don't really possess. I would love to see them together again to know that it was all a misunderstanding.

He pauses as though he's searching for the right words and decides to sit down beside me. "I hope it's ok to ask you this, but have you hooked up with Tynan before? You guys seem closer than friends..."

I cannot help myself. I laugh out loud. "Oh God, no! Tynan is gay."

"Tynan is gay? And yet he lives up here? There can't be that many gay men here."

This is a common reaction when newcomers meet Tynan. He seems as though he could not possibly belong, but the truth is he could fit in anywhere. He has a sense of how to be, what to say and to still somehow be himself. It's inspiring.

"He lived in Montreal for a year after high school and had a boyfriend. Guy was his name. The break-up was very messy. He refuses to talk about it and I don't push him."

"I see." Declan clears his throat, unwilling to drop the subject. "Why did he move to Montreal? To meet guys?"

I look around me almost as if to make sure Tynan isn't standing nearby, listening. "Well, he originally went to study music at McGill, but he only stayed for 2 semesters. Now he does some online marketing thing selling memberships to some website and he plays in a band." I pause and wait to see if he wants me to continue. His face is nervous and yet expectant, as if he is gathering information. Briefly, I wonder again if Declan is gay and my heart instantly sinks.

As if my thoughts are written on my forehead Declan says, "Sorry for all the questions. I was just curious. He...uh, he seems like an interesting guy; that's all." He's holding the wine bottle tightly in both hands, so tight that his knuckles are white. "So what about you? How do you meet guys up here?"

The question catches me off guard for a moment. I give a nervous laugh in order to buy myself some time. "I don't. In the summer there are lots of people here, mostly families though. The guys that come are usually in big groups here to camp, fish or dive." I shift my feet in some gravel on the sidewalk and let the noise distract me so I don't have to process what I say next. "I've always imagined living a solitary life. I have no plans to leave Tobermory. If I can just live here peacefully, do some soul-searching, work at odd jobs, I'd be a happy girl."

"And what if one of these divers takes an interest in you?" he says softly. I swear that somehow he is now sitting closer to me. His voice seems to resonate sweetly just inside my ear.

"Like I said, I have no plans to leave Tobermory." I feel myself pulling slightly away from him, a little uncomfortable with where he is going with these questions. I manage somehow to look him in his face and see it has taken on an air of confusion.

"So you'd rather stay here than take a chance and possibly find the love of your life?" A silence grows between us as he looks up at the sky. He almost seems upset. "And how can you know he wouldn't move here? If he loved you I bet he would," he says confidently. I'm taken aback by the conviction in his voice. It occurs to me that he must be in love and if he isn't now, then he definitely has been.

"Uh, you make a good point…"

"Sorry, now I'm the one being nosy."

"No, it's ok. I've never been in love. That's probably a good thing though. I have no idea what I'm missing. Whenever I think of marriage I just picture myself with a fisherman or a ferry captain. Someone who would love the water more than they loved me," I tell him. "But honestly it seems so distant and unreal. I imagine myself preferring to be alone." As the words come out of my mouth I realize how ridiculous they would sound to a stranger.

"Jesus, Ellie. That's not what I see for you at all. I mean, I understand the "no drama" thing but you're so…so fascinating," he says and then looks away aware he's probably said too much. He shifts the bottle between each hand and looks up at the clouds.

"No one has ever described me that way before. Although it's very possible I don't really know who I am." I have his attention now. "I'm twenty-two and don't know who I am! Is that even normal?" My insistence in embarrassing myself with this guy is beginning to astound me.

The wind picks up and I notice Declan wince. I want to reach out to him, put my hands over his ears and bring his head close to me. I want to feel the roughness of his jaw against my cheek. It seems unfair to have all these unspoken rules. I want to skip to the part where he's mine and I can touch him whenever I please.

"Listen, it's freezing out here…" he says, annoyed.

Ugh. My stomach does a somersault at his words. "Oh yeah, I'm sorry. I didn't mean to keep you. I was actually just heading to the pub anyways. You know, the Town Pump," I say quickly. I cannot blame him for wanting to be somewhere else. Try as I might, I cannot seem to be anything but awkward around Declan O'Shea.

"No, I just… You were?" He pulls out his phone and then puts it back in his pocket. "I was going to ask if you wanted to come to my room at the inn. It has a fireplace." And this time he's looking me in the eye. His hair hangs in his face and I suppress the urge to reach up and sweep it away for him. He hasn't shaved today, but the stubble suits him. Everything about him suddenly seems cloaked in magnetic perfection.

I'm unnerved, but I want to do this. This is something real. I can feel his attraction for me and I have no doubt of mine for him. I want to know how deep our connection is. "That sounds great. I will. Thanks, Declan." I manage finally.

"You're welcome, Ellie," he says mocking me with a boyish grin.

He starts walking toward the inn and I get up to follow him. Turning to me he smiles and takes my hand. Again I am surprised at the warmth of his body considering the cold. There's a change in him. He seems more comfortable, as if a bridge was crossed. I must have missed something.

What did I miss?

All of a sudden, another vision flashes in my mind…

He's holding a candle at his side. It's the only light in the room. I am in my bed, but I am wide-awake. He's looking at me with longing and yet I can feel his self-loathing. He has been drinking. I know I should tell him to leave, but I want him to stay.

"William?"

"Ellie? Are you ok?"

Declan's voice brings me back. I wince for a second and look up at him. The concern in his eyes momentarily distracts me. Realizing his arms are around me, supporting me, I actually consider asking him to hold me tighter and then silently scold myself for being so ridiculous. "I'm so sorry. I'm fine. I just keep having these dizzy spells," I tell him, squirming out of his grasp without a trace of grace.

He's still holding my arm and stroking it lightly with his thumb. "Is that normal?"

Neatly avoiding his question I start telling him about the history of the inn. He's politely listening, but I can tell he's still worried about my mini-blackout. I keep talking until we reach his room. It suddenly dawns on me that I have no idea what I'm doing here. What does he want? Are we just going to talk or did he ask me up here hoping I'd sleep with him? Where is his father? Does he have his own room?

I take a deep breath and remind myself that I trust Declan. I may not know him all that well, but my soul trusts his just the same.

He leads me into the room and puts his stuff on a chair. Looking around I'm pleasantly surprised at how quaint and cozy it is. The decor is dated, with pale pinks and forest greens, but it is clean and smells of wood. There is a kitchenette, a fireplace, a chair, a small sofa and of course, the bed. The window overlooks the bay. I walk over to it and notice the sun is already beginning its descent. The sky is a mixture of purples and oranges while the water is a vibrant blue. I've seen it a million times yet it still stops me dead.

"Beautiful, eh? I can see why you like it so much up here." He's right behind me. I can feel his closeness. It makes me shiver. "Can I get you something to drink? Wine? Tea?"

"A glass of wine would be great, thanks. It's not really that early I suppose," I say with a wink. His room is very neat and tidy. Looking down beside his bed I see he has brought one duffle bag and a guitar. I ask him how long he has played.

"Since I was ten," he answers. "It calms me to play it. I don't even care how good I am. I just play it for me."

"I like that. Somehow I think that's how it's meant to be…doing things because we love to and not requiring any other reason."

I sit down on the sofa. Declan hands me the glass of wine and settles in beside me, two cushions over. I tap the glass with my fingers, searching for an icebreaker.

"You should play with Tynan sometime... He plays the drums," I say, happy to have found a neutral topic.

He ignores my comment completely. "You're very beautiful, Ellie." I swallow hard. He continues, "I'm not trying to make you uncomfortable. It's just...it's obvious and I just wanted to let you know that I think so."

I feel myself go red. "That's sweet of you to say Declan, thank you."

"I'm not just saying it to be sweet."

The silence is loud now. I don't know what to do. I have made out with three guys and had sex with one in my entire life. None of these experiences are worth mentioning here. It's not that I didn't ever want to fall in love; it's just that it never happened. I know that I held back, but it was safer that way. It never seemed clear to me what guys wanted, other than the obvious. But what about afterwards? Was there room for love in their lives? Was there room for me?

Frances says it is the other way around...that I have been unwilling to welcome in anyone who I hadn't known at least half of my life.

"What are you thinking about?"

I shake my head. "Nothing."

"I don't want anything from you, Ellie. If you're not comfortable, I can walk you to the pub or even home and we can call it a night."

I'm sure the disappointment is written all over my face. I look down at my wine and say nothing.

Declan shifts over to the cushion next to me and takes the glass from my hand to set it down on the table. He puts his left hand on my thigh and with the other he sweeps my cheek. I feel my heart quickening and I hope to God I'm not blushing again.

His face is so close to mine now that I can feel his breath, warm and insistent on my lips. I dare myself to look in his eyes. He takes this as the green light he was waiting for and puts his mouth to mine. His kiss is soft and my head begins to spin. He gently pushes me back against the arm of the couch and positions himself on top of me. Instinctively I bring my hands to his back. I feel the strength of him.

I can't focus; I can't breathe. I let go.

Lifting his flannel shirt up, I make small circles on his skin with my fingers. He moans softly against my neck and moves a hand down to my hip to pull up my dress. The room must be moving because I cannot see straight. He kisses the hollow of my collarbone and I feel it throughout my whole body.

All I can think is: I want this.

It crosses my mind that I have never been truly attracted to a man until now and I have never felt so wanted, so required. Declan is turning my world on its head.

Bringing my hands to his hips I pull him to me, willing him closer and closer. There is a feeling that I could never get enough, and yet I still want more; I want as much as he can give. He is hard against me and I hear him gasp as I bring my hand between us. I am so caught up in the moment that I barely notice my phone ringing until Declan pulls back slightly.

"Did you want to get that?" His voice is breathless. It makes me think he wanted me as much as I wanted him.

"Um yeah…I guess I should." I sit up and reach for the phone and instantly remember where I was supposed to be. "Damnit! I totally forgot about Tynan. I'll let it go to voicemail and I'll text him back. Just give me a second."

I send Tynan a message saying there was a change in plans and that I'll call him soon. I look back at Declan hoping to continue what we started but he's gotten up from the couch and is pacing the floor.

"I feel like I should apologize. I don't normally do things like this…ask girls back to my place so quickly. I hope you don't get the wrong idea. I uh…I don't know…There's something so familiar about you, but that doesn't excuse…Anyway, I'm sorry, Ellie."

I feel my heart sink to the floor in an undignified heap. He regrets this. Am I supposed to feel like a fool because I don't? It's not supposed to be this confusing.

I scramble to pick up my phone and purse. "Oh, it's ok. I should be going…" And then all of a sudden I feel angry. Why the hell is he playing these games? I don't deserve this. "Wait a sec. So you wanted to ask me back here, you wanted to kiss me and now you don't?" There's a tone of bravery in my voice I barely recognize.

"Well, it's just…"

"Just what? What is it, Declan? What?" I ask, unable to contain my impatience.

"I don't know. It's messed up. I don't know you, but I feel like I do. More than that, I feel like I will only hurt you. But the really strange thing about that is I can't imagine how! All I want to do is take you in my arms and never look back, but this stupid nagging voice in my head says you're way too good for me."

He's worked up now. I can tell he wasn't expecting to blurt all of that out. His breathing is heavy, thick with fear.

"I see." I mumble, not knowing what else to say. I put my coat on and walk over to him placing a kiss on his cheek. "I'm all for slowing down Declan, but I like you. I'm confused too, but I do know that I want to see you again. I won't make you go against your gut though. If you want to see me, you know where to find me." I walk out the door.

I can feel him watching me; his helplessness is palpable. Part of me feels like crying and the other part of me feels like I should have expected this. It all happened so fast.

I take a deep breath thinking how hard it will be to wait two days to see Mrs. Dawes. I have a lot of questions that need answers.

Right now it seems like looking into the past is my best bet. I don't want to wait. I want to see.

Mrs. Dawes always said to pay attention to my intentions. I go to bed that night asking what my mother calls 'that still, small voice within' for a favour: To see more of my life as Louisa.

She is a sister soul; she is me. I am rewarded in dreams.

CHAPTER 11

William

Mr. William Mara could hardly believe where he was. Sitting in the drawing room of the home of Sir Thomas De vale on Turks Row would have been beyond anything he could imagine only five short years ago.

Upon finding the home he had counted fourteen windows on the facade alone. And now he sat in a room three times the size of his own drawing room with the largest hearth he had ever seen. The furniture was elegant and tasteful, nothing gaudy nor boastful about it at all. He had not known what to expect, but it was clear that the De vales, while wealthy beyond imagination, were not garish. They were comfortable in their station in life and it seemed, comfortable in their own skin.

William ached to know what that would feel like.

Growing up poor in London taught him many things, but foremost in his mind right at this moment was gratitude... gratitude and a solemn vow that all he had attained would never slip through his fingers. Working at the dockyards and apprenticing with an abusive fishmonger from the age of 13, William had gained many skills. He also had the good sense to know there was nothing dignified about struggle. He had seen what poverty had done to his parents. He had borne witness to the ugliness of it, the sheer helplessness. It disgusted him.

No, he would never be poor again.

William's father, Matthew Mara, was a gentleman and the second son of a wealthy and noble family in Ireland. The Mara family holds a great estate in the county of Tipperary as well as a town home in London. Matthew wanted for nothing. He attended Oxford and after his graduation had gone to London for the Season. While he was expected to marry well within his sphere, his family had not pressured him to find a bride quickly.

He was free to be a bachelor and took advantage of this freedom often.

Much to his surprise, William's father found love in London and in his own home. Olivia, a chambermaid, was in Matthew's eyes, perfect: An angel from Manchester with hair like a raven's feathers and lips the colour of poppies. She spoke softly though her accent was rough. She moved in long graceful strides as if changing sheets were a dance, not a chore. Matthew was captivated and soon Olivia was with child.

Their marriage meant that he was disinherited and they were forced to leave the house. Olivia had some small savings, but these quickly ran out. Matthew, being a gentleman, was not particularly skilled in anything. It had been his intention to enter the militia, but now he could not afford to purchase a commission. He eventually found work as a clerk in a bookshop and William's mother did laundry for some families nearby. Even though they were often cold and their meals were scant, William noted his parents never seemed unhappy. His father looked at his mother as if he were under a spell. Their love for one another was palpable.

Indeed, his parents had two of the most generous hearts he had ever encountered, but he noted bitterly that it got them nowhere. In William's eyes their love brought only destitution and disease. In the end they died when he was a mere twelve years old, within days of each other, feverish and delirious. William could only hope there was a heaven for if there was, they were surely there together.

"Mr. Mara? The master and Miss De vale will see you now," called the butler.

"Very good, I thank you." His voice was even, but in actuality his mind was racing. Miss De vale would be there too? Whatever for? The only thing that bothered him more than this news was his reaction to it. After all, why should it matter if a woman was present? What could she possibly have to say on the matter?

58

William was led down the seemingly endless hall to a large black door. The butler announced him and he entered. Sir Thomas was seated behind a grand oak desk and looked sincerely pleased to see him. Miss De vale was sitting on an ornate chaise lounge to the left of her father, her hair pinned becomingly and her hands folded neatly on her lap. She looked at him with an open smile that momentarily disarmed him. He had not expected her to look at him directly. Upon hearing Sir Thomas, he was brought back to the purpose of his visit.

"Ah, Mr. Mara! How good it is to see you again," he stood to greet the younger man. "Do have a seat. I am anxious to hear your proposal! You have not yet had the pleasure of meeting my daughter Louisa; am I correct?" Sir Thomas asked, sweeping his arm in Miss Louisa's direction.

"That is correct indeed, sir. It is a pleasure to meet you Miss De vale," he said bowing before her.

"The pleasure is all mine, Mr. Mara; I assure you," she replied bowing her head in return. She looked nothing short of lovely. Her dress was obviously made of the finest silk and its golden yellow colour brought out the green in her eyes brilliantly. She was pretty, that much was certain, but there was more to it. She had an ease and grace about her that said at once she was open to joy and yet she had more than enough to give.

"My dear, did you send for tea?" asked Sir Thomas.

"Yes, father." Louisa said with a knowing smile that had anticipated the question. It was clear that father and daughter knew and understood one another well. William was both pleased and envious to see it.

"Good, good. Alright lad, let us get down to business. Please, tell me more about this proposition," exclaimed Sir Thomas rubbing his hands together quickly. He had an easy joy about him that was infectious.

William heartily agreed and pulled out the plans for the fishing village from his satchel and spread them out on the desk.

The project was planned by the British Fisheries Society, who William was representing, but they needed more capital from private investors. He explained that the drawings came from Thomas Telford himself, a renowned Scottish engineer. Mr. Telford would be there to oversee some of the construction as well. He spoke slowly, deliberately so. It would not do for Sir Thomas to guess at his desperation. It would not do at all.

Louisa

Louisa listened intently as Mr. Mara described the intentions for the village. It was apparent he was a passionate man and keen on her father's participation in the project. She watched as he pointed out various areas on the plans and explained how much money he was expecting would be required. She noticed that from time to time he would look at her out of the corner of his eye, but would not actually address her directly. She took no offence. She knew men seldom sought the opinion of ladies. This was another reason she had no wish for marriage. Her father respected and trusted her and even desired her opinion. It was probable that a husband would want no such thing.

Trying her best to take in all she was hearing, Louisa found that she loved the sound of Mr. Mara's voice. At times she thought she detected a touch of cockney in his accent, but as quickly as it came it would then disappear. She also could not deny how handsome he was. She was again taken aback by the darkness of his eyes and the stunning likeness they had to his hair.

He was dressed well, though he did not seem exactly comfortable in his expensive clothes. At times he would fiddle with his neck cloth, though Louisa could not blame him. Cravats seemed constricting and entirely ridiculous as far as she could tell.

Her musings were temporarily interrupted by the tea being

brought in. She offered to pour it out herself and presented both gentlemen with a cup.

"And you are certain, sir that this is all the money that you are anticipating will be required?" Sir Thomas asked and then cooled his tea with a long breath.

"It is an estimate, sir, based on past projects though I am aware that weather on Mull is unpredictable. Of course it would be preferable to begin this project in the summer, but it cannot be put off any further, I fear. My fellow men at the BFS have tried other investors but to no avail. You are, it would seem, our last hope," finished Mr. Mara quietly.

"Well, Mr. Mara, I do think your estimate is a trifle naïve, but it is no matter. I will mention however, that Mull is known to be haunted..."

Mr. Mara looked like a child who had been caught stealing a sweet. "Sir, I..."

"Did you think I would not consider that aspect? Mrs. De vale had told me many a tale," said Sir Thomas, his mouth in a tight line suppressing a smile.

Louisa knew her father was teasing the poor gentleman. She was about to interrupt, but thought the better of it. With no small trace of guilt, she enjoyed seeing Mr. Mara needlessly anxious.

"My dear Mary told me that a strange spell can sometimes be cast upon mortals by fairies. This spell causes them to believe they must leave the island, be it by land, sea or death." Standing and pulling himself to his full height for dramatic effect he continued, "There is also the headless horseman and not to mention the Bean-nighe. You have heard of it, Mr. Mara?"

"I uh...a little, sir."

He pretended not to hear him. "Bean-nighe, some Scottish spirit or other who, it is said, can be seen washing the clothes of those soon to die."

Unable to contain it any longer, Louisa burst out laughing and quickly covered her mouth. "Father please, have pity on poor Mr. Mara."

William's look of confusion only spurred her further. She tried, in vain, to apologize but the words were muffled by her giggles.

"Yes, my dear!" he laughed and went over to Mr. Mara to clap him on the back. "Sir, I am sorry; I jest! Of course we do not believe in these ghost stories. And with regards to your proposition, I like what I see so far and I especially like the idea of investing in an area so dear to my late wife's heart." Her father paused to stroke his chin, pondering something. "I think though, I should like to be in Mull during the construction."

Louisa looked up suddenly, her reverie from staring at William now interrupted. "Father, you cannot be serious! Surely there is no call for that. Mr. Mara can communicate all the goings-on via Post. Can you not, sir?" asked Louisa as she turned to him.

Mr. Mara seemed unsure how to respond, as if trying to decide who held the power of decision, she or her father. At length he replied, "Yes of course I could do that, Miss De vale." He turned to Sir Thomas, "If however, you feel so passionate about overseeing the construction, sir, I could not deny you the satisfaction. And I hope it goes without saying that your counsel would be most welcome."

Seeing her father torn between what he wanted and what she asked of him, she decided to concede. And though he had not mentioned bringing her along for the journey, Louisa knew that he had always wanted her to see her mother's birthplace.

Louisa could not help but think that Mr. Mara underestimated her influence, however. She narrowed her eyes at him as she said, "Oh nicely done, sir. You have played that well. Mr. Mara, I hazard to guess that you are quite skilled at games of strategy. Am I wrong?"

"You are not wrong, madam" said William evenly.

Her mouth curled up slightly at his remark and Louisa knew he was stifling a grin. She did so enjoy a challenge. Yes, Mr. Mara would most certainly prove to be a worthy adversary.

Sir Thomas looked back and forth between the two of them. "Then it is settled? Will you not come with me, Louisa? You have never been to Scotland. You must wish to see it?" he asked, hopefully.

Louisa smiled at her father's attempt to appease her. He was such a dear man and she could never deign to disappoint him. A voice whispered in the back of her mind: "Go".

"Yes father, I believe I would." She glanced over at Mr. Mara. "Well, sir, when are we to leave?"

CHAPTER 12

Declan

I awake with the kind of headache that is totally unfair considering I only had one glass of wine. My body is punishing me and I deserve it. I wanted her like I have never wanted anyone and I let her leave.

It's overwhelming, but I haven't ever been so completely certain of anything like this: I will want her forever.

The problem is that I've hurt her. It's not clear to me how I have hurt her; it's not clear when, but I know that I did. Or maybe a new symptom of my insanity is that I now see the future. Maybe I'm sensing the inevitable epic mistake before I even make it.

It's best that she left.

But I don't believe that either. There's more to this; I know there is. Maybe it's up to me to make a pre-emptive strike on my usual fuck-ups. Perhaps there is still time to fix me. It's possible I'm not the hopeless case I believe I am.

She could help...Ellie could show me how to be, what to say. I could remember myself in her laughter and that incredible skin. I swear I could get drunk on her skin. There should be a Twelve-Step program for skin like hers.

More than this though, she is a light. I want to stand before her brightness and be consumed by her. Let her wash over me until I fade into it and become it.

Christ, that's desperate.

What could I possibly be to Ellie but a burden? I'm too sad, too broken. I can't let the promise of her be the thing that pulls me through. It's sketchy, temporary. She is not a lifeline; she is a woman even if the very word could never in a million years encompass her.

She has already given me so much.

Too much.

I take my phone out of my pocket to check the time.

Shit. I've got to meet Dad.

I pray that I see her today. Even if it's just glimpsing her golden hair across the bay, I will be a happy man.

Heaven help me, I will be a happy man.

Ellie

Waking at dawn was never a habit of mine, but I am excited. It feels so good to be excited about something again. Pushing aside the previous night, I move forward undaunted. It is as if my life has been on snooze for the past ten years and now I am finally ready to awaken. Before these past few days I had been nowhere, had no desire to learn new things or even meet new people.

Now I am thirsty for what lies ahead. I am on the cusp of a new life, or at the very least on the brink of looking at my life in an entirely new way.

My visions have always been something that made me feel separate from other people. Mrs. Dawes understood of course, but I always considered her a surreal being, someone who – by virtue of her understanding - was a freak like me and therefore didn't count.

Now though, the visions seemed to be bringing me closer to someone, to Declan. And while it was clear this threatened the serenity I had been trying to cultivate, I was willing to relent...a little...for now.

The dreams from the night before of Louisa and William leave me longing for more answers and even more than that. I want to see them again, to feel their connection and know it has been reborn in me and in Declan.

Without a thought for breakfast or even coffee I quickly dress and head downstairs to the front door.

A soft, loving voice stops me in my tracks.

"Where are you off to so early, Ellie? I didn't think your shift at the shop was until this afternoon," asks my mother. She's still in her pyjamas, a messy blonde ponytail on top of her head. Her early morning ease reminds me how young she still is.

"It's not. I'm going to see Mrs. Dawes," I tell her quickly, gathering my things. Frances leans against the wall, warming her hands with her mug of coffee. I can tell my brief answer will not satisfy.

"Mrs. Dawes? Why? Are your visions back?"

I drop my shoulders, preparing for a conversation I had been wishing to avoid. "They never left, Mom. They've gotten worse though. Well, not worse exactly, but much stronger and more vivid."

I tie my scarf around my neck and look back at my mother. I know she's concerned and yet she doesn't want to pry. I don't know how I would feel if I was in her shoes, but I know I can't ignore the look in her eyes.

I turn fully to face her. "Ever since I met this guy, Declan, the visions are more like movies in my mind's eye. I can sense how everyone in the picture is feeling, what they're saying and who they are. It's unlike any other vision I've had. And he's there," I tell her.

She looks puzzled. "Who's there? This Declan?"

"Yes. I don't know what it all means yet, but I know I'm supposed to help him. Or maybe we're supposed to help each other."

She considers my words. "Have you told him? Does he have visions too?"

I shake my head. "I haven't told him. As far as I know he doesn't have visions, but he has told me a few times how familiar I am to him."

My mom's eyes widen and her jaw drops. "Ellie, this is wild. What a mind-blowing gift! This is some pretty far-out shit. Who was this guy in the lifetime you're seeing? Is it just one lifetime?"

Her blue eyes are lit up and her ponytail bobs up and down as she speaks.

"Since I met him it's been the same lifetime. We're in England and I think it's the late 1700s. He's a businessman in his late twenties. He's very guarded and also very handsome. I'm the daughter of a wealthy gentleman. I look a lot like you come to think of it. It appears he and I end up having some sort of relationship, but not much has been shown to me yet. Something major happens though, Mom. That much I can tell. That's why I've got to get to Mrs. Dawes. She's been doing the regressions. I want to figure out all of these things before Declan goes back to London," I say opening the door to leave.

I'm running down the hill, past the inn. The sun is warm in my face and the wind is cold, but I barely notice. I cannot remember a time when I've felt more alive. I see now that I have been so afraid. There is a world that has been beckoning to me since I can remember, and I have been doing my damndest to shut it out. I have felt the peace of it, the loving endlessness and yet I have resisted it.

This physical world, this earth is so full of pain. And the other world, which I have only felt in silence, is so free of it. I have longed for something in the middle, somewhere to hide. I sense that one exists simply to steer me back to the other. There is nowhere to hide.

Running and floating at the same time, half-afraid and half-delighted, I almost run right into Declan and his father...

"Whoa! Slow down Ellie? Where are you running to?" asks Declan with a look of shock to see me. Thankfully he doesn't seem too disappointed.

"Sorry, I didn't see you guys there! I'm...uh, I'm going to the health food store."

Alistair looks mildly amused. "It's 7:30 in the morning, my dear. I doubt it's open yet. You are, of course, more than welcome to join us if you wish."

Trying to calm my breathing my words are clipped, "Normally, I would love to, but I'm meeting Mrs. Dawes...the owner of the store. It's important we have enough time... before she has to open."

Alistair raises an eyebrow at me. "Mrs. Dawes? I've heard a bit about her. She's some kind of a psychic right? Why are you going there?"

"Geez, Dad, leave her alone." He's embarrassed. There is something about seeing his blushing face that makes me long to have seen him as a child. How precious he must have been.

"Listen, I'm working at the shop until six. You can meet me there if you want and we could grab a bite," I say to Declan, holding his eyes hostage with my own. My daring amazes even me, but then I feel like it's not even me talking.

Alistair looks surprised at my bluntness, but says nothing. Declan smiles nervously. "Sure. Sounds good," he says. His hands are in his pockets, his eyes on the ground. I try to pretend not to notice that he cannot seem to face me.

I remind myself he doesn't know about our connection and what it all could mean. How could he? I feel as though I can barely fathom it myself.

Letting myself into The Natural Touch, I begin to feel calmer. There's almost a sense that I'm following a script and it's a relief. All I have to do is wake up in the morning and go where I feel pulled to go, say what I feel compelled to say. I'm on the verge of something here...some secret to living maybe?

I never thought much about it before, but it's like I'm suddenly aware of the tension I had been carrying because I feel the lightness now.

"Hi Ellie, how are you, love? Come in; have a seat. My, you look lovely today! You look...happier," says Mrs. Dawes. She is eating a crisp green apple that matches the colour of her T-shirt.

She wipes her mouth with the back of her hand and motions to the sofa. "So, any more visions since we met last?"

"Yes I..."

She closes her eyes and waves her hand. "Don't tell me, love! I think it's best that we get right to it. I'm glad you're making progress though. Remember, it's your mind. You can direct it as you wish. You are not at anyone's whim. If you want to know a date, ask that it be shown to you. If you want to see more of your surroundings, just ask. It's ok to be curious. Got it?"

"Got it," I say firmly.

I lay back and let my mind drift back to the time and place that is most helpful to me right now.

In the soft background of my awareness I hear her counting down from ten. My thoughts relax, a door opens and I am a new woman, now watching from above, patient and loving, ready to see.

CHAPTER 13

Louisa

Days of fog, rain and mud made for weary travels, but Louisa, her father and two of their servants arrived safe and sound in Oban, Scotland at the Pillar & Post to rest for the night. Mr. Mara had travelled separately as he had business in Manchester, but was to meet them this evening.

They would all take a boat to Mull in the morning and would arrive in the village by dinner. There was a small inn near the shore that would house everyone during the construction. It was unclear how long their stay in Mull would be. Sir Thomas reckoned it would be six months at least. Louisa had never been away from their London home for so long and never so far, but she felt safe and secure. Truly, she was beginning to feel that she was exactly where she belonged.

The Pillar & Post was a modest Scottish inn. The décor was minimal, but the fires were well-tended and the rooms comfortable. It was a welcome sojourn after some rather questionable establishments along the way. Louisa was unaccustomed to such rustic accommodations, but then she was unaccustomed to travel of any kind. Sir Thomas preferred to stay in London as their country home in Gloucestershire only reminded him of his wife.

Louisa was content to stay in town not only for her father's sake, but for her own. She felt the need to be rooted and stable. All she wanted was to read, to pray and to live quietly. Travelling here and there all the time would be distracting.

This trip to Mull however, felt different. London was so crowded, loud and yet vapid somehow. If she was honest, it had begun to feel as though it was closing in on her. As much as she had wanted things to stay the same, her intuition was tugging at her to embrace change. Louisa had always been unafraid to be herself, but lately she had felt guided by an inner voice, a voice she believed was Mary, Mother of God. She did not think it was God Himself, but she knew it was of Him.

Whenever she heard the voice, she closed her eyes and could see a faint outline of a woman, her head bowed in prayer, a halo of light atop her crown. The voice had been offering her wisdom and insight. She hoped to hear it more clearly. Perhaps this was why Mull was coming into her life. Perhaps Mother Mary was guiding her here, preparing her to learn how to better serve.

William

Miss De vale, her father and Mr. Mara agreed to meet in the dining hall and go over the plans for their arrival in Mull. The end of the journey was near and each was beginning to feel a renewed energy at the prospect of reaching their final destination.

William was the first to arrive in the hall. It was a relief to change out of his travelling attire. Only recently had he treated himself to some new clothes. It seemed almost surreal to purchase items from the finer tailors in London. He hardly knew what to buy and required much direction.

A woman's opinion would have been most welcome.

The truth of the matter was that he rarely met women who were not barmaids or servants. Of course he would visit a brothel every now and then, but conversation was rarely had or desired. Many of his business associates had daughters, but it seemed to be the prevailing opinion amongst them that he was far too young to consider settling down.

William took a table and waited for the rest of his party. He spotted Louisa coming down the stairs and entering the room. Trying to push away the flutter in his chest, he waved to her discreetly. She saw him and smiled immediately and as William rose to greet her, she settled herself directly across from him.

"Good evening, Miss De vale," he said attempting to keep his gaze at her face. She wore a simple, light blue dress that flowed and swayed effortlessly. She was effortless. "It is a pleasure to see you again. May I inquire about your journey? I know the weather has been uncooperative. I hope you have not been overly put out."

"You are indeed kind to inquire, Mr. Mara. I will admit that I have been chilled often, but I know it is my own fault for not bringing proper gloves. And I hope I am not being too open in telling you that my bottom has been quite sore from all the bumps in the road. I have to laugh at myself. It is an adventure though is it not?" she said giggling. "But I see I have shocked you with my frankness. I do apologize, sir. I suppose I feel as though we are friends already."

William looked down at his lap and shifted uncomfortably in his chair. Was she in earnest or was she teasing him? It annoyed him that she had the power to unnerve him so. "I am sure that is a compliment, madam," he replied calmly.

She laughed at him, "I am not altogether sure that it is! Would you choose to be friends with the likes of me...someone who says every little silly thing in her head?"

"I would be honoured I am sure."

She smiled widely at his diplomacy. "Yes well, Mr. Mara I can honestly tell you I am finding this trip thrilling. Indeed sir, comfort or not I am grateful to be here. A lady such as myself is rarely treated with this kind of excitement!"

William could not help but smile at her declaration. It was refreshing to see someone of high society put propriety aside just a little. Miss De vale, it would seem, was not silly. She simply did not take herself so seriously. He knew he could learn from her. "I believe it is good to laugh at oneself from time to time. I know that I have a penchant for severity. It is a fault perhaps, but it does often help me in business," said William trying to keep the conversation somewhat formal.

He knew if he let his guard down with her, he would be lost. He had already caught himself staring at her long neck accented with a simple opal cross as well as her graceful hands. He longed to reach for both. Yes if he was not careful, Louisa De vale would know his every secret in under an hour.

"Does it really? I had no notion that the members of the British Fisheries Society were so severe," she winked at him lightly. William pressed his lips together to stifle a laugh. "You do not find it helpful to relate to your clients in a less formal way? Are you afraid, sir, that they will not like you? Or are you afraid that they will think you do not know what you are doing?"

William felt his face grow dark and he looked away for a moment. She reached across the table to gently touch his arm. "Sir, I meant no offence. I was only teasing. Can you forgive me?" she pleaded.

He looked down at her hand and she quickly removed it. The warmth of her touch still lingered. "Yes of course, Miss De vale. You did offend me I suppose, but it was true what you said. I am afraid. I am afraid of being poor again. That fear drives me to keep going, so in that respect I am grateful for it. To have it pointed out to me by someone such as you is…I do not know. I suppose it stung a little harder," he replied but he could not bring himself to look her in the eye.

"Someone such as me, you say? I hope you know Mr. Mara, I see you as an equal. I do not know your background, but it does not matter to me. Truly, it does not." She leaned toward him as if to convey her earnestness. "It is obvious that I have no knowledge of what it is like to be poor and so I will make no attempts to comment on that aspect of your life except to say I admire you. My father had told me that you have built yourself from nothing. It cannot have been easy to achieve what you have. I am in awe of you, sir," she said softly.

William looked down, suddenly uncomfortable. "I did not

mean it in that…" he began, but then stopped himself. "I thank you, Miss De vale. You are too kind."

"Now I seem to have offended you once more. Allow me to make one general apology and if you would be so generous as to apply it to the remainder of the evening I would be most obliged to you. I fear I cannot be trusted!" It was clear that she only wanted to bring him comfort. William allowed himself to chuckle briefly and she continued, "Do you know, sir I don't believe I even know the name of the village we are headed to! Does it have a name yet?" she inquired.

"It does indeed, madam. The local folk call it "Tobermory". Apparently there is a well dedicated to the Virgin Mary in the village. It comes from the Scottish Gaelic, Tobar Mhoire, which means "Mary's well".

"The Virgin Mary? How wonderful!" Louisa paused a moment. "I pray to her often. And lately I have been able to hear her guidance. I know it is unusual, but I will say it has been most helpful to me, especially since my mother's death." She dropped her head a moment, afraid perhaps that she had said too much.

"I am happy to hear that you found comfort during such a difficult time." He studied her for a moment. How could a young woman be so lively, so lovely and yet so pious? He had never before witnessed such a thing. "Miss De vale, you are a curious young woman."

"Strange is the word I believe you meant to use, Mr. Mara." He started to protest but she stopped him, a mischievous grin playing about her face. "No, no! It is quite alright. I am a strange young woman."

She was doing it again, reeling him in and enchanting him.

This was not a good sign.

As embarrassing as it was to be undone by this lady, it was even more embarrassing that he did not want it to stop. He had designed his life for business and prosperity. Flirtation with a nobleman's daughter did not figure into his equation. Still, he could not be rude to her, but was there really any sense in engaging her? It would go nowhere and he could not risk disapproval in any way from Sir Thomas.

"You mistake me, madam. I was thinking no such thing," he replied politely.

Louisa sighed and looked about the room. She appeared disappointed.

It occurred to William that she must long for some female company. "Forgive me, Miss De vale, but I had thought you would have a lady's companion with you on this trip and yet I find you here alone..."

Louisa interrupted, "I have no companion. Father wished me to procure one to accompany us to Scotland, but I saw no need. We have brought two servants, Janey and Edward. Certainly that shall suffice."

William shook his head in bewilderment, "But, how is one maid possibly apt to serve your needs?"

"I beg your pardon. You have an inkling of my needs, sir?" asked Miss De vale with a stifled smirk.

Collecting himself before he was any further embarrassed, William took a deep breath. "I meant only, madam that I assume you are accustomed to a certain lifestyle. Mull will be isolated and unrefined enough as it is. With only two servants, you may have to carry out some tasks yourself and..."

"Heaven forbid!" she declared with mock severity.

And William had to laugh at that. Though she may not have any idea what she was in for, he could do nothing but admire her willingness to try. He hoped it would not end in disaster. The last thing he needed was for Sir Thomas to change his mind about supporting the construction in Tobermory because his daughter had, at length, decided she could no longer tolerate styling her own hair. If he was honest with himself however, he would admit that Louisa De vale did not seem like such a woman. Quite the opposite...indeed she appeared to be the sort of woman who could do anything.

William saw her flush from cheek to chest bone and realized it was because he had been staring at her. He shuddered to think what his look bespoke. He reached up to tug at his cravat which seemed to choke him all of a sudden...even more than usual.

Miss De vale appeared to search for something to say, "Yes, well, I do believe my father shall be joining us any minute now." She spoke quickly and motioned for the barmaid to attend them.

CHAPTER 14

Louisa

The next morning Louisa was escorted by her father to the coach that would take them on to the dock where a boat would be waiting to ferry them all to Craignure, a small port village on the Isle of Mull.

As Louisa entered the coach she saw that on one of the seats lay a cushion and a pair of fur-lined gloves. She looked about the coach as if to spy a clue as to how the items appeared, but everything else looked untouched. With a mixture of satisfaction and confusion, Louisa sat on the cushion and tried on the gloves. Each was perfect. Her father gave her a questioning glance, but she was not offering any answers.

Settling in to her newfound luxury, Louisa allowed her thoughts to drift back to all she had seen on her travels. So much of Scotland appeared to be untouched by man. She liked that. It was thrilling to be venturing into such virgin territory, full of silence and plenty of room to breathe. Spirit could be heard in these wide, open spaces.

She closed her eyes and after a moment she heard: *You are free.*

She inhaled deeply and felt a gentle smile spread across her face. The risk of Scotland was paying off.

None of her London acquaintances, she thought to herself, would appreciate the landscape that was before her. Louisa had glimpsed what looked like eagles and had even spotted a pack of sea lions, animals of which she had only seen drawings in books.

She could feel herself surrendering to this country, not willing it to change but instead allowing it to change her.

Stepping onto the questionable boat that would take them to Mull, Louisa was admittedly cold, but full of excitement. She looked about her and allowed the wild and rugged shores to fill her senses. She resisted the urge to spin round and round.

Biting her lip, she tasted salt. It baked itself into her every pore, as if the sea were trying to claim her as its own. The wind was relentless and she had given up on her hair days ago. Strands of it stuck to her face, smothered by the joint forces of water and air. Looking back at Oban she noticed what appeared to be a castle that she had not seen while they were waiting for their vessel.

"That is Dùn Ollaigh. It belongs to the infamous MacDougall clan. They no longer live there, however." Mr. Mara had materialized behind her and read her train of thought. His voice was low and gentle, causing Louisa to feel as though he had been observing her for some time. "Are you warm enough, Miss De vale?"

Louisa nodded in reply. She could swear she detected admiration in his manner, but she refused to think about that right now. These were ideas she could not be overwhelmed by just yet.

Her gaze moved to her father who was staring across the sea wearing a look of longing. She knew without question that he was thinking of his wife.

"My father misses my mother every minute of every day, I think." Louisa lowered her eyes at the confession. It was personal information, too personal perhaps, but she had no one else with whom to share these things. "I know not how to comfort him except to simply be myself."

"That seems most wise." His hand was flexing next to his thigh as if he wished to reach for something, but was schooling himself to pause.

"I was young, you know, too young one might say to know what love looked like, but I swear to you, Mr. Mara, my parents had love. They respected one another. They were companions of the truest kind."

He smiled slightly at her words. "*Anam cara*" he whispered and let his voice trail off.

Louisa searched his face. "I beg your pardon?"

"*Anam cara*. It is Gaelic. It means friend of the soul, one who sees you exactly as you are."

She smiled and reached for his hand, squeezing it gently, briefly. "Yes," she said with a deep breath. "That's it exactly."

William's hand relaxed. Indeed, his entire manner seemed to relax, as if he had wanted to speak to her of this long ago. "I suppose it is not so romantic," he said with a half-smile.

She shook her head. "Who could possibly require romance after forming such a connection? What else could be more important?" She spoke as if she was offended at his comment. When he looked away from her, she knew she had once again gone too far. What was it about Mr. Mara that let her thoughts escape through her mouth unchecked?

Louisa resolved to hold her tongue and just simply breathe. She had learned many things today, but more important, she now had the words for all she longed for.

William

Arriving in Craignure, the party was led into two carriages: one for the servants, the other for Sir Thomas, Louisa and William. Sir Thomas helped his daughter into the coach and got in himself placing a large satchel on the seat next to him. When Mr. Mara poked his head into the coach he could see the only empty seat was next to Miss Louisa. William cleared his throat in hopes of bringing the older man's attention to the matter, but he did not appear to hear him. Sighing loudly, William decided to relent and settled himself in beside Miss Louisa. When the coach started moving, Sir Thomas looked up, eyed Mr. Mara strangely and then shrugged it off.

Silence fell around the party for a while until the gentle rhythm of Sir Thomas' snoring took over. William decided this was a good time to engage Miss De vale in conversation, but she anticipated him.

"Mr. Mara, I have not yet had the opportunity to thank you for my gifts. You see for yourself that the gloves do fit perfectly. I am in your debt, sir."

He looked away briefly and then revealed a quick tight smile. "Think nothing of it, Miss De vale. I merely did not want to be the source of any discomfort you may have."

She laughed at him. "How could you be the source of my discomfort? Are you responsible for the rain? The cold? You do appear to be quite talented, Mr. Mara, but I fear the weather is beyond even your superior abilities to control." She tried to catch his gaze, but he kept eluding her.

Trying to hide his discomfort he ventured, "I meant only that I am the one who invited your father to participate in this venture, madam and through him you are here too. I implied no black magic on my part and I think you know that." Her joking was relentless and he could have no part of it. Even if he did love to see her eyes light up when she looked at him, it was all for nothing.

Though perfectly lovely, Miss Louisa had nothing to do with the task at hand. He had to stay focused.

"Do not make yourself uneasy, sir. I am here because it is where I am supposed to be. That is all," she said, her tone now serious.

"Yes, of course. I did not mean to imply that you should be separated from your father." He had caused her smile to vanish and it left him with a pit of regret in his stomach.

Seeing his reaction, Miss De vale seemed to take pity on him. "I know you did not. I am always where I am supposed to be and at this moment, that means I am supposed to be with you."

William started at her words. Her benevolence was plain. It was a hard feeling to shake, but she reminded him so much of his mother and this thought both comforted and disconcerted him. Clearing his throat he attempted to rid his mind of these thoughts and began a new line of conversation. "Miss De vale, do you and your father often spend time at your family's manor?"

She appeared to be momentarily caught off-guard. "Overfield? No sir, not at all. I spent more time there as a child, but of late father prefers town. You can imagine how surprised I was when he was so eager to agree to this. A jaunt all the way to the Isle of Mull is very much out-of-character for him. I do see the wisdom in it now, or at least I am beginning to."

Was she again referring to him? William looked down at her hands clasped neatly in her lap. She was so close to him. If he moved his leg but an inch it would grace hers.

Was it worth the torture?

He decided it was and allowed his knee to brush hers briefly. He shuddered and coloured, hoping desperately she could not tell though she seemed to hide a satisfied grin.

William reached for his cravat in an attempt to loosen it and lessen the heat with which he was now overcome. When exactly had he transformed into a thirteen year old boy? This would not do. He sighed loudly and vowed that he would rein this in, this silly inclination...this doomed infatuation.

CHAPTER 15

Ellie

"Well then, love!" exclaimed Mrs. Dawes as she brought me back to the present day. "This keeps getting better and better. It may seem slow, but we're building to something. I know it. If you like though, we can set intentions at our next session to fast forward to the hurt or pain in this lifetime. What do you think?"

I sat up and pondered the suggestion. "I think this is all unfolding exactly as it should," I say quietly. I am feeling humbled by the experience. It is an honour to witness the lives of these people, to feel their happiness and their struggle. "Let's keep going the way we have been. I feel that would be best."

"Of course, Ellie, if that's how you feel. I think that is very wise. You have an intuition; we all do. For Louisa, it is the symbol of Mother Mary that represents her inner wisdom. Yours may just be a gut feeling, or you may also have a guide. Just use it, whatever it is. When you use it without fear you learn; you grow and you heal. There is a current that carries you, my child. Ride it and be unafraid. You are taken care of," she says almost wistfully. I could swear her eyes were moist with unshed tears.

She sits back in her chair and looks at me as if it were the first or the last time.

"I sense that too." I reply. "In these short few days I feel like I've been able to control the visions so much better. I'm not getting those painful flashes every time I'm in his presence anymore and that dream last night...I asked for that."

I had to smile. I was getting this. However small my progress, I was getting it. "Thanks so much Mrs. Dawes. I'll come back tomorrow. I'm going to see Declan tonight. That seems to incite very vivid memories. I imagine there will be lots to reveal tomorrow." I put on my coat, gather my things and bend down to hug her. "Really, I cannot thank you enough."

Her voice is gentle: "Ellie, think nothing of it."

Declan

There is not enough liquor in the world in which to drown myself so I dump the wine down the drain. Frustrated, I walk over to the window. The wind is fierce and what little leaves remain on the trees will surely be shook free tonight. I am safe inside. Ellie is safe, or she will be at least.

I already know that I'm a total chicken shit. I know it. Telling myself that she would try and change my mind, I opted to stay here, stand her up and piss her off. She is going to hate me, but really that's what I want. That will make it easier for both of us.

And she will be ok.

It is unbelievable to me that her blond-haired, blue jean-loving friend hasn't spilled the beans. He will though. Especially now. He will be the one to hold her, brush her hair from her face and whisper love in her ear. At least I know he has no desire to take my place.

Someone will though...someday.

I can see the same part of the bay that Ellie is looking out onto from the dive shop. Maybe we are even looking at the water at the same time. That makes me feel better for a minute. That we may, for a short while, share a private moment before she realizes I'm not coming makes me smile. It brings me a modicum of peace and I wonder why I feel like I am saying goodbye to my oldest friend in the world. I have known her only a few days.

But that's not true, is it? No, even I know that isn't true.

If I were a stranger to her, this would be simple. I would be that jerk who stood her up, a frivolous story she would tell her friends at the bar when the silence grew too deep.

But I am not a stranger.

Strangers don't feel the earth move when their eyes meet. She knows me in a way so ancient, so instinctual it frightens me. Her memory of me is surely far superior to my tiny, mad reality. I can't live up to it. There is so much she doesn't know...the details that mar me like pockmarks on an otherwise flawless face.

I couldn't bear to see her disappointed. I could never stomach knowing I was the source of her sorrow. We need a clean break, as clean as could ever be possible.

I will make the break.

There's a knock on the door.

"Yeah?" I call.

"Don't 'yeah' me, laddy, it's your father. Open the door, please."

Oh Christ. This is the last thing I need...

Ellie

The shop is quiet my entire shift. There was a large group going out on charter today and they had already disembarked by the time I started work. Looking out the window I think I can see the boat and imagine all the excitement of those aboard. They are all ready for adventure, to try something new. Declan's father would be on it. Would Declan be there too?

I try to distract myself with tidying the shelves and counting stock, but my mind is on William and Louisa. I try to see me, Ellie, as the same soul as Louisa, but it's difficult. She seems to have been so comfortable in her own skin. She opens her heart and mind effortlessly and just knows that the best thing to do is to surrender.

I've had those feelings, but I bury them. Has Declan come to help me dig them up again?

But I know better than that. He is the catalyst, not the reason. I can't place all my hope in him. I'm better off with the wind. The wind knows where I'm going.

It is now a quarter past six and there is still no sign of Declan. I'm beginning to get anxious. Did I tell him seven by accident?

Did I say I would meet him at the inn? I know that I didn't, but allow the thoughts to grace my mind anyhow.

I resolve to walk to the Town Pump in the hopes of bumping into him along the way. Walking into the back room to grab my things, I hear the door.

"Ellie? Are you still here?" It's Alistair. I make my way to the front to greet him. This can't be good.

"Hi! I'm here. Where's Declan?" I ask trying unsuccessfully to hide my concern.

Alistair hesitates a moment. He face looks grim. "I'm really sorry but Declan won't be meeting you tonight, my dear." I'm disappointed and he knows it. "Can I buy you some dinner? We have a lot to discuss. I'm afraid there's a lot you don't know about Declan, but I think that you deserve to," he says kindly, but I don't appreciate his implication.

"I know that." I said sharply. "Don't you think I know that? We're practically strangers, Alistair. Everyone knows that. But we..." I trail off. My breathing speeds and my heart is racing. Passion seems to come from nowhere when I talk about Declan.

He immediately reaches out to gently touch my arm and give me his reassurance. "It's alright, Ellie. Just come with me. Maybe what I have to say will shed some light for you. Ok?" He is being so nice...so calm and nice, and yet I'm hesitant to trust him. Why? Alistair has always been kind. He and Declan look so alike and of course I can see William in him too: daring, proud and Irish.

I have to relent. That much is clear. I have to hear what Alistair O'Shea has to say.

CHAPTER 16

Ellie

Leafing through the menu at Town Pump, it dawns on me how ridiculous it is to be looking at the menu at all. It has been the same for the past ten years. I know it by heart. I put the menu down and take a gulp of water. Whatever Alistair has to say I will be ok. I tell myself this the whole way over and I continue now. The funny thing is I am actually beginning to believe it.

I order French fries with a salad, and get treated with listening to Alistair explain to Noelle, our waitress, that the food on his plate is not to touch.

"I will send it back if it does, Miss. I'm not threatening you, merely warning you…" he says with a tender earnestness.

I giggle. He'll get his meal on three separate plates, I think to myself. Hopefully, he has a sense of humour.

Alistair turns to me as Noelle plods off, his mood quickly becoming serious. "Ok, Ellie. I'm going to give you a brief history of Declan. Are you ok with that?" he asks.

My heart is in my throat, but I don't want him to know. "Yeah, absolutely; I'm ready. I want to help him, Alistair. I mean that."

"Right, well I'm not sure what you think you can do for him, but I'll just tell you the story and let you decide." He leans on the table and looks me in the eye. "Declan has always been a very sensitive guy. Even when he was little, he was quiet and always seemed to be easily affected by what was going on around him. You could just tell he was listening, but he was feeling too. His mother, Jill, and I separated when he was five years old. The year leading up to our separation he had six ear infections. I swear to you, Ellie, the wee boy just didn't want to hear our fighting anymore. It was awful. It got better after I moved out of the house, but he was still shy and withdrawn. He walked around as if he was carrying a guilty secret. Now you tell me, what could a child possibly have done to feel so much shame? I would joke with him sometimes and try to coax it out of him, but it seldom worked and never for very long. His mother took him to see specialists. For a while there we thought he might be autistic, but he had no problems expressing emotion. He laughed at times, smiled; he enjoyed drawing, playing his guitar and riding his bike. It was just that he had this burden of infinite sadness… like he was mourning something. I've asked him repeatedly over the years if it had to do with his mother and me breaking up. He says no every time. Perhaps it was unfair of me to ask in the first place." Alistair looks away, sad for a moment and then continues.

"He said he knew his mother and I were better off apart. High school seemed to help him a bit. The school he attended had a great music and arts program. Declan really excelled there. He even had a girlfriend for a while. Corinne was her name." He catches my eye as if looking to register jealousy. I nod, urging him to go on. He waves a hand, dismissively, "It never seemed that serious to me, but when they broke up, Declan went into a deep depression that lasted nearly four years. We eventually had him committed to an institution because we were afraid he would hurt himself and we knew he couldn't take care of himself properly either. It was the hardest thing Jill and I have ever done." He paused to take a drink of water.

"He did ok at the institution. It took a while to find the right medication for him, but when they did, Declan seemed to get a little better. I'll never forget the day his doctor called me to tell me that Declan was drawing again. What a relief! He was finally coming around. I asked the doctor what he was drawing and he said that most of the pictures were of a young woman. My heart sank. I knew they must have been of his ex-girlfriend, Corinne. At least this was progress, I thought. Perhaps this was part of his healing process. I decided to go see him the next day and maybe try to talk to him about his drawings."

Alistair pauses as Noelle sets our salads down in front of us.

I have no idea how I'm going to eat any of it. My stomach is tense, as if holding a breath of its own.

"Go ahead," I say. "Continue."

He picks up his fork, but begins his story again before taking a bite. "Ellie, I remember sitting in his room and asking him to look at what he had drawn like it was yesterday. He reached under his bed and pulled out what must have been fifty pieces of foolscap with charcoal sketches on them. I looked at the pictures and they were stunning. The detail and the raw emotions of the girl depicted were exquisite. I looked at every one; I was so impressed and yet really confused. Not one of them was of Corinne, but they were definitely all the same person. I did not recognize the girl in the drawings at all."

He took a deep breath as if willing his voice to still. "That is until one week ago when I walked into the dive shop."

My eyes shoot up to meet him in surprise. I have a vague premonition of what is to come, but I blink it away, needing the words. "What are you saying, Alistair?"

"Ellie, I can't explain it, but my son had drawn countless meticulous pictures of you years before he had even met you."

My throat closes up and I have to struggle for air. So that is why he recognized me! "Alistair, he knows me now! He said he recognized me. Why hasn't he told me about the drawings?" I ask bewildered.

Alistair hangs his head and considers what to say next. It is clear he's caught between protecting his son's secrets and honestly answering my questions. "Ellie, he may remember your face, but I highly doubt he remembers drawing it. A month after I visited him, another patient found his pictures and ripped them to shreds. Declan was beside himself. He even went catatonic for a while and the doctors had to change his meds all over again.

"Apparently he doesn't remember much from his stay at the institution these days. We don't speak about it very often either. He finds it embarrassing and I try to respect that. The past two years have been better. He's living in an apartment in one of the buildings I own. It helps that I can check in on him on a weekly basis. I know that he is twenty-five and shouldn't need a babysitter, but I'm his father and this works for us."

I nod reassuringly at him. It hadn't occurred to me to judge their situation. In fact, I was relieved that Declan had a father who was so concerned.

Alistair's face takes on a shade of pride that had been absent. His smile is gentle as if recalling a pleasant memory as he says, "He's even started playing guitar again. And he's really good. He hasn't drawn in almost three years though. It's a shame. He is really talented."

I take a deep breath trying to absorb all that Alistair has shared. It's mind-boggling and yet not that surprising but it still doesn't explain why Declan stood me up. "Why didn't he come tonight? If he doesn't really recognize me then why is he hiding?"

"I don't know, Ellie. I really can't say. All I know is that when I went to his room he was totally withdrawn. He said he couldn't meet you. He said he knew he would hurt you."

Not that crap again. I can feel the tears in my eyes, but don't have the heart to cry in front of Alistair. "I'm so sorry," I say and put my hand on his arm. "This is all pretty upsetting, but I have to say it's not very surprising." Gathering my courage I resolve to continue, "Alistair, I have to tell you about what's been going on with me since I met Declan, since before that even. Will you hear me out?" I ask.

He nods and I confess everything. I even tell him about the night Declan and I first kissed. It's embarrassing and yet I know that it's necessary. Alistair listens patiently and when I finish he almost seems relieved.

"I don't know what to make of any of this," he says quietly, playing with his fork. "Honestly, I want to just write it off as one big coincidence. Anything beyond that seems...overwhelming."

Putting his fork down, he runs his hands through his hair and says, "Perhaps it's enough already with these visions. What can it help?" When I don't respond he adds, "I'll leave it up to you," and looks down again at his plate.

I look at Alistair closely. His handsome face drawn and worried, I want to reach out and stroke his cheek just to have him look up.

Look up! I want to shout at him.

But I don't. Instead I eat my salad and pray that Noelle brings my fries quickly so I can get the heck out of there. Alistair may be unwilling to go deeper with this, but I'm not. I am more determined than ever to find out what all of this is for.

CHAPTER 17

Louisa

The party was to stay at an abandoned stone cottage not far from the village after all and not the local inn. Her father was dubious at first, but Louisa reassured him.

"Let us consider it as part of the adventure, Father! We are here together. We are safe. Surely comfort can be created. We need only be willing to make the best of it," she said cheerfully. He smiled at her. She knew that his grumblings were always short-lived. It was easy enough to help him see the light.

The first night was unfortunately spent among the dust and the mice, but there was nothing to be done for it. They each knew it was temporary. The next day, the servants cleaned the cottage up well enough and killed as many mice as they could. Even Louisa assisted. She was determined to be useful while her father and Mr. Mara were down in the village overseeing the beginnings of construction. She set her sights on the small kitchen located on the main floor at the back of the house. They had brought some vegetables with them from one of the stops along the way, but all of that had yet to be unpacked. She decided to start.

Though Louisa had been trained in many things; art, music, languages etc, she found that none of these skills were particularly useful outside of society. In Tobermory, they appeared to be frivolous indeed. She laughed at how she could describe a perfectly delicious meal of guinea fowl and roasted vegetables in French, Latin and German, but was at a complete loss as to how to prepare it.

Her predicament grew more ridiculous by the minute. Looking about she realized she had no idea where vegetables were kept. She heard footsteps in the hall. "Hello there?" she called. It was Janey, the scullery maid they had brought from their London home. She was a kindly woman of about forty who had never married. Louisa had interacted with her only a handful of times before this journey, but she always proved to be kind, capable and opinionated. It was a combination that Louisa adored.

"Janey, thank goodness you are here! I am wondering if you could help me." Louisa raised her hand to brush some loose strands of hair from her face, but upon seeing the state of her fingers she thought the better of it. Wiping her hands on an old apron she had found she continued, "I am trying my best to make myself useful and I've just realized I know nothing about kitchens or food or cooking at all. Can you help? I know that I'm keeping you from your other duties, but I thought if you teach me now, I'll know what to do from this point on. What do you think?"

Janey was a head shorter than Louisa and a little wider. Her light brown hair was pulled tightly back into a bun, but her blue eyes shone bright. She had no problem holding her own. "It's not for a lady of your status to be working at all, mum, nor to be asking my opinion now is it? If you want to help though, I can't say no to you." She said with a wink and brought her hands to her hips. "I'll show you where the cellar is and after that I'll take you out back. There are some root vegetables growing in the garden. We're very blessed for that, we are."

Louisa clapped and beamed, "Oh indeed we are, Janey! I am your student. Lead the way if you please!"

She was determined to learn new skills. It was not that she minded the duties of a lady; she did not. She loved running her father's home and felt enormous gratitude for her situation in life. Here now though, was a chance to see her character in a whole new light, to face challenges. She would take advantage of this opportunity and she knew she would be a better and stronger woman for it.

Following Janey to the cellar, she was surprised by the foul smell, but then gently chided herself. London had smells much worse than an old, dingy cellar, to be sure. Janey led her to the wild and overgrown area outside of the kitchen. There was indeed a small garden of what seemed to be yams, onions and carrots. She bent down to dig through the earth and delighted at the feel of the moist soil in her hands. Perhaps they could plant even more!

She was confident that with Janey's help she could create an excellent vegetable garden. It gave Louisa an indescribable sense of satisfaction to be able to contribute to the family meal. This was something that had never crossed her mind before in London. It was not that she was spoiled, more that she had never before been in a position to question where her meals or her clothes or any of her comforts came from.

Rising again and looking about her, the scene took her breath away. It had been nearly dark upon their arrival and so she had not had the opportunity to take in the prospect around the house. The cottage itself was on flat, low ground, and the yard behind it was nothing but a hill that seemed to climb straight up.

She called out to Janey declaring that she would scale the hill to see where they were. Louisa would have to scale the incline using her hands to help her, but she was determined. She had climbed trees as a girl (much to the dismay of her governess), and she was not so much a lady as to find distaste in getting a little dirty.

Reaching the top of the incline she could see that it levelled out for a fair distance before dropping again to the sea. They were along a cliff-side! Louisa had smelt the sea strongly since their arrival, and had thought maybe that was the nature of this island... that the scent of the sea followed you wherever you would go. The hill and the cliff were covered in mossy rocks and heather. At the top of the hill over to her right she glimpsed a pack of red deer eating the moss peacefully, unaware they were being observed.

"Beautiful," she muttered to herself.

Looking out across the sea, she could see for miles. There was a ship in the distance with three great masts and sails. She wondered: who was on it and where were they going? There was a whole world that seemed to beat on without her and when she stepped into it she made it real. By witnessing it, she brought it to life.

The wind whipped her dress and she could feel droplets of salt water on her face. Walking over to the edge of the cliff she looked down at the sudden drop and the jagged rocks below. For a brief second she wondered if the wind would carry her. If she felt with all her might that she could fly, could it happen? Would she be supported by the loving force she was beginning to feel was with her always?

Louisa rolled her eyes in spite of herself. She believed in the divine, but she was not an idiot.

Her hands and feet were filthy and the sight thrilled her. For the next few months she would live anew. She loved this land already and had been here but a day. Raising her eyes to the sky she took a deep breath and felt at peace. Louisa thought of her mother and mused that she was looking at the same sea that her mother would have witnessed. She was walking the same earth and breathing the same air. The idea made her a little sad and yet brought her some sense of comfort. Mary De vale was a force, Louisa remembered that much. She would have given as much strength to this wild place as it would have given her. Louisa smiled at the memory of her mother's blond, fair face. She saw it smiling at her, proud and encouraging. The wind loud in her ears, she did not hear the approach of someone behind her.

William

His breath caught in his throat when he saw her. He had heard of ghosts on Mull, wandering the moors mourning lost loves and lives cuts short. She looked like a spectre there looking out over the sea, half here on earth and half in a world beyond.

William swallowed hard. She was also incredibly close to the cliff! What on earth was she thinking? He ran to her and without a thought for propriety, called out her name.

"Louisa! Louisa! Come away from there!" He waved his arms wildly at her.

Her mien was so casual, as if she was doing nothing wrong at all. "I am quite alright, as you see. I was just enjoying the view. Have you seen it?"

William was grateful that she not did mention his thoughtless use of her Christian name, but what was she doing? "Miss De vale, your father is worried. Janey told him you climbed the hill to come up here. You could have fallen! And standing so close to the cliff's edge? What were you thinking of? It is not safe," he scolded and grabbed her by the wrist to take her back with him. Louisa pulled her arm back and took a deep breath, as if to calm herself.

"Mr. Mara, I thank you for your concern, but as you see I am fine. And there is no need to drag me away as if I am a child," she said kindly, yet firmly.

William's hand still took the shape of having her arm in its grasp. He flexed it to remove the feeling. "I apologize Miss De vale, but seeing you so close to the edge was… was… well, it was very unpleasant. The winds of Tobermory are so strong and you are so… what I mean to say is you need to be careful," he lowered his eyes to his shuffling feet as he spoke.

He had been terrified to see her putting herself in that kind of danger. Why did she do it? Did she not realize the risk she was taking? What would her father do without her? One day, he thought to himself, her over-confidence would be her undoing.

Granted, William knew very few ladies of the *ton*, but those he was familiar with would never dare scale a hill! At this thought William looked down at Louisa's hands; they were covered in mud. What lady would dirty herself so? Come to think of it, what sort of lady would venture off to Scotland without any reassurance of her comfort? She had not even brought a lady's maid. Her defiance made him want to laugh at her, reprimand her and kiss her soundly all at once.

Louisa De vale was indeed singular.

"I will be more careful, Mr. Mara for the sake of my father. I promise you," she said.

He took a step towards her. "Yes of course, for your father's sake. Shall we?"

Louisa took the offer of his arm and they slowly climbed back down the hill using the odd jutted rock as steps. Tentatively taking a step onto a slick stone she quickly lost her balance. William reached for her immediately, but instead of re-positioning her at his side he swept her up and over onto his shoulder. Louisa screamed and he merely grunted in reply. "It's easier this way, madam."

William felt her concede and relax. He focused on each step as much as he could and pushed away the awareness of her body and how it felt to hold her this way. He would lock that memory for now and come back to it later. Right now, he only wanted her safe, unsullied and in one beautiful piece.

CHAPTER 18

Louisa

The first dinner at their temporary home was a rather informal affair. Although it had not been as informal as Louisa would have liked. She had invited the servants to dine with them - to her father's shock and momentary discomfort - but Janey and Edward had politely declined. As Louisa sat down to the table across from her father, she noticed that it was set only for two. When Janey brought out the soup, Louisa inquired as to the whereabouts of Mr. Mara. She was informed that he was to take his meal in his room.

"In his room? Whatever for? Is he ill, Janey?" she asked.

"I don't believe so, mum."

Louisa saw her father lift his spoon and attempt to eat his soup. "Father!" she admonished. "We have not yet said grace and Mr. Mara has not yet joined us."

Sir Thomas sheepishly set down his spoon, disappointed.

"Miss Louisa, I do not think Mr. Mara has any intention of joining you for dinner," said Janey gently.

At this, Sir Thomas once again attempted to eat his soup and once again was halted by his daughter as she levelled a look of warning at him.

"We shall see about that." Louisa set down her napkin and strode up the stairs with purpose.

William

William Mara looked about his room with a mixture of relief and anxiety. It was a comfortable space indeed. The wood-plank floors were pleasantly worn, well-loved. The ceiling was slanted so that he had to duck his head whenever he moved about the room. The furniture, a bed, writing desk and chair, was simple and functional. These things were all good. The anxiety he felt was that their current situation was born out of a comedy of errors.

Several days previous, when he had been in Manchester, he received word that the so-called 'inn' in Tobermory had only two rooms to let and that neither was available. Scrambling, he had written to one of the engineers who was already in Mull to see what could be worked out. Thankfully, a letter reached him in Oban that an abandoned cottage had been let and furnished for them.

This is not how it was supposed to have been. He should be somewhere else, staying with a village family perhaps. He should not be here with the De vales. It was not right.

He heard a knock on the door and called to Janey to enter. The voice on the other side however, was not Janey's.

"It is Miss De vale, sir. May I speak with you a moment?"

William felt his pulse quicken and his heart beat loud in his ears. What was she doing at his door? He rose from his chair and opened the door, bowed quickly and saw her standing there, arms crossed.

"Well, I can see for myself that you are not ill. So enlighten me, Mr. Mara, why will you not join us for dinner?"

Her daring nearly caused him to fall backward. This was not done. William was not accustomed to having his actions questioned, never mind having unmarried ladies appear at his bedroom door.

"I know not how to respond to that query, madam, except to say that I believe it best to take my meals in my room."

She would not be deterred. "Why is that?" Her tone was gentle and genuine, as though she really had no inkling as to the wisdom of his choice.

William sighed loudly. "Under normal circumstances, it would be highly unlikely that we would share a meal. I am not even a guest here. I have imposed upon you and your father."

It was Miss De vale's turn to sigh. "I will not even dignify that statement with a response. It is my dearest wish for you to join us for dinner, Mr. Mara. Will you honour it?" Her arms were still crossed and now she was tapping her foot, awaiting his answer.

William raked his fingers through his hair in defeat. "I will."

These two simple words brought a smile to her face. "Good. I shall see you downstairs."

He shook his head as he followed her. Louisa De vale was accustomed to getting exactly what she wanted.

"Is the food to your liking, Father? I helped Janey with the vegetables myself," said Louisa with pride.

Sir Thomas raised his eyebrows. "You did what?" He shifted his chair to look directly at her. "My dear child, while I expect that you will have to do some things for yourself out here in the wild as we are, there is no call for you to cook and clean like a common servant." Throwing up his hands he declared, "I still cannot believe I let you talk me into bringing only a maid and a manservant." His tone was severe but he did not seem to be truly angry.

Miss Louisa reached out to him and squeezed his hand affectionately. "Father, I want to learn. I want to be of use during our stay here at Cliffside. Please allow me this," she pleaded. Her father looked at her, shook his head and smiled. It was clear she had won.

"Cliffside?" asked William.

"Oh yes! I forgot to tell you both. I have named our humble abode here in Tobermory. Gentlemen, I formally welcome you to 'Cliffside Cottage,'" she announced beaming and raising her glass.

William smiled widely at her. It was becoming agonizingly difficult to hide his admiration. Her happiness was infectious. He had been so anxious at the prospect of bringing her here. William had no idea what to expect, but felt there was little chance it could live up to Miss Louisa's standards. To see her now so happy, so at home and even naming this small, dusty place, he was delighted to be wrong.

"Mr. Mara?" she said softly.

William cleared his throat and raised his eyes to hers. For a moment he feared she had read his thoughts. He replied, "At your service, madam."

"I hope you do not think I am prying sir, but may I inquire after your family? You have not spoken of them before, but I should dearly wish to know about them," she said gently.

William looked down at his plate, unsure how to respond. He did not want to disappoint her, nor did he want to relay the tale of his poor parents. "I thank you for your interest in my family. Sadly, my parents both passed away when I was but twelve years old and I have no brothers or sisters," he said hoping to close the subject.

"I am sorry to hear that, lad," said Sir Thomas quietly.

"As am I," echoed Miss Louisa.

William thanked them both. His mood turned grave at the mention of his parents. He was now wandering down a dark hall of thought and knew not how to bring himself back to the light.

Sir Thomas clearly felt the tension in the room and attempted to lessen it, "Shall we play cards after dinner? I would like some amusement after such a long journey."

"I must apologize again, Sir Thomas, for intruding on yourself and your daughter. It was my intention to stay at the inn. I had n-no idea it would be so small..." stammered William.

"Think nothing of it! Louisa and I are more than happy with the arrangements are we not, my dear?" he asked kindly looking to his daughter for confirmation.

But she could not let the matter drop. "Sir, I must say you are a mystery to me. Why you keep insisting on this imaginary barrier between yourself and us I shall never understand!"

"There is nothing imaginary about it, madam!" William was

nearing the end of his patience on this subject. How could she not see the disparity between them? He looked to Sir Thomas who seemed uncomfortable with this line of conversation. William schooled himself to calm. "Though I may have some wealth now, it was made in trade. Yes my father was a gentleman but he…In any case, I am not your equal in society, nor do I ever expect to be. You are very kind, Miss De vale, but I cannot accept your notion that we shall ever be peers in that sense," he said with feeling. His heart was racing.

Her face softened at his declaration. She paused before she answered him. William felt halfway between pulling her to him to quiet her with his mouth and bolting from the room altogether. In the end, he was silent, waiting for her reply.

"I thank you for your honesty, sir," she said finally. "I am sorry that our situations appear to bring you pain. May I make a suggestion?" He looked up at her. Her eyes were so kind, so full of compassion. William nodded. Louisa continued: "May we play a game while we are here? Might we pretend that we are equals? I should have liked to have had an elder brother. And here you are, three years my senior! What say you? I would like so much to get to know you, sir and I am sure my father feels the same way."

Sir Thomas readily agreed. "Certainly, lad! I understand why you feel the way you do, but we are in a small island village. I see no harm in leaving certain society rules behind us in London so that we may better enjoy the company we have. Now, what do you say?" he asked, slapping William on the back.

William smiled as he looked from father to daughter. It was becoming impossible to doubt their sincerity. He had not felt a sense of family since the passing of his parents. Here now were two kind people offering him just that. It would be foolish of him to think his feelings for Louisa were akin to that of a sibling, but he knew how hopeless the alternative was.

"You are both too kind. How could I refuse?" He looked at

Louisa meaningfully. She was changing him. Whether she knew it or not (though he was fairly certain she did), she was changing him. It was an uncomfortable feeling, though not an entirely bad one.

CHAPTER 19

Declan

Hope is a dangerous word. It's fully loaded with potential joy and possible heartache. There is risk in hope.

I've never had any use for it myself.

I was a moment-to-moment kind of guy, a victim of circumstance. I always let the world tell me who I was and what my struggles were. It was as if I only existed when noticed by someone else. Every person became a mirror in my life to remind me I was still here and that I hadn't fallen into some black hole of nothingness. So many people I know have been kind too, if not a little preoccupied with their own shit. I've been supported, helped and loved.

I should not perhaps, have been depressed but I was. I was. And now it seems...It seems I have hope. Hope born in a beautiful girl with golden hair dressed in oversized knit sweaters and black tights.

It is as if I have wandered the earth feeling like a fragment and have finally found where I fit. She is a thousand-piece puzzle, and I the thousandth piece. I feel like I would follow her anywhere and believe me, I know how that sounds. So many years spent being so vulnerable has helped me to let go of the fear of looking like a wimp. This is how I feel.

And I dreamt of her last night. She looked different, but it was her. She had desire in all her looks, a photo booth reel of attraction and acceptance. She told me that I had been mistaken and there was so much I did not know.

I want so badly for it to be true. I have hope.

I've got to go get her. There's nothing left to do but say I'm sorry and ask for her forgiveness. It is worth the risk I am sure. I can't have her thinking I'm a jackass. There is a whole new lens with which to see myself through her. I have to wipe it clean.

I splash water on my face and rub my chin. I would rather not shave. A big part of me just wants to meet her as I am, to test the waters in a way that will leave no room for questions.

I'll just show up and lay it all on the line.

I am a desperate man.

I'm in love.

Ellie

Coming back to my own time and place I can't help but feel annoyed. If I was ready and willing to wait out this story before, I wasn't anymore. What if the answer to his depression lay deep in my subconscious? What if looking into the past could help him heal? I get up and start pacing the room.

"What is it, Ellie? You look upset." Mrs. Dawes watches me with concern.

"I am upset. I'm pissed! I know I said I was happy to wait but things have changed. It's worse than I thought with Declan. He was in a mental hospital, Mrs. Dawes. Did you know that? A loony bin! What if I send him back there? What if I'm too late with all of this stuff? He...he was catatonic. Can you believe that?"

I collapse back onto the couch and let myself cry finally. I've been holding so much in, trying to be strong. In an instant it all comes pouring out of me. "Why is this happening?"

Mrs. Dawes rises from her chair and sits down beside me. She rubs my back and pulls my hair back from my eyes to rest it behind my shoulder. "It's ok, Ellie. It's ok to be overwhelmed. You've charged yourself with a huge task."

"What is that supposed to mean? I didn't ask for the visions! I didn't ask for any of this!" I shout.

"I know, love. I know that. But you're assuming that you are being asked to heal him. It's clear to me that it is your own heart and mind that needs healing. Declan has his own path. He deserves to walk it the way he is guided to. That is not for you to decide. As you heal, you help him to heal."

"I'm fine! I know I'm supposed to help him. You don't see what I see."

She pauses, holding my eyes with her own. She means business. "Yes I do, child. Believe me." Her voice is gentle.

I roll my eyes at her. "I don't have the time to sit here and listen to you be all cryptic. I have to go see him. I have to do… something!" I grab my coat and bag and scramble towards the door. I'm behaving like a petulant child, but I don't care.

"Ellie, wait! You often describe Louisa as listening to some kind of inner voice. Remember I said that you have it too. We all do. You are just as guided as she was. You and she are the same soul. You can do it too."

"You forget, Mrs. Dawes that something really awful is going to go down between Louisa and William. I can feel it. I'm pretty sure you can too. Whatever this voice is she listens to, whatever guidance she received, it seems to me she would have been better off tuning it out." I surprise even myself at how frustrated I am.

"I have to go. I'm sorry," I say and walk out the door.

Putting my coat on and tightening my scarf, I leave the store with a direction in my mind.

Walking along the harbour I find myself thinking of my father. I never knew him. My mom said he was an older guy in his twenties who came to Tobermory for a week to do some ice fishing. They got drunk, had sex and that was it. She didn't even get his last name, but told me his first name was Chuckie. I don't think Chuckie when I think of him though. I think Charles. He sounds like less of a jerk that way.

I want to see where he is. I want a glimpse, a sign that he is out there. I know he doesn't know about me, but does he ever wonder if he has a child somewhere? Would he like me? Would I like him? I never let myself think about these things but now, it seems, the floodgates are open.

And then in a flash I see something...someone.

I see Pelee Island and somehow I know that I am seeing my father where he is or where he will be very soon. The air is mild and comforting as he grasps a mug of coffee. He sighs with resignation and disappointment as he looks at his car: a beaten-up, old Chrysler LeBaron. I can feel him thinking he will have to let it go.

I smile. That was cool.

My father is ok. That, for now, is all I need to know.

The moon is full and I am thankful for it. I use it as my guide. The wind whistles around me so hard I can barely hear, but somehow I manage to notice someone calling my name behind me. It's Tynan.

"Ell! Hey! Wait up," he calls.

He's running toward me. It's not easy to run in denim. He looks so awkward I actually start to laugh. But by the time he reaches me, I'm in tears again.

"Geez, Ellie what's going on? I thought you were laughing at me; I was ready to smack you! I won't smack you now though; I promise. What's up?" he asks putting his arm around my shoulder.

I sigh and lean into him gratefully. "I don't have a clue! I'm a mess, but I need to see Declan. I have to talk to him, but I have to calm down. He can't see me like this."

He breathes in sharply. "Are you sure you want to be hanging out with that guy?" I shoot him a dirty look and he backs off. "Ok, alright. I'll walk you there. Can you tell me what's going on? Did you guys do the deed or something?"

I punch his arm hard and he pretends to be hurt. "Tynan! No, ok. No! We didn't. It's much more complicated than that."

"Ellie, in my experience, there's not much more complicated than sex...maybe death, but at least that's final."

I look away and say, "Yeah, it's not though. Final, I mean."

He gives me a questioning look and so I elaborate. "Tynan, I am ninety-nine percent sure that I had some kind of love affair with Declan in a previous life and I think it messed him up pretty bad." I've got his full attention now.

"He was a "rags to riches" businessman and I was the daughter of a baronet. It was the late 18th century and we were in the UK. I'm not exactly sure what happened yet, but I know it can't be good. And Declan knows about it too except he can't remember like I can. He's drawn pictures of me though, and he drew all of them years before he ever met me." I look up at Tynan and he's stunned, silent. "I've been asking Mrs. Dawes to regress me through hypnosis and that's how I see all the memories, but I've also had dreams."

Tynan is, for perhaps the third time in his entire life, speechless. He stares at me for a full minute before finally exclaiming, "Holy crap, Ellie! What the hell are you talking about? Does this have to do with those blackout things you have?"

I pause. I hadn't meant to confide in anyone else in so much detail. "Yes. They are visions... past-life visions. As soon as I met Declan they got stronger, clearer and they were all from the same lifetime." I tell him. He looks unsure of what to say. My stomach is in knots fearing that he is judging me...that his soul is slowly inching away from mine, reconsidering our friendship. Looking up at Tynan I ask him to say something, anything.

He shakes his head and his eyes are still wide in amazement. "This is kind of mind-blowing, Ell. I don't know what to say." I take a deep breath and put my head on his chest. He holds me close and strokes my hair gently. "I believe you. Does that help?" he asks hopefully.

I half-laugh and half-cry at his simplicity. "Yes, it does. Believe it or not that helps a lot." Squeezing him tighter and tighter, I begin to feel tears in my eyes and I let them come. It's too late to be embarrassed and much too late to care. Tynan doesn't say anything. He just keeps stroking my hair and holding me tight. Faintly he says "Shh," in my ear.

I relax easily into the comfort he provides. Breathing in his citrusy cologne I am grateful for his embrace. I know he has questions, but for now he keeps them to himself. His arms and his silence give me everything I need.

CHAPTER 20

Ellie

Climbing the stairs that will take me to Declan's room I stop suddenly. Something pushes me back for a second. It's like a force, some kind of an energetic warning. It's not alarming, just a gentle heads-up. I reach his door and raise my hand to knock when it opens. There he is right in front of me. We're both startled, but I'm clearly the one who is nervous.

"Sorry," I say. "I didn't know you were going out." He looks surprised, but not upset to see me and I am relieved. That's one fear put to rest.

Declan smiles warmly and reaches out a hand to my cheek. "I was just going out to find you," he says. "Come in." He steps aside to let me pass. I walk over to the sofa and sit down. There's something about him, something so calm and composed. It's as if he's made a decision.

"So, I've been thinking..." he starts. "Wait, no. I should have started with; I'm sorry, Ellie. It was a shitty thing to stand you up last night. I shouldn't have done it. I'm really sorry," he says and moves to sit beside me.

He takes my hands in his. "Wow, your hands are freezing. You're freezing! How long were you outside?" I look up at him, but I can't bring myself to say a word. "Have you been crying, Ellie? Your eyes are all red and your makeup's all smudged. What happened?" His voice is like a thick, warm blanket of comfort.

I consider telling him that there's nothing wrong and that I'm just happy to be here with him, but it seems better to go with the truth. "Your father came to see me," I tell him quietly.

"Oh."

"I hope you're not angry with him. He was genuinely worried about you. He told me about your time...away," I say looking down at our hands.

"Away. Yeah, that's one way to put it." He takes a deep breath. I want to know what he's thinking.

"Are you mad at him?"

He shakes his head. "I'm not mad. I kind of figured that's where he went after I told him I wasn't meeting you."

He's drawing circles in the palms of my hand with his thumb. "I'm sorry you had to hear all of that. I was pretty messed up for a while. In a lot of ways I still am, but at least I can tie my own shoes and play guitar again. That's definitely progress for me," he says smiling. He gently lifts my chin and looks into my eyes. "Did it change anything for you? Hearing about my past, I mean?"

I shake my head. "What is there to change? We're friends, right? A friend doesn't leave because of a shady past. And it wasn't even that shady. You were sick," I tell him. My voice is cracking. There's something so peaceful and gentle about him now, like the anxiety is just melting into nothingness. I wonder if he took his meds.

Declan frowns slightly and I notice a dark look in his eyes that leaves me with a heady feeling. "Friends..." his voice trails off and I swear my heart in is my throat. "Right, well, as I was saying before Ellie, I've been thinking. I feel like I haven't breathed a full breath since I met you and my heart pounds so hard that I can barely hear. You do that to me. I want to see you every moment, but it's more than that. I want to know you. I want to know you better than anyone else does. Your hands will never be cold again if I can help it. You will never be cold again."

I'm beginning to feel devoured by his gaze. I have to look away.

He continues, "I remember you said that you didn't think a guy would move here for you, but I would. I will. If you ask me to, I will." He's serious, but he's also radiant somehow, lit from within.

I have to clear something up before I let things go any further. "Can I ask you something, Declan?" He nods and I still cannot bring myself to look him in the eye. "Are you high right now?"

"What? No! Shit, Ellie," he shouts, clearly offended. He releases my hands, turning away.

"Well, I'm sorry but you seem so different. You seem...peaceful," I say putting my hand on his elbow. I can't regret asking him. We have known each other for such a short while, I barely know him at all. He feels familiar, but there's a sense that his mood could change at the drop of a hat. My intuition begs me to be cautious.

He turns to face me. "I'm peaceful, Ellie, because I made a decision to take a chance and it feels good to not be tortured by fear anymore." I nod, encouraging him to continue.

"When I first met you I recognized you. That's what I thought at least. Now I know it was more than that. This may sound silly, but it wasn't 'me' that knew you. It was my soul, something bigger than me and it wants you. It has to have you." He runs his hand through his hair and exhales loudly, forcing himself to continue. "And I had a dream last night...and in my dream you wanted me too."

He blushes. "I know you haven't said you like me in that way. This is me taking a huge risk; I know that. You don't have to say anything tonight. I just had to tell you. It was killing me to keep all of this in." He says the last part quickly as if trying to confess every last thought.

I don't take time to think. I just step closer to him, reach my hand to his cheek and kiss him.

He sighs and softly pushes me back to look at me. "Is this your answer?" he asks.

"You told me I didn't have to answer tonight. Not to mention, you never actually asked me a question." I smile and raise an eyebrow at him.

"Let me ask a question now then: will you stay here with me

tonight?"

I move my head slowly up then down. Yes.

It's all instinct. There was never a plan to fall in love with this man. I've spent the past week thinking about him, wanting to help him, trying to see our connection through time. It never occurred to me to just be with him, to just let him hold me.

Declan reaches up to cradle my head in his hands. His gaze is heavy. "I'm sorry, Ellie. I have to hear you say yes. I have to see the shape your mouth takes when you say it."

"Yes," I say softly, biting my lip. "Yes, I will stay with you tonight. I don't want to be anywhere else."

He brings my face to his and kisses me. My mind feels light and I surrender to it. Our kisses begin slow and soft and then become hungry. Declan reaches his hands under my sweater and pulls it up over my head. I shake out my hair and smile at him. I reach for his shirt and begin to unbutton it.

My hands are trembling. It's been so long since I've been with a guy. As if reading my mind, Declan puts his hands on mine and undoes the buttons for me. The look on his face tells me we don't have to go fast and I am relieved. I can't remember feeling so safe. Kissing his chest, I breathe deeply and whisper "I think I love you."

I feel him tense and then relax all at once. He leans down to kiss my temple. "I know that I love you. It's something I couldn't help if I tried. You've got me."

He stands and leads me over to the bed. "There's something so wrong about crowding you on a couch. I want you to be comfortable. Get under the covers. I want to kiss your body while you tell me your story." His mouth is at my neck.

"My story?"

"Yes, I want to hear whatever you want to tell me. Will you do that for me? We won't go any further than what you are ready for." He reaches his hand to the side of my breast and traces a line down to my hip.

My body is willing to fall into this headfirst, the traitor. My thoughts however, are a jumble of confusion and hesitation. Declan is handsome and mysterious, and I feel myself wanting to know more and more with every move he makes. I love him from a place that I don't yet understand.

Damn. I can't even enjoy what his mouth is doing to the spot behind my ear. My hands are clutching his waist, distracted, ready to still him.

As much as I would love to think that William and Louisa don't matter, I know deep down that isn't true. The closer I get to Declan, the more all that happened back then will come to the surface. There is something there that I don't want to look at.

A voice whispers: *You're not ready.*

I know the voice is right.

"I'm not ready."

Declan calms and then tilts my chin so that I am looking up at him. "Ok. I understand." I put my head to his chest and feel tears in my eyes. I am confused and ridiculous. He sweeps my hair out of my eyes. "I'd still like you to sleep next to me, if you're okay with that. And I still want to hear all about you."

I sigh with relief and a realization that I barely know myself. "I'll tell you everything I know."

CHAPTER 21

Louisa

Autumn in Mull was beautiful even if the wind was not. Trees seemed to bend to near breaking every day, and if things were not tethered to the ground, they were lost to the whims of the breeze. It did not bother Louisa though. She loved the wildness of it. There was no pure beauty in this world, for without fail, some kind of darkness would follow. She knew that for certain.

Louisa considered herself a good and kind person even though her status in society dictated that she had no real need to be. She often thought of the welfare of others first and foremost, though she did have her character defects. She could be impatient, especially when she was sure of the outcome. It was not so much a lack of faith as it was a burning desire to experience the good (or not-so-good) without delay.

Louisa also had a tendency to force her opinion on others. Although she found it difficult to explain to people, she sensed things before they occurred and could often tell how people were feeling without them having to express it. The only problem was other people didn't always follow the advice she so generously relayed. This frequently frustrated her even though she knew it shouldn't. As Mother Mary would remind her: I am responsible for myself alone.

The other character flaw she felt she possessed, which had been especially troubling to her lately, was her curiosity with men. She found them fascinating and incredibly pleasing to look at. While she was definite that she would never marry, she was intrigued by the relationship that was expected between a man and a woman in that arrangement. She had heard that these relations were more for the man than the woman, but her cousin Margaret had told her something very different.

Margaret had said that it was actually very pleasant if your husband took his time. She also said that kissing was divine. Louisa recalled Margaret lighting up at the description. Ever since that conversation with her wiser, married cousin, she found it hard to think of other things when in the company of a man she found particularly attractive.

William Mara was such a man.

Every time William spoke, Louisa caught herself staring at his mouth. It held a world of wonders soft and whispered. Thankfully, most of the time she could recall enough of what he said to form a proper response. It seemed unfair that she should have to go through the great trouble of getting married in order to discover the pleasures a man could bring. Then she would chide herself for thinking this way. Louisa was acquainted with more than a few wealthy women who stayed single their entire lives. It was a safe wager she reckoned, that these women never entertained such thoughts.

She wondered what was wrong with her. Why did she have to be so strange?

Her interests and pursuits were mostly related to philosophy and prayer. There had always been little that was of this world that interested her. She loved her father dearly, of course, but until Mr. Mara appeared, she never questioned her ability to move through life with discovering its meaning as her sole objective. He was an anchor to earth when heaven was her goal. It was perplexing. How could she possibly have both?

"Miss De vale?"

Louisa was seated by the fire and had not heard him entering the drawing room. She was startled and hoped he had not noticed the blush that was so plainly now on her cheeks. "Oh I'm terribly sorry. I've interrupted you while deep in thought," Mr. Mara said kindly.

Taking a deep breath and shaking her head she replied, "It's a welcome interruption, sir I assure you. My thoughts were doing nothing but troubling me." Louisa stood to greet him and hoped he did not notice her discomfort at his joining her. Finding her courage as she again sat down, she ventured, "And Mr. Mara, if we are to be treating one another as brother and sister, surely you can begin to use my Christian name?"

William took the armchair across from her and coughed nervously. "I suppose I could do that. Perhaps it is best to keep that between the two of us, however. In front of the servants and your father I will still refer to you as Miss De vale." He laced his fingers together and leaned forward, awaiting her reply.

"And may I call you William, sir?"

This request appeared to make him uneasy, though Louisa could not think why. It took a moment before he finally replied, "Of course you may."

She tilted her head to study him. "Have I made you uncomfortable? I realize I often impose my will upon others. This is done frequently by people in my own sphere of acquaintance of course. However it is a trait that I am nevertheless ashamed of. If using each other's names makes you ill at ease, I am prepared to surrender the idea," she said quietly, looking down at her hands as she smoothed her skirts.

William observed her strangely, as if he did not understand her. "I promise you Louisa, if I was uncomfortable with anything you suggested, I would tell you straight away. It may not have always been so, but I feel acquainted with you sufficiently for this to be the case now."

Louisa was relieved. "I thank you, sir. You have eased my mind."

The silence of words unsaid hung heavy. Louisa began to feel nervous at the strength of feeling between them and decided she must say something. "Tell me about your friends, William. Are most of them married?"

The sound of her voice brought him back to the present. "I uh...yes, madam. That is, I have one married friend. I am but five and twenty so many of my friends are still bachelors."

"Why is that I wonder? I mean, I am twenty-two and am close to being considered an old maid. My dear friend Laura, who is the same age as I, recently wed a Mr. Kelly, a man of forty-five! It rather unnerves me that he could be her father. Why is it alright for men to wait and not for women?"

William considered her question for a moment. "I don't believe I've ever really thought about that. I suppose it has something to do with children. The younger a woman is when she marries, the greater chance she has of having many children, especially male children."

"Yes, of course. Males are important. What is a woman after all but a means of bringing them into the world?" There was bitterness in her voice. It surprised her a little.

William sighed loudly, but his tone was kind. "What you must understand, Miss De vale is that many men have trades to support their families. A male heir means that the living can pass on to the next generation; it all but guarantees for a man that his family will be provided for should he die. You cannot begin to comprehend what a relief that is for him."

"It is not as if a woman would not do the work of her father though. One has already assumed she is incapable."

"You have proven yourself more than capable, Miss De vale. Every day it seems you have mastered a new skill. I find it inspiring. Indeed you…" William stopped himself.

"Pray continue, sir," said Louisa quickly. He had spoken to her with such feeling. She did not want him to stop.

William's smile was restrained. "It is nothing," he said lightly.

"And you have ceased calling me Louisa, sir!" she countered. "Have I offended you?"

"No indeed. I thought it was I who had offended you." He cleared his throat. "Did I?" He tipped his head purposefully to better see into her eyes. It was as though he desperately needed to know she still approved of him.

"You did not," she said honestly. In truth the conversation

had unnerved her a little but she could claim no real feelings of insult. She had never shared her opinions with anyone other than her father. If Louisa was honest with herself, she would admit that she was concerned that she had gone too far with William. She did not wish to lose his good opinion. Thinking it best to change the subject she said "Tell me about your friend who is married then, is he happy?"

William appeared momentarily confused, but obliged her. "He is, very much so. He and his wife played together as children. They are friends as well as man and wife."

"How lovely for them both."

William nodded and then gave her a questioning look. "I must say, I am surprised at your interest in marriage. Your father has told me of your resolve to never marry."

Louisa went white at his words. She looked away from him to stare into the fire. "Never is a very long time." She paused and exhaled slowly. "While I do not wish to be under the control of a man, I could be persuaded to marry by one whom I loved and who would consider me an equal," she said quietly.

"You could?" he said quickly. "I think that wise. Indeed, never is quite permanent." William wore a half-smile and Louisa longed to know what he found so amusing. He leaned forward to pick up her hand and place it in his. She could hear her pulse loud in her ears...almost deafening. "I must tell you how much I enjoy your company, Louisa. Indeed, I prefer it to anyone else's." He brought her hand to his mouth and kissed it gently. His lips lingered there for a moment until the clock began to chime.

She began to say thank you, but he rose from his chair and left the room.

What just happened, Louisa could not say. The exchange, however, seemed to be far from what occurs between a brother and his sister.

CHAPTER 22

William

It was the striking of the clock that made him stop. As soon as he left her, he knew he had to get outside. Stalking through the kitchen and out the back door he stopped again to gather his thoughts. The taste of her skin had been sweet indeed, but to sit there any longer and pretend he did not want more was preposterous.

It was enough now, no more.

William burst through the back door and was greeted by the rare assault of sunlight on his weary eyes. He really must seek out living quarters elsewhere. In truth, he knew that he could ask any family in the village for accommodations and he would not be turned away. The problem was she would not be there.

Pacing in the back garden, William felt the wind cut him where he stood. It seemed to sweep up his jacket and overcome his warmth with its chill. He winced at the sensation and at the thought that it was no less than he deserved. He heard a rustling coming from around the side of the house and decided to follow the sound. It was Edward. He was holding an axe.

"Good day to you, sir." Edward bowed at William's approach. "I was just about to cut some wood for the hearths. Is there something I can do for you, Mr. Mara?"

"Not at all Edward, I...that is...May I assist you?" he asked. Edward observed him strangely, speechless. William understood that his request was unusual, but if he did not do something to quell his nerves soon he would surely go mad.

"Of course you may, sir, if you wish to." Edward handed William the axe he was carrying and told him he would go back to the house to fetch another.

Off to the side of the cottage, just before a small copse of trees there was a pile of logs underneath a large piece of thick black cloth. He picked up several and brought them to the wood block. Setting down the axe he removed his topcoat, followed by his dark brown vest and finally his ever-constraining white cravat. He brought his shoulders back and pushed out his chest.

He felt freer already.

William picked up a log and placed it on the block, balancing it with one finger. He picked up the axe and raised it above his head, ready to strike. With teeth gritted and all the force his body could muster, he brought the blade down hard in one fluid motion, splitting the log in two.

He heard footsteps behind him. "Looks like rain, sir." Edward went to the wood pile and added casually, "I do hope Miss Louisa isn't caught in a storm."

"I beg your pardon, Edward? Has Miss Louisa gone out?"

Edward eyed him queerly, as if William should know already. "Yes, sir...gone to the village."

William saw a dark cloud moving across the sea towards their port. When it arrived, he would seek her out. He knew he should send Edward, but he could not.

He hoped by then she would have returned. It was uncertain how much longer he could keep secret the feelings he had for her.

Indeed, it could not be long.

Louisa

Louisa decided she needed some air. It had been nearly a week since she had walked into the village. In London she would not dare to venture outdoors unescorted, but here on the island things were different.

She noticed a wild dog following her at her side, but at a distance. As she walked the beaten path, the dog kept pace with her walking through the woods to her left. She did not feel threatened. It was as if he stayed with her to protect her, to ensure she arrived at her destination safely. Louisa looked over at the dog and mouthed "Thank you". He seemed to acknowledge her briefly.

She was in awe of the majestic animal, with his tall and lanky frame and brown matted fur. She imagined he hunted deer and other large animals. She could see him stalking the forest with his pack. Where was his pack? He was a warrior and yet his presence and demeanour clearly spoke of protection.

Reaching the clearing that led to the village, she looked over her shoulder and saw he had stopped and was sitting, waiting for her to continue. Louisa waved good-bye and walked quickly towards the village market.

The market consisted of three stalls. One sold bread, cheese and eggs. The second had cured ham, fish and some freshly slaughtered lamb. And the last stall sold root vegetables and a few spices. She bought a leg of lamb, some pepper and onions and then a few loaves of bread. She and Janey planned to make a stew for dinner. Though Janey would prefer to make the stew herself, she was kind enough to indulge Louisa's desire to learn to cook. There were many skills she wished to learn. She wanted to return to London a different woman than the one who left it.

Louisa's perpetual habits of reading and quiet contemplation were no longer serving her in Tobermory. Try as she might, she could not banish the thought of William Mara. There was something that seemed to set him apart from any other man of her acquaintance. He seemed to be able to see her. It was as if being in his presence meant she never had to explain herself, he would always understand. Louisa found herself longing to be close to him.

She decided it was time to quiet her mind and listen to her inner guide. Walking towards the shore she breathed in the sea air deeply. How clean and fresh it was compared to London. Louisa found a rock to sit on and look out at the sea. She closed her eyes and put her hand on her heart.

Be honest is what she heard. *Hide nothing and trust him* came shortly after.

She stayed a while longer just looking out across the water. The waves were rough; they rose and fell with a vengeance. She felt the spray of water on her face. Thinking it was from the ocean, she made no move to leave. Soon though, it was clear it was beginning to rain. The wind picked up and the sky burst open. Collecting her things, she got up and ran toward the nearest shelter. As if on instinct, she changed her mind quickly and made her way back to the cottage. She ran as she had never run before, with purpose and propelled by fate.

She could barely see a thing as she moved. Looking to her right she saw her faithful companion running at her side. His presence both amused and concerned her. Through the driving rain she did not see the fallen branch in her path until it was too late. She tripped and fell, crashing to the ground in a heap.

The dog ran to her in an instant. Licking her face and nudging her body, he inspected her. He lifted his head as he heard footsteps coming quickly toward them.

William

William and Edward were running and spotted Louisa on the ground. "Louisa!" William cried out. The dog moved toward them with a growl and flared his teeth.

"The dog is wild, Mr. Mara! You shall have to stay back. I will run back and get my gun," yelled Edward turning back toward the cottage. William didn't know what to think or do. It was clear Louisa was hurt. He wanted nothing more than to gather her up in his arms and carry her home, but the dog was clearly untamed and capable of ripping him to shreds. Without thinking he dropped to his knees on the ground.

His breathing was heavy from the run and from the sight before him. How badly was she hurt? Had the dog attacked her? He could not assess her injuries from this distance and the rain blurred his vision in any case.

The dog eased his stance and began to pace. He then slowly approached William who dared not move a muscle. Sniffing the man and deciding he posed no threat, the animal wagged its tail and rushed back to Louisa. William got up slowly and made his way toward her. He saw no blood on her though her ankle was clearly bent. She was covered in mud. He said a silent prayer of thanks that she still breathed, although she did not appear to be conscious.

He scooped her up and ran back to the house, the wild dog leading the way. He sailed past Edward who was holding his gun.

"Leave him!" shouted William. Edward obeyed and followed him into the cottage calling for Janey. William carried her to a room just off to the side of the kitchen. There was a small cot and a table there. He placed her gently on the bed and knelt at her side. Janey was there almost instantly with hot water and rags.

"Leave her to me, sir; she will be well," said Janey calmly. William did not move. He only stared at Louisa, almost willing her to awaken. "Please, Mr. Mara, her father is upstairs resting. You must go to him and tell him what has happened. He will want to see her," she pleaded.

William rushed out of the room and climbed the stairs to Sir Thomas' chambers. He knew she would be ok as long as it was just her ankle that was injured, but who could be certain? They needed a doctor. Before reaching the older man's room, he called for Edward and sent him out to the village to look for help. There was no doctor, but there was a midwife who served as the village's apothecary. She would have to do for now.

CHAPTER 23

Ellie

I awake suddenly not knowing where I am for a moment. It is obviously late morning because the sun is already high in the sky. I look down beside me to see Declan sleeping peacefully and I smile in recollection. Of course, how could I forget? I am with Declan. We talked about scraped knees, bush parties and past life visions until our eyes refused to stay open. I shared with him my pseudo-psychic gift, but I didn't mention his role in everything. I haven't yet found the courage.

Today is a new day. In my pale yellow tank-top and underwear, I do a silent celebration that they match and my legs are shaved.

I look over at Declan. Gorgeous stubble peppers his jaw. I reach out and feel it with my fingertips.

"Good morning." His voice is low and scratchy. He pulls me to him and kisses my forehead lightly.

"Hi," I say, shyly. "I hope that it's ok I'm still here."

"Of course, Ellie; I want you here. How did you sleep?" He's stroking my hair gently and I close my eyes to enjoy the sensation.

"I slept really well. I forgot where I was."

He smiles and it makes me want to take a mental picture of him. His stern, serious face breaking free for a moment, letting a lightness settle upon it. "Do you dream of your past lives too or is it just visions you get?"

"I've dreamt of the future a few times. And yeah, lately I've dreamt of the past. Usually though, I just get the flashes."

"It's kind of a cool talent you have, eh?"

I am not sure if I agree that it's a talent, but I keep that to myself. "Tell me about a skill you have...there must be one you haven't mentioned yet." He's still stroking my hair and it's so soothing that I'm tempted to fall asleep. Talking is helping me stay lucid.

"Hmmm, well I'm not sure it's a talent, but I can speak Gaelic."

"Really?" My eyes light up. My English is fine, my French is crap. Gaelic seems like such an exotic, romantic language. "Say something in Gaelic."

"Like what?"

"Anything"

He pauses. He's looking at me intently, his hand cradling the side of my face.

"*Tá tú go h-álainn.*"

I ask him what it means. "You are beautiful," he says slowly, emphasizing each word.

I blush. It's uncomfortable to be so analyzed, even if it's with admiration. I know that it could be so fleeting. What Declan loves today could be old and boring in a month. Of course, I want to believe him. I do. And then an inner voice says: *It's more than beauty. You know this.*

He continues, "Oh and speaking of you, I want to draw you! Is there a place in town that sells art supplies?"

"Not really, but we can go to Jack Bailey's place. He's an artist and my mom's ex-boyfriend. He's cool. He'll hook you up." I haven't spoken to Jack in over a year, but I know he will help us out. I also know he still loves Frances.

"Why did they break up?"

I pause. I remember how sad Frances was, and how she said it was just "over", that there was nothing left to keep them together. It didn't seem that way for Jack, but Mom had been adamant. It was done. "My mother just wanted to see other people," I tell him. "Do you want to go now?"

"Yes! We can grab a coffee from downstairs and go. Is that cool?" Declan is already out of bed and putting clothes on as he asks. I nod at him and proceed to get dressed myself.

Downstairs we see Alistair and he seems to study me with an air of disapproval. It annoys me slightly. I mean, he is the one who set us up!

"Good morning, son. Good morning, Ellie," he says and motions for us to join him at his table.

"Sorry Dad, we're on our way out. Ellie's taking me to the studio of a friend of hers. I'm going to pick up some supplies. I want to start drawing again. I'm feeling inspired!"

Alistair sips his coffee slowly before he replies, "Is that so? That's good to hear, Declan. And what are you thinking of drawing? The harbour? The trees?"

"Ellie," he says and I can feel Alistair's eyes on me, but I don't dare look at him. Guilt washes over me, but I say nothing.

Declan grabs my hand and we both wave good-bye to his father. I look back at Alistair and shrug.

He shakes his head. Nope, he does not approve.

We huddle together for comfort against the wind as we walk down the hill toward Jack's apartment / studio. Jack is a full-time artist who has found his success selling paintings of The Bruce Peninsula's nature and wildlife. That's what he painted for a living, but I know that his passion is painting nudes. I frequently saw women of all shapes and sizes climbing the steps to his apartment. I had even glimpsed a painting or two. The pictures were always tasteful and yet erotic at the same time. I found his work brave and fascinating.

I know he painted Frances. I always felt fortunate to not have stumbled across any of those pictures.

As if conjured out of thought, my mother appears, coming out of the Foodland with cloth shopping bags in either hand. Her wavy blonde hair is covered by a blue kerchief and she is dressed in black yoga gear. Even at this distance I know her eyes light up when she sees me. "Hey baby!" she shouts.

Declan and I walk toward her arm in arm and I can feel his

tension, his anxiety. "Mom, this is Declan. Declan, this is Frances, my mother."

"It's nice to meet you, Mrs. Stewart. Can I help you with your bags?"

Frances looks at Declan, sizing him up and shoots me a glance that says: 'Nicely done'. I sigh inwardly: Frances, Frances, Frances...

"Nice to meet you and it's Ms. Stewart, Declan. I've never married. And no thanks, I can manage."

She turns to me, "So is this where you were last night, Ellie? With Declan? You could have texted me."

I feel the heat rising in my cheeks and it annoys me. I am a twenty-two year old woman.

"Baby listen, I know you're an adult but you still live with me and so I worry. Just text me next time, okay? Just so I can sleep?"

I know she's right. "Sure Mom."

"Thank you." She exhales, relieved. "So where are you two off to?"

Shit. I have to tell her the truth because she'll find out anyway. "Um, well...I was taking Declan to Jack's place." Frances visibly tenses. I can see her holding her tongue and breath. "Declan sketches and paints. He's been inspired lately." I trail off with that last sentence and again, feeling uncomfortable. Declan is looking anywhere but at my mother.

"Has he now? I see. Well, Declan, I'm sure Jack will be able to help you out. Say hi to him for me."

My eyes grow wide at the request. "Really? Are you sure, Mom?"

She rolls her eyes at me. "Of course I am, Ellie. He's a good man."

And my mom just stands there. Her peace and her wisdom just stand there and I see it for the first time. I really see it. She loves everyone and even if she tried not to, she would love them anyway, fully and completely. She had the courage to let go when she knew it wasn't working anymore. My mother's bravery is just now obvious to me and I cannot help but feel a teeny bit ashamed.

It occurs to me that I never saw the relationship from her point of view and I feel childish. At least I'm seeing it now. I feel compassionate understanding taking the place of irrelevant teenage cynicism and it's good. I have taken one more step down the corridor of adulthood.

I walk over to her and hug her tightly. I just squeeze her until she laughs. "I love you too, baby," she whispers in my ear. "I love you too."

CHAPTER 24

Ellie

The stairs to Jack's are behind the shop and just past the Coke machine. As we climb up I briefly wonder if I should have called ahead. God knows what or who he could be doing.

Too late now.

I knock on the door and he answers almost immediately, as if he knew I was coming.

"Ellie! How are you?"

He's wearing a blue bathrobe and, I suspect, nothing more. His thick gray hair sits high atop his head in a wave and his eyes are made small by his dark-rimmed, thick-lens glasses. He's smoking a hash pipe.

"Jesus, Jack it's ten in the morning!"

He waves off my comment, "I am not bound by time, Ellie. You know that. Come in! Who's your friend?" He cocks his head to observe Declan.

We enter the apartment and it's exactly how I remember it: sunlight streaming in through dingy windows, paint-spattered newspaper strewn over wooden floors, half-empty wine and water glasses hastily left in random places. It's comforting to think that some things can be predictable.

"He is why I'm here, Jack. This is Declan. He paints too. He's been feeling really inspired lately and I thought maybe he could buy some supplies off you."

Jack looks Declan up and down with a dreamy smile on his face.

One thing I forgot to mention to Declan: Jack is bisexual. And forward. And very, very open.

"Well, yum-yum! You don't have to pay, Declan. Just let me draw you." His eyes are bloodshot, but wide now with excitement. He scratches himself beneath his robe and then darts off, presumably to grab a sketch pad and a pencil.

Declan looks confused. "What just happened?"

"He wants to draw you," I say, collapsing on an old red velvet couch with a loud sigh.

"Should I let him?"

I have to laugh at that. "He's harmless. It will take twenty minutes and then we can go. Ok?"

Declan nods, but he still looks nervous. Jack returns from wherever he was and it's not a sketch pad in his hand, but a camera.

"Changed my mind," he says quickly.

He asks Declan to sit in the windowsill and to look outside. I watch as he snaps photo after photo and it strikes me how quickly sadness can reign over Declan's features. I begin to think that melancholy is his set point and that happiness and deep depression are each just a heartbeat away.

I observe Jack in action and it reminds me how brilliant he is, how open to inspiration. His face is lit and yet concentrated. I had nearly forgotten how handsome he is. His features are chiselled and decidedly masculine, his body strong.

"Perfect! I'm going to paint one of these. Your look is so...intense. I want to contrast it with the light coming from the sun. Thank you for indulging me." Jack waltzes over to Declan to shake his hand and as he stands, the difference in height is almost cute. Jack is only an inch taller than I am. "You have very well-built hands."

Declan's voice is unsure, "Um, thanks."

"You are stunning, Declan. You've got that whole 'Black Irish' thing going on."

"Ok, Jack. We've got to go. Can you just pack up a few things for him?" I know Jack is truly kind and would not hurt a fly, but this could take forever. He loves and is fascinated by everyone.

"Yes, yes. A deal's a deal." I look over at Declan as Jack hurries off to pack some things and he just smiles back at me, amused.

"Oh, Ellie? I meant to ask you, how is that beautiful creature you call Mom?" he calls from his bedroom.

"She's fine, Jack. She's teaching Yoga and Nia. And she still paints."

He returns wearing an oversized grey t-shirt and jean cut-offs and hands the stuff to Declan. "Good to hear. I miss her." The longing in his face is impossible to miss.

I nod and reach a consoling hand to his arm. "I know you do." And I do.

I walk away with a flash of a scene: a mother, tall, dressed in burlap with black hair streaming down her back wandering the hills of Northern Ireland a thousand years ago. She is screaming for her son who has gone missing. He never returns. Jack is the mother. Frances is the son.

My heart feels tight for a moment and then understanding dawns on me. He's mourned her forever.

I breathe in and then out. I let it go.

Declan

I want to jump out of my own skin I'm so wound up! For the first time in years I want to draw. There is something itching within, a silent tug that won't be ignored. I look at her and I must re-create her. There's something the eye is missing that I need to bring out, to show. Looking over at her as we walk back to my hotel room, I notice she's been watching me.

"What?" I ask.

She shakes her head. "Nothing, I just like seeing you so excited."

And all I can do is smile...smile before the darkness creeps back. It always feels like a race against the clock when I start to feel good. Sadness has speed, joy only brevity.

I unlock the door and grab her; kiss her. I take off her thick, woollen sweater leaving her only in a pale pink tank top and black tights. Pushing her gently onto the bed, the scene before me is a beautiful mess of sheets and she, Ellie.

I kneel above her on the bed and take out the sketchpad from Jack as well as a thick charcoal pencil. I start with her mouth, pouty and delicious and then something takes hold. It is no longer me drawing. My eyes go blurry. I don't resist. I let it take over. My hand and pencil move furiously. The hair is long, but pulled back. The face is heart-shaped, eyes large and expressive. The image unfolds from something deep within. I don't recognize it, and yet I do.

The face staring back at me is not Ellie's.

"What the fuck?" I drop the sketchpad onto the bed, stunned.

"What? What is it, Declan? Did I move?"

I shake my head and motion for her to pick up the pad. She grasps it tentatively, her hand shaking slightly.

"Shit," she says succinctly. "Louisa."

Ellie

I make tea for us both and ask Declan to come sit beside me on the couch. He's quiet. Part of me wonders if he's worried he's gone nuts again.

"Your father told me a little bit about your time in the institution. You know that already," I say and he nods. "Well, he also told me that there was a period of time where you drew... a lot. And your drawings were all very similar. It was almost obsessive. In fact, he said that at one point another patient found a drawing and he ripped it. You apparently attacked him because of it," I said searching his eyes for any recollection.

"Ok. I believe him. I don't remember much about this, though. I know that I drew while I was at the hospital and then I stopped," he says warily.

"Right, so here's the thing: the drawings were all depictions of the same person. They were all of me." And even though my words are gentle, he draws in a breath sharply and pulls his hands from mine.

"What the hell are you talking about, Ellie?" he shouts. "That's impossible! Wait, were you in the hospital too? Did I know you there and forget you? Was this Louisa chick there too?"

"No, Declan. It's a little more complicated than that. I think...I'm not sure, but I think we're like soul mates. There was a part of you that already knew you were going to meet me, that we would fall in love and help each other. There's something else..." I start.

"What? Tell me. I don't want any more secrets, Ellie! This already makes me feel like you and my dad have been treating me like a child." His tone is chilled, defiant.

I swallow hard, preparing for the sudden weight of truth. "You know that I've had visions since I was a little girl. A friend of my mom's told me they are memories of past lives."

"Right, I know."

"Ok, well, I used to get them as quick flashes. Sometimes the scene would be in a hut in Africa, then it would be in a temple or on a canoe in a lake...it always shifted. They were completely random and made very little sense at all. That is...until I met you. As soon as you came into my life the visions got stronger, clearer and were of one specific lifetime." I pause looking at him, trying to assess his feelings. He takes a deep breath; I can tell he's processing all I'm telling him. "What I see is like a movie and I'm a character, or at least my soul is. And you're there too. I was the daughter of an English nobleman and you were a tradesman. We fall in love in Tobermory, Scotland in the late 18th century," I tell him.

"We've been together before?"

"Yes. And that woman you just drew looks exactly how I looked in 1790...when I was Louisa De vale."

He shakes his head violently as if he cannot believe what I'm telling him. I sigh. I knew it wouldn't be easy to explain this. Taking a deep breath I start from the beginning. He listens intently, never taking his eyes off of mine. I tell him about all that I have seen so far, about how I think we've come together to heal and how important it is to me to see these visions through. Declan is overwhelmed.

"This is nuts. I don't know if I can do this. It's too much!" he shouts. "What if you see something from back then that makes you hate me? What if I totally screwed you over?"

I reach for him, but he pulls back and stands. "I don't think that is where this is headed, Declan. I think we're supposed to forgive what happened in the past, no matter what it was."

He's pacing and is not willing to look at me. "I've got to go Ellie. I've got to get out of here. I'm not saying I don't believe, but it's just, I can't believe you kept this from me. I'll call you later," he says getting up to leave.

"Declan, wait! Why don't you see for yourself? Meet me tomorrow at the health food store by the Town Pump at seven in the morning. Mrs. Dawes, the psychic who I mentioned, she's the one who helps me to remember these things. We do what's called a past-life regression. Can you do that for me?" I ask.

He looks at me and my heart breaks at what I see in his eyes: sadness, confusion and regret. He leaves without a word.

I collapse back into the chair with my head in my hands.

That did not go well.

The next morning I walk into Mrs. Dawes' store with my heart on my sleeve. I tell about all that has happened. Relief washes over me as I look at her and see only love in her eyes, love unconditional and complete. She calls me to her and hugs me tightly. "What's this world without a little forgiveness, eh love?"

Tears are stinging my eyes as I say "Thank goodness for you, Mrs. Dawes."

"Are you sure you want to go ahead with this?" she asks

"Yes. I'm not sure what I'm looking for. I just know that I have to do it."

She winks at me and leads me to the back room. I tell her that I asked Declan to join us, but that I saw no sign of him as I came into the store.

"Oh he'll be here, Ellie. That I know for sure," she says with a smile.

CHAPTER 25

William

William and Sir Thomas paced in the kitchen waiting for Mrs. Young, the midwife, to appear with news of Louisa. William felt helpless and it was clear that Louisa's father felt the same way. His only child was in another room without even a proper doctor to tend to her. He had berated himself for bringing her here. He called himself thoughtless and selfish. She was a lady accustomed to the comforts of London, he had said. Nothing could prepare her for the wilds of a Scottish isle. William assured him that it was most likely just an ankle sprain, but it did not seem to ease his mind.

Just then, Mrs. Young appeared in the doorway. She was a short, stout woman of about fifty with the curliest brown hair William had ever seen. Her face was kind and full of humour.

"The ankle's not broken, gentlemen, but she has a wee bump on her head. She's sore alright, but she'll be right as rain in no time. You can send for Dr. Maclay in Craignure if you like. I'd say she best stay in bed for a few days to heal and then I reckon she'll be good as new," she bellowed good-naturedly. "I'll have to take me leave of you, gentlemen. Mrs. McCann is starting with her pains. She'll be needing me, this being her first babe and all."

"Yes, of course, Mrs. Young. We cannot thank you enough for coming so quickly," said Sir Thomas with a bow. His face visibly relaxed and he was smiling once more.

"You can go in if you like. She was asking for you." Mrs. Young was looking at William.

"For Mr. Mara? Are you certain?"

"If his name be William then aye, sir," she said with a curtsey and quit the house.

Sir Thomas narrowed his eyes at the man before him. William could think of nothing to say and instead, coughed nervously.

"I think I shall go in first, lad. Even if she did ask for you by name, I am her father. I believe she needs me."

William shifted uncomfortably, finding it difficult to look the older man in the eye. "Of course, sir," he said with a bow. He was overcome with feelings of both guilt and joy. She had asked for him. The thought made his hopes soar, but he quickly reeled them in. He needed to remember himself, his place. "Please convey to her my wishes for a quick recovery. I think I shall take my leave. I shall find somewhere else to stay tonight," he said finally mustering the courage to look Sir Thomas square in the eye.

The older gentleman breathed deeply, observed William for a moment and then said, "No, Mr. Mara you must stay. If my daughter has asked for you, you must stay. I do wish to see her first, however. Wait here, if you please."

Louisa

Louisa greeted her father with a wide smile. She had been changed into a white nightdress and her long, red hair was loose at her shoulders. As much as she would prefer not to be fussed over, she heard Mother Mary say gently, Rest, listen and be honest. She would try her best.

"How are you my dear? What happened out there?" Her father asked, grasping her hands in his.

Louisa told her father about the storm, about her decision to run back to the house and even about the dog. She assured Sir Thomas that she was sore, but otherwise no worse for wear.

"Mrs. Young said that you asked for Mr. Mara. She said you called him William. What is going on, Louisa? Has he asked to court you? Has he…imposed upon you in any way?" His eyes were full of concern, but also trust.

"No indeed, father. I asked Mr. Mara to call me Louisa. He is a friend. He gave me leave to call him William. There is nothing more. He has not imposed upon me in any way. He has been a perfect gentleman," she told him.

Sir Thomas smiled at his daughter. "I am pleased that you have a friend, my dear. He seems a very good sort of man. I enjoy talking with him myself." He stood up, bent down and kissed her forehead. "Shall I send in Mr. Mara?" he asked.

Louisa nodded and reached up to embrace him. "I cannot tell you father, how happy it makes me to know that you trust me so. I carry that knowledge with me wherever I go and it gives me strength. It helps me to try things and indeed to say things I ought to not otherwise dream of. Your faith in me helps me to be who I am," she declared.

"I am speechless. The change in you since leaving London has not been lost on me, you know. I have witnessed your emergence. Though it is not easy to let you go, I fear I have no choice." He paused for a moment as if deciding whether or not to proceed. "Will he make you happy?"

Louisa smiled warmly and shook her head. "No. He will not. That, dear Father, is a task all my own."

William

William looked out across the incredible scene before him. Never had he born witness to such wild beauty. He could now see why Louisa had been drawn to this spot, why she had been mesmerized by it. He walked closer to the edge and looked down at the staggering drop. Below were rocks: jagged, unforgiving. The sea foam tangled, only to be swept up by the next formidable wave.

The weather on the Isle of Mull was not what he expected. It was highly changeable. Many of the villagers had said that you can experience all four seasons in a single day. Today seemed to be such a day. The sun had felt so close a moment ago and now it was far away again. The sea spray was like ice-cold pin pricks, assaulting his face. The wind blew straight across, threatening to cut him where he stood.

Nothing to do up here but surrender, he mused to himself. Louisa was so good at that. She adapted to any situation in a heartbeat, with grace and ease and without a word of complaint. William raked his fingers through his hair. How was it he was unable to think of nothing else but her? He wanted her in every way. She was so incredibly close and yet painfully out of reach.

Could he propose to her? What would she say? She did not wish to marry. No, what was it she had said? She did not wish to be under the control of a man. Yes, that was it. William knew he would not do that to her. He could not crush her spirit thus.

And yet she did not need him. Indeed, she was in the rare position of needing no man. Possessing both a father willing to leave her his fortune and the wherewithal to manage it, she was as independent as any woman could ever hope to be. He could offer her nothing but his love and fervent devotion. He breathed a heavy sigh. It would only be worth something to her if she loved him back. Who could tell? She was so kind to all she met, though she did not have to be. He had never before witnessed someone who could treat a servant as an equal and yet have her distinction of rank remain intact. He was humbled by her.

"You are terribly cruel, sir!" William turned quickly to see Sir Thomas amble toward him, bent over and out of breath.

"Sir Thomas! Are you alright?" William shouted and ran to the elder gentleman.

"I am well, lad. What are you doing up here? I believe I asked you to stay in the kitchen. Our dear Louisa wishes to see you. Shall you keep the lady waiting?"

"No indeed, sir. You are certain you are well?" asked William helping Sir Thomas to stand upright.

"Yes, Mr. Mara. I am well. Go to her. I am well." He looked out over the Cliffside as if seeing it, really seeing it for the first time. "This is a favourite spot of hers is it not?" he asked absent-mindedly.

"I believe it is, sir." He waited until Sir Thomas spoke again before he made to leave.

"Yes, well, she is waiting," he said softly and turned to walk to the cliff's edge. "I will stay up here for a few moments. Send Edward up if you like. Either way, I shall be fine."

"As you wish, sir," replied William. He would indeed send Edward. He did not trust the winds of Tobermory. They seemed to have a mind all of their own.

Louisa

She heard him enter the room before she saw him. She wanted just to listen for a moment, to hear his movements and the sound of him breathing. She wanted to feel the shift in the atmosphere of the room with every step he took. He had a presence that commanded attention, an intensity that longed to be eased. Louisa heard William sit down beside her and release a long-held breath. After a moment, he shifted his chair closer to her bed and touched her hand lightly.

"William?" she whispered as she opened her eyes.

He looked up at her, eyes shining. "I am here, madam," he declared. "Tell me, are you well?"

She smiled. "I am very well indeed, sir. I thank you. I am especially so now that you have come"

He looked away for a moment. "I am glad to hear it."

She cocked her head slightly to observe him more closely. "Are you glad that I am well, or that I feel better because you are here?"

William tugged at his cravat and cleared his throat. "I..." He paused and then said quickly, "What was that dog?"

At this Louisa laughed out loud. "I hardly know, William! He followed alongside me as I walked into town earlier this afternoon. He took it upon himself to protect me I think. And as

I ran from the village to home during the storm, there he was again. I am much indebted to him, you know," she said studying his face. "Are you upset, sir? Your eyes are red."

He swallowed hard. "I am not upset."

"I see. Well, I wanted to thank you for your great service to me." It was clear he was uncomfortable. She did not want to do anything that would make him more so.

William leaned back in his chair, and removed his hand from hers. "It was nothing Louisa, I assure you. When I asked Janey where you were, she replied that you had gone to the village. Seeing the weather, I asked Edward to accompany in searching for you. I only wanted to ensure your safety," he replied evenly.

"And that you did. I am in one piece as you see." Her tone was light while his look was heavy. He looked down at her and his gaze seemed to take in her entire body at once. She shivered and he looked away. "William, have I done something to cause offense?" He shook his head. "This is not going the way I had imagined!" she declared with a laugh. "Will you not look at me?"

"Louisa" He exhaled loudly, painfully and leaned closer to her. "I hardly know what to say to you! If I were a gentleman, if I were your equal…" he trailed off.

"If? Sir, how many times must I tell you? You are my equal in every way that matters!" She placed her hands on either side of his face. "What is it, William?"

He lowered his head and began his tale. He told her of the origins of his father, an Irish Nobleman and his mother, a chambermaid from Manchester. His speech was hot with shame, as if it burnt him to utter every word.

"My father turned his back on his family and was disinherited because of it. I grew up in poverty because of his stubbornness and my mother's unwillingness to release him."

Louisa listened with an open heart. William was still hurting over his childhood. She wanted only to comfort him. Sitting up, she placed her hand on his arm. "You judge them harshly. Your father turned his back on his family? I'm sure it was the other way around, William. Your parents, they passed away when you were quite young if I am not mistaken?" she asked.

"Indeed, they died within days of each other when I was twelve years old," he replied looking down at the floor.

"Again, I am so very sorry." She squeezed his arm gently, willing him to look at her. And then a thought occurred to her. "William, you never did mention, how did you know my mother was from Mull?"

He raised his head swiftly; his face blanched at the question. "Did I not?"

She shook her head.

With hesitation he proceeded to tell her that his mother had worked for a few months at the Boyle home in London. William explained that his mother had observed Mary Boyle from afar and thought her most kind. And then one day, his mother had fallen down the stairs accidentally while carrying linens. Mary had heard her cries and rushed to help her. She insisted on staying with her until the doctor arrived to examine her, and while she waited she had related stories of her beloved Scottish Isle; of fairies and spectres and ghosts. Shortly after the incident, Mary was betrothed to Sir Thomas and William's mother obtained a new position at the London home of the Maras.

Louisa delighted in knowing that their two mothers had met and had shared such a moment. Would they both be happy to see them now? Would they encourage Louisa and William to further their acquaintance? She felt certain that her mother would. At the mention of his father's family, Louisa had a question, "And the Maras, do they know of your existence?"

William eyes turned cold as he said forcefully. "They do not and they never shall. What would be the point, so that I may be an object of their derision? No, I have made a life for myself. I do not need them."

She blinked at him. "So, you like being alone William? I know we are very merry here the three of us, and Janey and Edward too, of course. What will you do when it is time for my father and me to return to London? Will you stay here in Tobermory?"

William's mouth tightened, his eyes grew cold. "I do not yet know. I will have to stay here for a few months at least, after your father has gone." The bite in his voice still remained.

"I do not like to think of you all by yourself," she said softly. His eyes remained fixed on the floor. "If it were up to me William, you would never be alone again."

He would not look her in the eye. "Yes, well I thank you for your concern, but as it happens, solitude suits me. I shall never marry, if that is what you are alluding to. I saw what that kind of dependence did to my parents."

"I did not mean to imply…"

"You implied nothing. I am simply stating that I will never put myself in a position of such reliance. It is pathetic." He nearly spat the words as he said them.

Tears came to her eyes as she listened to him. She had not realized how angry he was. And that much of his anger was directed at the people who had given him life was very troubling to Louisa.

Seeing that she was close to weeping, he rose to leave. "I have upset you. I am sorry. It was not my intention," he said quickly and quit the room.

Louisa tried to get up to go after him, but found she could not. She sighed forcefully in pain and frustration.

It had not gone well.

CHAPTER 26

Ellie

"Three, two, one, and when you are ready Ellie, you can open your eyes to the room," says Mrs. Dawes softly.

I open my eyes slowly and sit up. Scanning the room, I see no one but Mrs. Dawes. The disappointment is surely plain on my face.

"He was here, love. He's waiting for you outside. I think this was a lot for him. He arrived just after you went under and so he heard everything."

I stand up and put on my coat and scarf. My hands are shaking. "Should I go after him?"

Mrs. Dawes walks over to me and takes my chin in her hand, smiling. Her glittery pink scarf clashes softly with her bright red hair. "Of course you should."

My chin is quivering beneath her grasp. "He wasn't ready..."

She rolls her eyes, a sign I'm taking this all too seriously. "You don't need me to do this anymore, Ellie. It's becoming a bit of a dog and pony show anyway. You can remember all of this on your own. Louisa is with you; she is you. You can access her love and guidance at any time because they are yours," she says gently, placing her hands on my shoulders. "This has always been her. It's a part of your mind that is tenderly calling you to wake up. This is not about Declan or William. It's not even about your parents. This is about you waking up to your true nature. Sometimes we need these mystical experiences. They act as a reminder that there is more than this...more than this world of seeming joy and perceived pain. Listen Ellie; listen to that inner guidance. You may not hear it perfectly every time, but if you are willing to listen you will know what is yours to do in any situation most of the time. That is how you will heal and learn to let go."

I hug her. Even though I am not clear on everything she was saying, I know that clarity will come. I so want to be fearless and I wonder: is my willingness enough?

A gentle whisper comes: *Yes, it is everything.*

The chill of the air hits me like a brick wall and yet the sun is so bright above me I am temporarily blinded. It's as if the weather is conspiring against me. Looking from side to side, I cannot see him.

I close my eyes, take a deep breath and hear: he is in the alley behind the dive shop.

Running toward the shop I know that he will be there. I am sure of it and it occurs to me that Louisa is teaching me this. She, a part of me, is speaking to me through these memories, reminding me of what is possible. She reminds me that my life is not a mystery to be solved, but a tapestry to be unfolded and learned from. The people in my life will teach me everything I need to know. That is why they are here. And though they seem separate, they merely represent parts of me, fragments. It is up to me to piece them together and remember we are the same.

I approach the alley and of course, Declan is there. He looks up at me and I know what we have to do.

"Hey," I say.

His look is unreadable, but I know he's not angry with me. There's heat between us despite the weather and I wonder if I'll ever get used to it. Will I be given the chance to?

"I'm so sorry." My voice is high, unsure.

He looks down at his feet and shuffles them. I know he doesn't know what to say.

Reaching out to touch his arm I tell him, "I don't want to talk about what happened. I want to take you for a hike. It's cold as hell today, but the sun is out and we can keep each other warm. Let's explore."

He smiles with relief and stands up, pulling me to him. "That sounds amazing. Where are you taking me?"

The words are spoken with as much mischief as I can muster, "The Devil's Monument!"

The sky's ceiling is low and grey as we pull onto Dyer's Bay Road. Declan has barely spoken a word and I decide that maybe silence is best for now. He stares out the window of my rusty, old Ford Ranger and I wonder what he is thinking. I desperately want to know if he identifies at all with William or if it all sounds like some far-fetched fairy tale. My intuition says he will tell me in his own time.

Winding our way down East Road, I think about how long it has been since I've been out here. I was in high school and came out here with a boy to fool around. Why we felt we needed to go further into the middle of nowhere I cannot recall.

"So that regression thing was kind of weird," says Declan quietly.

He's still staring out the window, but I take this as my opening. "I can see how it seemed strange. Did it bring back anything for you? Do you remember being William at all?" I ask. I am trying to sound casual, but it's not easy. Right now, there is nothing I want more than to be able to share all of this with him.

"No, but it didn't seem unlikely. I don't know anything about this past life stuff, but I see how it makes a kind of sense. It also helps explain to me how you seemed so familiar. I'm just not sure how I knew what you would look like. How was I able to draw those pictures before I knew you?"

"I don't know, Declan. Maybe it was like a premonition? I mean, if we can see backward, maybe we can see forward as well?" I say, trying to be helpful. It all seems so foggy and difficult to explain. I want to tell him that the clarity comes from faith, but that seems so vague too. All I can do is trust my intuition.

"Yeah, I don't know...can't analyze it. I believe you, but I want to see for myself. I've made a decision. I want Mrs. Dawes to regress me," he says.

I pull to the side of the road; stop the car and turn to look him straight in the eye. "Declan, are you sure? There's no guarantee it will work. You may not see that lifetime; you may not see anything!"

"I want to try. I want to see what you see...even if it's not exactly the same pictures. I want to know what you're experiencing." He sounds serious. Who am I to tell him he can't?

"Ok, let's do it. We'll meet her at the store first thing in the morning. Now are you ready to hike?" I ask, clapping my hands. He smiles at me in a way that tells me he loves seeing me so happy. "It's not very far. I just have to drive us down this one-lane road and then we'll get out and it's about three miles from there. November is a great time to see Devil's Monument because the leaves are off the trees."

We walk down the muddy trail, hand-in-hand. I slip in the mud and curse myself for not wearing my hiking boots. We could walk on the stones, but most are covered in moss. As if reading my mind, Declan whispers to me that he'll catch me if I fall.

I let him walk ahead of me a bit so that I can look at him. I suppress the urge to come up behind him and pull him to me. I want to be overwhelmed by his skin and his strength. A breeze blows past us and I catch his scent: leather and incense. Heaven.

We reach a fork in the trail and decide to follow the right side of the trail because it's shorter. I grasp his hand and lead the way. His hand is enough for now.

All of a sudden we both hear a rustling in the trees up ahead, followed by a deep growl. I squeeze Declan's hand and we both freeze. We watch in horror as an enormous white dog comes out from the trees baring his teeth and growling. Declan pulls me to him. I let out a scream.

"Shh..." he whispers sharply and draws me as close to him as possible.

I had heard that there was a wild dog on the trail, but I had never seen him before. It never even occurred to me we would run into him. My thoughts are racing, trying to remember: had it ever attacked anyone?

That voice whispers: *You felt safe in coming here.*

I am safe.

"I think we can run. I don't think he'll chase us," I say slowly.

"You run, Ellie. I'll make sure he doesn't go after you."

My eyes are fixed on the dog as I tell him, "We can make it. You have to trust me." I feel rather than see him nod. "On the count of three."

On three, we are off. Racing back through the trail, we don't skip a beat. Regardless of our shoes and mossy steps, neither of us slips. The dog doesn't follow us, but that doesn't slow us down. We run the whole way back and collapse into each other against my truck. We are safe, laughing and exhilarated.

A look of intensity takes over Declan's face and suddenly he's not smiling anymore. His hands are in my hair and his mouth is claiming mine with desperation. I grasp him back, tightly. His emotions become his body. His sadness is in his kiss; his fear in his hands, his longing in his chest. I pull back for a breath of air.

"Sorry," he says quietly, breathless.

"Don't, don't be."

He takes me by the hand to the passenger seat and buckles me in. "I'll drive us back, ok?"

I nod, "Ok."

"I knew we'd be fine," he tells me as we drive away. I look at him and smile. I know I don't have to tell him I felt it too. He knows.

We decide to get something to eat and I text Tynan to meet us at Haddock's for fish 'n' chips and beer.

It's high time for some fun.

CHAPTER 27

Ellie

B.B. King's "There Must Be a Better World Somewhere" is blaring as we walk into Haddock's on Bay Street. Melissa, the owner of Haddock's, loves all the blues greats and plays them exclusively, unapologetically.

"Hey Ellie, where's Tynan?" she asks me, white rag slung over her shoulder. Melissa always looks the same. Black hair cut short, bright red lipstick, knee high boots with fishnets and both arms covered in henna tattoos. It strikes me that she seems more like the type of girl Declan would be attracted to than I am. They're the same age too: twenty-five.

"He's coming. This is Declan," I tell her, pulling him closer to me.

They shake hands and I tell myself to chill out. Yes, she's cute but so am I. Jealousy is the oldest form of paranoia.

We grab a table near the back where it's a little quieter. Declan orders a pitcher of Guinness and I begin to relax. It's been a long day, but there is something in me that refuses to dwell on the drama. I want peace and I'm beginning to realize that it's always up to me. In any situation I can choose to see a crisis or an opportunity to trust. It's as if my soul is tired and just doesn't want to fight anymore. It's a wise and loving surrender, not a fearful letting go.

"What are you thinking about Ellie?" Declan asks me with a warmth in his eyes I want to wrap myself in.

I reach across the table to grab his hands. "I'm just so thankful that we've met. I know I'm still in the fog a bit, but I'm beginning to see the light. We planned all of this, like our souls did, you know? Do you feel that too?"

"You must be right. We must have wanted to be together again. I'm not sure why we did, but I'm happy we did. I can learn so much from you." He leans over to give me a kiss and smiles. "So when is Tynan coming? I'd really like to get to know him better. I don't think he likes me too much." Declan looks away.

I laugh lightly. I can't tell if he's looking for reassurance or giving me a warning. "He's a little protective, that's all. You don't have to worry. He'll love you because I do."

At that moment Tynan swoops in chest first, his head held high and his hands grasping the strap of his leather messenger bag. He cannot seem to do anything subtly, ever. We exchange hugs and he settles in next to me.

I can feel that Declan is nervous. Tynan is studying him, almost searching for something in his demeanour. As I start talking about the wild dog incident, it's clear that Tynan is not listening to a word. Completely ignoring me, he turns to Declan.

"So what do you do?" His tone alerts me. This is a loaded question.

"I uh, well I'm not working right now. Actually, I've never worked," he says, observing his hands as they play with his glass.

"You've never worked? Wow. Are you rich or something?" asks Tynan with disdain in his voice.

Declan shifts uncomfortably. I can tell he doesn't want to talk about it. Being in the institution for most of his adult life probably put a cramp in his career plans. I had never considered that he didn't work and the thought makes me embarrassed. I don't like feeling that there are things about Declan I'm unaware of it. It's silly, but it's how I feel. I want to be the one who knows him better than he knows himself.

"Tynan! There's more to a person than what they do for a living and how much money they make," I admonish.

Tynan grins, "So that must mean you're an artist."

And I'm thinking: Um, Tynan you know this already. Where is this going?

Declan looks up briefly, not amused. "I am; I guess. I play guitar and I used to draw pretty good," he says.

"You play guitar, eh? I'm a musician too you know. We should all play together sometime. We'll throw Ellie a tambourine and turn down her mic; it'll be amazing," he jokes, eyes wide with jazz hands.

Declan laughs at this revelation in spite of himself. Tynan loves to mock my musical inability.

"So why do say you used to draw?" He's turning the conversation serious again.

Declan shifts again in his chair. He appears to be cursing himself for mentioning that he could draw at all. "I haven't done it in a long time, that's all. Ellie's been helping me get back into it."

Tynan is still looking straight at Declan. It's obvious I underestimated his resentment. I'm beginning to regret inviting him tonight. "So what did you draw then? And why did you stop?" he asks.

Declan looks from me to Tynan, unclear of what to say. I blink slowly and smile. In my mind I tell him he is safe. "Is there something you really want to ask me, Tynan?" asks Declan trying to remain cool.

Tynan doesn't skip a beat. He's calm but intense. "Yes actually. I'd like to know if you really think you're ready to be with Ellie, because I gotta be honest with you, man. I don't think you are."

It's as if the rest of the room has ceased to exist and these two men are alone, righting wrongs, clearing the air and I'm completely in the dark.

Declan pauses and then raises his stare to meet Tynan's. "I want to be. I will be," he replies evenly.

"You will be? What the hell does that mean? You expect her to just wait around while you get your life together? That's pretty damn selfish if you ask me." Tynan stops, takes a deep breath and starts again. For a brief moment I feel like maybe there is hope after all. "Listen man, I know what it's like to be in love. Sometimes you want to keep the other person in your life so much that you're blind to how wrong it is... how bad it is for them."

I can feel the fear rising in me, as if I had stored it away in some pocket of my gut and now it had burst free.

"You're not well, dude. You know you're not. Is it really a good idea to be pursuing this when you're still so sick?"

Declan goes white. I look from him to Tynan wishing that all of this could be unsaid and yet also to know what I'm dealing with.

"You can't look to her to save you. People can't save other people. You make a decision and you save yourself, period." He takes a deep breath, apparently considering his next words. "You have to tell her, man. You have to or I will," says Tynan with a kindness in his voice that had been absent all night.

I decide I have been silent long enough. "What's going on? Declan, what is he talking about?" I ask, now desperate to know.

Declan closes his eyes as if in pain. He looks as though he's lost everything in an instant. Glancing at me briefly he then looks down at his lap. "I'll tell her," he says quietly. He gets up from the table and offers me his hand. "Not here," he says in a tone that says there will be no arguing this point. "Let's go outside."

Declan

My heart is beating fast and loud in my ears. The reality of my madness is rising to the surface and I feel like I can't breathe. I take Ellie's hand and lead her outside, seating her on a park bench just outside. Tynan follows us, arms crossed. I consider telling him to piss off, but I leave him be.

I should have told her.

"I'm listening, Declan. You can tell me anything." Ellie's so calm and love seems to just drip from her lips. I want scoop her up and run away. Her eyes are clear and trusting, but I know she's scared.

I'm in front of her, pacing. Tynan stands beside her like a watchman. I force myself to speak, "Ok. Listen, I didn't hide this from you because I was afraid. It just didn't seem necessary and I didn't want to scare you."

I move to sit down next to her. I want to hold her hands, but I stop myself. "The night before I met you at the store was a really crappy night. I was low, like epically low. I went walking because being alone with my thoughts was making me crazy." Pausing, I look up at Tynan but his face reveals nothing. His arms are still crossed. "I walked over to Big Tub Harbour and climbed up to the lighthouse. I thought about… jumping."

Her hand shoots to her mouth in shock. I keep talking for fear of stopping. "Tynan was leaving the Big Tub Restaurant and he saw me up there. He talked me down. He was so calm, it was weird. He didn't freak out at all. I, on the other hand, was a mess."

Tynan's voice is barely above a whisper. "I've been there, man. It wouldn't have helped me to have someone freak out."

I continue and now I'm talking to Tynan, "As soon as I got down, I ran. I hoped you hadn't seen my face, but the night we met it was clear you had." I look down for a moment, squeezing my eyes shut, feeling the shame all over again. "I can only imagine what you both think of me. I'm just…I'm so ashamed."

"Declan, man, listen. Cut that shit right now. It's not what you've done, but what you're going to do. Are you going to get help?"

Ellie cocks her head as if to echo his question and it nearly breaks my heart. All I can do is nod.

She brings a hand to my cheek, cradling my heavy head. "We've all thought about it, Declan. We've all wanted to jump off bridges at one time or another. You came back down. You're safe." She sighs and gives me a puzzled look. "Where does all this sadness come from? You seem so guilty, why?"

"I don't know," I say and I really don't. "I wish I did. I wish I felt like I deserved to live, but honestly, Ellie, I don't. It's like I carry a weight with me every day and it's only a matter of time before I'm crushed beneath it."

"Are you taking your meds? That must help you feel better."

And then I can't look her in the eye. I stand up and take a few steps away from her. "They make me a zombie. I can barely feel! I sure as hell wouldn't be able to feel loving you. That I know for sure. Is that what you want?"

"Dude, you can't yell at her like that." Tynan's voice is firm bordering on ready-to-kick-ass.

"I'm not yelling at her. And what the hell are you still doing here? You got what you wanted. She knows!"

Ellie is biting her lip. "Declan, I want you to feel well."

"You make me feel well! You do that. Even when I feel I don't deserve you; you are my medicine!" She starts to say something, but I cut her off. "I already know what you're going to say. You'll say that's not healthy, that you can't fix me, but Ellie, all I can say is that you've given me something to live for. I feel hope when I'm with you. I feel like in the corners of your mind lies my salvation. Whatever it is that you're seeing when you see, I'm meant to see it too." I'm talking fast and ignoring Tynan's presence. As long as she's here, as long as she's listening I'll tell her all. "Do you believe me? I feel like my sickness started before I did...before I, Declan, did. I know it sounds crazy..."

She puts her fingers to my lips to quiet me. I finally breathe a strangled breath. She says, "Let's regress you, then. I know I could probably do it for you at this point, but I think it's best if we see Mrs. Dawes in the morning. Does that sound good?" I whisper: yes. She continues, "I love you... beyond time and space. It's overwhelming at times. I just have to remind myself that we've always been together and it's impossible for us to be apart, no matter what happens. When I believe that, I am at peace. When I remember that, I am happy."

I grab her. My hands are in her hair, my mouth on hers.

Pulling her as close as possible, I hear her gasp. I cannot get enough of her and yet I feel her exhaustion.

No more talking. Tynan can find his way in the dark. I'm taking this girl home.

I clutch her body, encouraging her to lean into me. Her breaths are shallow. I push my guilt aside. Thoughts of her perfection threaten to drag me down low. I grit my teeth and recall that no one is perfect. She hiccups loudly as if to illustrate my silent point and I crack a smile.

I whisper to her that we are almost there.

Walking through the threshold, the house is silent. Frances must be asleep. I ask Ellie if I can carry her up the stairs and she nods weakly, her fatigue now overtaking every cell of her. With each step I hug her closer, taking a moment to kiss her forehead. She makes a little sigh.

At the top of the stairs I turn my head to the right spotting a door with a wooden "E" hung on it. Taking her into the room, I flip the light switch and set her down onto the bed. The comforter is thick and soft. Ellie spreads her arms and grasps pillow corners in each hand. I could stare at her all night, just being close to her could be enough, but I know I have to go.

"I'll take your boots off, ok?"

Her eyes are softly closed, but she nods with a dreamy smile. "Just take it all off."

I laugh. She doesn't. "You're kidding, right?"

She shakes her head.

"Ellie, I..."

She raises an eyebrow lazily in challenge.

Has she any idea how cruel she is? I'm just supposed to strip her bare and leave? Maybe she thinks she's giving me a gift, displaying her forgiveness.

I grip the comforter nervously, debating. Her breaths are slowing, deepening. She's drifting off. I wonder briefly if I should just leave.

And then, as if of their own volition, my hands reach for her feet and unlace her boots: one, and then two. Her wool socks are next, revealing two long feet with a delicate pink polish on her toes. I rub her arches. She sighs. I breathe deep and move over her. Bringing my hands to her waist, I dip my fingers into the top of her tights and tug them down. Her knees are pink and dry. Her legs: pale and smooth.

Her underwear is white cotton. It's taunting me. I want to remove it with the rest but I don't. I reach for her sweater and slowly bring it over her head which has now lobbed ungracefully to her shoulder. She's out.

Her t-shirt is light blue and way too big for her. It's giving nothing away. I decide to leave it, but reason that she'll be much more comfortable without her bra. My hands reach up and underneath her, grasping for the clasps. Nothing. I have to peek. The clasp is there at the front, hiding beneath a cream-coloured ribbon. With great care and more time than the task probably requires I allow her bra to fall open. I glimpse her breasts: soft, round and perfect and then remove the garment completely.

Ellie curls up, her knees rising to her tummy as her arms and hands clutch her pillow. I bring the blanket over her and press my lips to her hair.

Shaking with a broad and bottomless longing that is doomed to go unsatisfied; I get up and leave her. Turning her light off, I trod down the stairs quietly, shutting the door behind me and walking once again into the cold, dark night.

CHAPTER 28

Ellie

I awake to Frances smoothing my hair out of my eyes. Her face is relaxed, the edges of her blurred as if surrounded by warmth and love. It could be the sleep in my eyes.

"Morning, baby," she coos. "Declan is downstairs. He says you're going to see Mrs. Dawes."

I stretch out and yawn loudly. "Yeah, he wants to be regressed."

She leans back slightly, almost disappointed. "Does he? I see. And how is Mrs. Dawes?"

I raise an eyebrow at her. "Still not a fan, eh?"

She shakes her head. "It's not that, it's just...I wanted to be the one to help you through all of that, you know?" I nod at her and put my hand in hers with a clap. "And what about Jack, how's he doing?"

I laugh, "He is as he ever was mother, as he ever was."

She smiles wistfully, a look in her eyes that I haven't seen in a while. "Good." She smacks my leg. "Now, get dressed! He's waiting."

Of course Mrs. Dawes knew we would be there. She even had some warm apple cider waiting for us. Taking the place I normally am Declan lays down on the couch a little unsure of himself. Mrs. Dawes kindly explains the process and it's clear it will take a little longer to calm his mind enough for him to accept. She leads him through a lengthy guided meditation and he begins to be soothed. Counting backwards from ten she leads him back into the nether-regions of thought. His eyes are fluttering gently as she asks him where he is.

"I'm wearing a linen shirt and weird, tight pants. I think they're called breeches. I'm drinking...a lot," he says and his body tenses.

"Ok, I'm going to ask you to rise out of that body and watch the scene from above. Can you do that?" asks Mrs. Dawes, softly. He gives an almost imperceptible nod and then visibly relaxes. It's on...

William

William downed another gulp of Isla whisky. He stopped appreciating the fineness of the spirit three glasses ago. It was doing its job of numbing the pain nicely. He had wanted to escape to the inn, but the weather was poor to say the least. He ended up in his room. All that was certain was that he had to get away from her and she would not dare to look for him here. His head hurt, but it was nothing compared to the pit of despair in his stomach. How could he have raised his voice at her?

It was like exquisite torture to be in the same house as Louisa. He desired her almost as much as he loved her, but he could not have her. It had been so long since William had been with a woman and the drink wasn't helping.

He stood and began to pace the room. How did it happen? He went to her room with the notion of gauging her feelings about him and left with declaring he would never marry. He was a fool. He had ruined any prospects of sharing his life with hers. Furthermore, after his brutish display, it was doubtful she would allow him to stay in the house any longer. Yes, he would have to pack up in the morning and leave. John Sinclair had a shack at the back of his house where he made whisky. Perhaps he would let him sleep there. He deserved little more than a shack.

Slugging back another drink, his mind grew fuzzy and his sadness rose. He would miss her. Would he still see her from time to time in the village or would she take Janey and go home earlier because of him? That is most likely what she would do. How could she stand to see him after the spectacle he made of himself?

Louisa was far too kind to make him feel badly, but he was certain she disliked him now. It would be too painful to face her and have her pretend she still cared for him. William decided it would be best if he avoided her.

He sat back down and cradled his head in his hands. Could he see her one last time? Surely she was asleep by now; it was after midnight. Could he not just look in on her? She would never have to know.

Emboldened by love and by drink, William shakily made his way down the stairs, candle in hand and cursed himself for consuming so much. He checked the hallways to make sure Edward and Janey were in bed. Noticing the fires were out, he concluded they must be. He made his way to the kitchen and stopped in front of her door. Deciding he had come too far to stop now, he opened the door and quietly stepped inside. He raised the candle to eyelevel and saw her sleeping soundly.

For a moment it was as if the world had come to a standstill. Swallowing deeply, he could only stare at her. Just being in her presence soothed his soul. Her beauty was so much deeper than her pretty features. Louisa had a peace and compassion to her that he found intoxicating. He wanted nothing more than to climb into her bed and wrap her body around his, to fade into her and never look back.

His breathing became heavy. He was thick with longing. William dared to inch closer. For a moment of insanity he believed he could have her right then and there without waking her. He closed his eyes briefly to imagine it and moaned involuntarily. She stirred.

"William?" she called.

In panic, he blew out the candle, but her eyes were accustomed to the dark.

"William, it is you. Is everything alright?" Though she must have been able to hear him breathing, he made no answer. "William, I know you are there. Will you not come closer? I wanted to speak to you." Her voice was groggy, yet kind.

Reluctantly he stepped toward her bed and fumbled for the chair. Sitting down he said: "It is unspeakable that I am here, madam..." He prayed she could not smell the whisky on his breath.

"William, all is well. I must apologize to you." He could not have heard her correctly. Why should she apologize?

"Louisa," he interrupted. "This will not do. I am the one who has been drinking. I am the one who has raised my voice and I am the one who has invaded a lady's room so disgracefully in the middle of the night!"

"I am in love with you, sir," she said quickly, perhaps afraid he would keep interrupting her. "I have been for quite some time. This is not easy for me to declare since I know you have no intention of marrying and that you prefer solitude, but there is no use in hiding it any longer."

William could not credit what he was hearing. How much had he imbibed? "You are joking. I have been so cruel to you! Louisa, no, this cannot be true." Was she mad? Or was she trying to take revenge on him? No, she was much too kind for such tricks. Too kind...

"Are you accusing a woman of not knowing her own heart? I love you. You are thoughtful, intelligent and...pleasing to look at. Shall I go on, sir?" she declared with a quiet laugh in her voice.

He felt tears in his eyes and his throat closing up. He was overcome. Never had he felt so much hope and despair at the same time. She loved him, but he did not deserve her love. Not five minutes earlier he had been fantasizing about taking her body against her will. "You don't know me Louisa," he croaked. "I am not a good man. If you knew the nature of the thoughts in my head, you would think me the most despicable scoundrel."

"William," she uttered softly. "I do not know what you think you were going to do to me while I laid here, but I know you well enough to be sure you could never go through with it. And, in any case, how do you know that your advances would not have been welcomed?" He was silent. "What have you to say to that?" She reached for his hand and placed a kiss in his palm. He breathed in sharply at her touch.

"Louisa, I...I am drunk..."

"I know," she continued to kiss his hand and trailed a line to his wrist. "You are also beginning to make me nervous. I have professed my love for you and you have said nothing of your feelings for me."

"You want the confessions of a drunken man? You know not what you ask for," he said quietly reaching for her hand and bringing it to his lips. "I am...taken with you." The words sounded barely adequate, even to his own ears.

He attempted to start again, "I...I love you Louisa. It is painful how much I do. You are second to no one in my eyes. Your beauty, your kindness, your wisdom... you are unequalled. I cannot have you and that is unbearable. It makes me want to rise above this world, to take you to some far off star and hide," he confessed. His heart was heavy. He did not like feeling so vulnerable, but there was nothing to be done for it.

"You can have me William. You need only ask," said Louisa. She placed her hands on his arms and gently pulled him toward her. "Will you not come closer? I fear I need your comfort right now."

Though it was highly improper, William could not bring himself to refuse her. Louisa shifted herself to allow him room and he lay down beside her. He wrapped his arms around her and pulled her near. The feeling of her body so close to his made him lightheaded. He found it difficult to focus, but knew he had to tell her his fears. "Louisa, you are out of my reach. We are in two very different spheres. I want nothing more than to...but in any case, my pride and my circumstances make it impossible," he declared, his voice shaking.

Her eyes grew soft and her entire being seemed to glow as she declared, "I see the light in you. And I am being taught that I am meant to see the light in everyone. I believe that I do. The difference with you William is that I would spend this life with you. You are not this body, this darkness. You are your light."

"I see only dark but with you."

She smiled at his severity. "You are being ridiculous, but I have not the strength to argue with you. Knowing that you love me is enough for now." Reaching for his shirt, she gently pulled it up and out of his breeches and brought her hands underneath it to the bare skin of his back.

William shivered and sighed. He sought her mouth and kissed her. Louisa yielded to him so easily. It was intoxicating and for a man who had already passed the threshold of reason, it was dangerous. He knew he could not stay another moment without compromising her irreversibly. It was his greatest desire to stay and do exactly that, but he respected her too much. Even in his inebriated state, he could not treat her thus.

He pulled back. "Louisa, I cannot stay. I shall leave you now," he said, determined.

"I do not want you to go," she said burying her head in his chest. After placing several kisses on the bare part of his neck she finally lay back and released him. "Good night, William."

He felt cold suddenly as she pulled away. He wanted to reach out and hug her to him once more, but knew the impossibility of releasing her again if he did. William rose, fumbled for the flint lighter at her bedside and re-lit his candle.

The neck of her night dress had been pulled down past her shoulder. Forcing himself to look at her eyes he said: "Good night, Louisa. Rest assured, I will dream of you tonight as I have done every night since seeing you in London. Though I have done nothing to deserve it, I am overwhelmed at the idea that you return my regard. I only wish things were different."

She studied his face. She appeared to be thinking of something that pleased her. "I love you," she uttered in a hush.

"*Anam cara.*" he whispered.
And he was gone.

Louisa

She found no sleep that night.

Putting her fingers to her lips, she closed her eyes to recall the moment when they kissed. She thought about how she had wanted more and could not bring herself to feel ashamed of it. Being with William was as natural as sleep, as breath, as heartbeat. It was not something she could repress, nor did she wish to.

Her mind raced with excitement and possibilities. She would write to the family lawyer in the morning and all would be well. They could be together. She would take care of everything!

Her inner guide whispered: *You need do nothing*, but she silenced it.

This was different, she reasoned. This time she needed to intervene. All would be well.

CHAPTER 29

William

He awoke from a half-hour's rest with a pounding in his head and a pain in his heart. He could scarcely believe the events of last night. Louisa loved him. She offered herself to him and he refused her. And she so much as asked him to propose to her. He could not credit it. Not only that, he could not agree to it. He had not yet been introduced into society and he could not enter through his wife. What a laughing stock he would be! No, if she could wait five years for him, perhaps he would have amassed enough money and clout so that he could enter society through his own merit and connections. He could not take a handout. He would not. Louisa deserved a man of worth.

Breathing deeply, he forced himself to get out of bed though his entire body ached at the effort. He walked over to the small, dusty looking glass hanging on the wall and studied his reflection. He desperately needed to shave. Rubbing his chin, William's thoughts drifted back to Louisa's beauty and the softness of her body. Could he wait five years to hold her like he had? Could he suffer half a decade of not being able to kiss her again? The desire to take her and make her his wife was overwhelming, made his mind run rampant with irrational possibilities.

He was fooling himself if he thought he could stay here any longer. He needed to get away for a while and think. He would feign a business emergency and return to London for a few weeks. Construction had been going well and he knew Sir Thomas planned to stay for a few more months.

It was decided. He would go.

He dressed himself and forced down a gulp of whisky: Hair of the dog.

He would leave tomorrow. Outside his window he could hear

the wind whipping the cottage. A tree branch scratched the pane and reminded him of Mull's wild weather. It was not good for travel to be sure, but it could not be helped. Perhaps he might take a ship to Harwich. That would keep his mind off of Tobermory, off of her. He needed to think of London. London would bring solace and ideas to solve his dilemma.

William stepped toward his bedroom door and stopped in an attempt to rein in his thoughts. Resting his forehead on the door he chided himself. There was surely no man who deserved Louisa less than he. Why did she love him? He was the son of a chambermaid, a mere tradesman, and last night he had acted vilely!

But it was obvious she had sensed his love for her. She knew him so well that he would swear she knew him before they met. When William had first spotted her in the ball room she appeared to look right through him. He was done for right then and there. Her beauty was obvious and her worth only slightly less so.

William raked his fingers through his hair and stomped his boot in frustration. He hated this confusion. His pride was leading him to London, but his desire for peace was beckoning him to stay. Would her love for him improve her life in any way? William was not convinced. She was so good, so pure and ready to forgive in an instant. If they did marry and she realized her mistake afterward, she would never complain. He could not bear to see her suffer in silence. It would wound him irreparably to suspect she felt indebted to him.

The more he thought about it the more he was convinced that Louisa's feelings for him were more likened to a vague inclination than love. She barely knew him after all. While he did not doubt his admiration for her, he also knew that was different. Louisa was perfection. Everyone loved her. William was only too aware of his many faults. Melancholy took hold in his mind once more. It was unfair to take her now and it was unfair to make her wait. The best thing to do was to end this whole mess before it even begun.

He could feel traitorous tears stinging his eyes and sniffed them back in an effort to regain control. It is for the best, he told himself. She would be happier without him.

Louisa

Louisa knelt at her bedside in prayer. William was pulling away. She did not need to see him to know it, she felt it. She knew him better than he knew himself. She felt as though she could recite word for word the tall tale he was spinning in his imagination. Surely he was convincing himself of his unworthiness. He was concocting some kind of escape. She was well aware of his propensity for guilt and misery, but she also caught glimpses of its retreat. William did have moments of hope...of allowing himself the happiness he deserved. She would concentrate on that. She would give that to the wind and pray for its return tenfold. But it could not hurt to help things along a little. Louisa would follow through with her plan. She had to...for William.

Louisa's ankle felt sufficiently better and she turned Janey away this morning in favour of dressing herself. She dressed in a plain white day dress and pearls. She styled her hair simply and pinched her cheeks.

She was ready to face him.

Was it too much to ask that he hold her? Kiss her? She hoped not. It felt as though they had crossed a bridge of understanding last night. She did not wish to go back. Indeed, she could not. William reaffirmed her faith. And though he mostly identified with darkness, his light was bright. She saw it. She recognized it at once and knew it to be her home.

A knock came to her door and she hobbled to answer it. William greeted her solemnly on the other side. Her stomach fluttered. Though she knew relatively few men, her intuition told her she observed near-perfection when she looked upon him.

"Louisa! What are you doing on your feet? Come; let me carry you back to bed." William swept her up into his arms before she could protest.

"I believe it is good for me to try and walk a little. I have only gone between my bed, my dressing table and the door, sir!" she laughed. Louisa soaked up the feel of being in his embrace. It was only mere seconds before he placed her on the bed.

"How are you feeling this morning? You look well," said William with a kind smile as he settled himself into the chair at her bedside.

"I am well. I will only get better, you can be sure. Will you not come sit beside me again William? My father has gone to the village and Janey will not disturb us," she said hopefully. She watched him consider her request and then lean back away from her. Louisa's heart sank.

"I see," she said almost imperceptibly. "May I ask you something, William?" He nodded his assent. Louisa brought his hands to her lap. "Will you ever allow yourself to be happy? Will you ever be able to let go of these insane notions of unworthiness and allow yourself to experience the peace and comfort you so deserve?"

William looked at her with a strained expression. "Madam, I am afraid I do not have the pleasure of understanding you. Have I given the impression that I am unhappy? And if I have, is there reason to believe that you could be the remedy?" His words held no warmth.

"Why must you grasp onto so much pain? It only begets more pain," she said bringing his hands to her lips.

He removed his hands from hers under the guise of needing to adjust his waistcoat. She had clearly struck a nerve.

"Louisa, I have business that needs my attention. I will have to leave for London in the coming days."

She ignored him. "William, dare I ask you about us? Many

women would have hopes for an engagement after what transpired between us yesterday. I fear I know you too well to expect that, but any insight into a future together is welcome, sir," she said softly trying to catch his eyes.

"Louisa, you have every right to demand marriage after..."

"You know I will not," she interrupted.

He softened at her declaration and his voice grew tender. "You are too good. I wish you knew what I know."

"Interestingly enough Mr. Mara, I wish for the very same thing," she replied. It seemed impossible to be angry with him. He suffered so, even if it was at his own hand.

Louisa breathed deeply, parted her lips and willed him to kiss her. He appeared to be watching her, helpless. He leaned in and put his mouth to hers. Her hand went to the back of his head to deepen the kiss leaving her in a fog of desire. William rose from the chair and lay down beside her without their lips parting.

Louisa shifted slightly to allow him room and then moved her body closer to his. She could feel his force as he put his arms around her. She moaned softly and momentarily brought him back to his senses. He pulled away slightly and apologized. "Forgive me," he said bowing his head. He attempted to rise from the bed, but was restrained by Louisa.

"There is nothing to forgive. I want you here with me. Is that so wrong?" Perhaps it was unfair to ask, but she knew he would leave no matter what. Because of that, she felt entitled to confessing her heart's desires. She felt it imperative that he know exactly how she felt, even if part of him did not believe her.

"I must go," he said unfeelingly. Looking up at her face though, he seemed to relent: "Louisa, I admit I am at your mercy. I will not make a speech. You know my heart and I suspect you know my mind, my reasoning... everything. I ask that you trust me. I may be a miserable soul, but I am one who would die to see you so. My love for you outweighs my need for you. I must leave you now." He stood up from her bed and she let him go.

She took hold of his hand one last time and kissed his palm softly. "You are a ridiculous creature, William Mara. I will not succumb to the torture you so readily embrace."

"I would not have you do it," he replied, his words heavy with despair.

"Yes, well I have seen too much to be anchored to such hopelessness. However, when I say I love you, I mean it. In you I see myself, the shadows and the light. There is an undeniable perfection beating strong in your heart. Know that."

William bent down and kissed the top of her head. "I make no promises."

And he left her.

Louisa lay back and closed her eyes, willing herself to calm down.

She pictured Mother Mary in her mind's eye. She smiled at Louisa and opened her arms wide.

Just let go, whispered the spectre.

Louisa took a deep breath, allowed a few tears to be shed and then finally surrendered to sleep.

CHAPTER 30

Ellie

Mrs. Dawes brought Declan out of hypnosis slowly and gently. Listening to him and experiencing William and Louisa from the other side was all-encompassing. I felt drawn in. I could sense William's pain so vividly. It was like I was remembering it.

Throughout the whole regression I had heard whispers, like a melody hummed soft and low tugging at my memory of a song sung long ago. There was a part of me, an intuition, that was asking me to awaken.

Declan opened his eyes gradually and looked around. I could tell he had gone deep and was finding it difficult to adjust to his surroundings. I would help him.

"Declan?" I call softly. "Are you ok?"

He sits up slowly and locks his eyes with mine. "I've loved you a long time."

He's looking at me as if we are the only two people in the room. All of my senses are on alert, completely attuned now to him.

His voice is intense, assured. "That was unlike anything I've ever done. I could feel how everyone was feeling. I knew what Louisa and William were thinking. William's fear and guilt were just so obvious and then Louisa...never have I been around anyone who had such compassion and innocence. Never until I met you, that is. You have her kindness and generosity, Ellie. You have her beauty."

I could feel myself blushing as he continued. "I can tell this experience is about more than just how cool it is to know about a past life. We're meant to learn some things here. I kept hearing the words 'Forgive yourself' while I was under," he said.

Mrs. Dawes rubs her hands together quickly, as she leans forward in her chair. "That is incredible, Declan!"

Pushing his palms into his lap, he stands. "I agree Mrs. Dawes, but I don't know what to do with it."

She nods at him sympathetically. "Spirit does. Have you prayed before?"

Declan looks down at her, uneasy. "In desperation, yes...not really for any kind of guidance."

"Right, well it's not that hard. You have all you need already. Just declare you don't know what all this is for and ask for help. Bring it all to the light. And you'll be shown," she says, her voice without a trace of doubt.

"I'm sorry, that seems so vague."

Mrs. Dawes laughs. "We want the mysteries of the world to be so goddamned complex so that we can give a reason for our resistance in learning about them. It's simple; and you -everyone for that matter- have all the answers within. Just ask. That's what intuition really is."

Declan goes to her, offering his hand to help her up. He tells her that he is still unsure, and yet he's willing to figure it all out. The two of them paint an endearing picture. He: tall, severe, lean and clad in black. She: petite, pear-shaped, bright and unapologetically loving.

Declan was tired and decided to head back to the inn for some rest. I tucked my head beneath his chin as we embraced and whispered: "Sweet dreams."

There was something about that session. There was something else in his manner, something I had rarely seen in him. It was hope.

I asked Mrs. Dawes for some privacy so I could meditate. Suddenly I needed hope too.

CHAPTER 31

Louisa

A few days passed and finally Louisa was given leave by Mrs. Young to walk out of doors. Upon hearing the good news, she immediately asked a favour of the midwife. She wanted to see her mother's old home and asked Mrs. Young to take her to it. Louisa knew that her mother lived in her. She hoped she came to her in dreams. She seldom remembered her dreams so the hope was placed there blindly: there was little chance of confirmation or contradiction. She missed her mother so much sometimes that it hurt. There was a physical ache, a longing that was subdued only by closing her eyes...breathing.

And then the Mother of God would whisper: *How can you yearn for that which has never left you?*

She let herself bask in the possibility of that and then shrugged it off. Today was the day; the day she would find her mother's home. Louisa was grateful for the words of wisdom, but this pursuit was already meant to happen. If God had written the script, then Louisa was following the stage directions, saying her lines. Finding this house would help her. It would lead her to exactly where she needed to be. And of course, the Blessed Mother would be her guide. She would not go anywhere without her.

Louisa reminded Janey and Edward in a brief and decisive manner that she was walking into the village. She was meeting Mrs. Young, the midwife, at her home in the village. She knew the servants would not approve, telling her father had been challenging enough. It was not a matter for discussion however; Louisa was determined.

When Mrs. Young had been treating Louisa for her sprained ankle, she had confided to Louisa that she had known her mother. It had been all Louisa could do to keep calm. Of course she always had her father to glean from, but here sat a woman who knew her mother as a girl!

She had grabbed Mrs. Young's hand right out of the washing basin. "Tell me about her, please! What was she like?"

Mrs. Young laughed at her young charge. "Aye, I will. Depend upon it child. I will tell you all I know about your mother. She be right pretty that one. She didn't talk much, but she said a lot if you catch my meaning. She was wise. Though she was but two years my senior, I felt as though she could have been my own mother. I wouldn't dare cross her for fear of disappointing her. We all loved Mary Boyle."

Louisa's eyes welled up at this. She had always felt safe with her mother, but that seemed a natural symptom of being her daughter. It warmed her heart to know that she made others feel this way too.

Continuing down the tree-lined path, she reached the clearing to the village. It was a fine day in Tobermory. The sun shone brightly and its rays bounced joyfully off the glass-like surface of the sea. Louisa breathed deeply, savouring the scent of salt and fish. The wind was a mere breeze today, the perfect setting for her quest. She said a silent prayer of thanks.

She approached the door of Mrs. Young's tiny village home with an excitement difficult to contain. Laughing out loud at her silliness, Louisa took a moment to calm. She raised a hand to knock on the door, but was surprised when it opened revealing Mrs. Young who was apparently preparing to quit the house.

"Oh, Miss De vale! I am so sorry, but I just received word that Mrs. Brown is having pains. It looks like her wee babe will be coming early," she declared good-naturedly. Louisa tried unsuccessfully to hide her disappointment. Mrs. Young touched her arm reassuringly. "Fear not, love. My boy, George, will take you to your dear mother's house. And you needn't worry, he'll be a gentleman. I put the fear of God in him!" she announced with a laugh.

It was then that Louisa noticed someone standing in the shadow of the doorway. Mrs. Young grabbed the young man and lovingly pushed him forward. Apparently this was George. She had to strain her neck to look at his face. Indeed, he was the tallest man she had ever seen and yet he could not be more than nineteen. His girth, it seemed, had yet to catch up with his height. He was so shy and his manner so gentle, that Louisa dropped any fear she may have had. She introduced herself quietly and curtsied before him. George immediately went red and bowed to her to be polite, but perhaps also to mask his embarrassment. Mrs. Young kissed them both and hurried away.

"Er…follow me, if you please, Miss De vale," said George in a voice barely above a whisper. Louisa now noticed that he was quite handsome although it was clear from his demeanour that this would be news to him. His brown eyes were soft, with long dark lashes and his chestnut hair was well-kept and shone youthfully in the midday sun. Louisa smiled. He would make some young lady a fine husband one day.

"I thank you, Mr. Young, for agreeing to take me to my mother's family home. Though I am sure you had little choice in the matter. Am I right?" she asked archly. George's eyes were fixed on the ground as they walked out of the village, but Louisa could tell he grinned at her comment. "I promise I shall not linger long. My mother has been gone these ten years and I miss her. To see a part of her past will bring me comfort, but it is not my intention to keep you from your affairs."

Mr. Young breathed in sharply. Looking up briefly he uttered "It is not a bother, madam. It is an honour; I assure you." Now it was Louisa's turn to blush. His voice was quietly intense and he gave the impression of knowing her.

"Have we met, sir?" she asked on impulse.

Her question seemed to catch him off guard. "No, Miss De vale…that is I…I have seen you in the village. You were singing one day with my younger sisters," he replied nervously.

He really was a sweet young man. Louisa could not help but feel affection for him and therefore her penchant for teasing rose to the surface. "Ah-ha! I have caught you, sir. You have been spying on me. Worried I am not a worthy friend for your dear sisters, eh?"

Immediately Mr. Young retreated. He was clearly worried that he had said too much. Putting his hands in his pockets, he quickened his pace to put distance between he and Louisa.

"Mr. Young! Come now, I was only jesting. I know you were doing no such thing. I apologize if I offended you. I seem to have a knack for offending. Perhaps I should take it as a sign to speak less…"

Mr. Young stopped suddenly and in a moment of bravery, offered his arm to her. Louisa felt her heart give a little jump. He reminded her of Mr. Mara. The thought made her sigh and curl her lips slightly into a saddened smile. For a moment she forgot where she was. Mr. Young turned and guided her up the path that would lead them to the cottage. Silently, Louisa asked Mother Mary for strength. It was then they heard a shout from behind them.

"Louisa! My dear!" called Sir Thomas. Louisa and George Young turned in unison to see her father and Mr. Mara at the bottom of the hill.

They had met with the engineer earlier and appeared to be on their way back to Cliffside. The two men climbed to meet them. William looked distracted and seemed unwilling to meet her eyes. Louisa introduced Mr. Young to the gentlemen.

"I had thought that the midwife was taking you to the house, my dear," said her father.

"As did I," said William sharply, his gaze now intensely fixed on her. She wanted to roll her eyes at his stern tone. Had he forgotten himself? They had no understanding to speak of. She was not his.

Mr. Young found his voice, "My mother had to visit Mrs. Brown and asked me to show Miss De vale to the house." It was obvious he was speaking to William, but William did not take his eyes from Louisa.

"Perhaps I may join you?" he asked.

Mr. Young started to reply, but Louisa spoke first. "I do not believe that to be necessary, sir. Mr. Young seems quite capable to escort me. We shall not be long." If he was jealous, she would make it clear she would have none of it. She would insist on complete trust.

William was seething. He looked to Sir Thomas as if seeking his support, but found none. "Really, Miss De vale, I must insist"

"No sir, I insist," she interrupted with a voice that would not be gainsaid. "Come Mr. Young. Farewell Father…Mr. Mara." And with that the two turned back toward the path and walked away.

CHAPTER 32

William

George Young looked back briefly at the gentlemen with a slightly smug look that made William's blood boil. "Over my dead body," he muttered to himself.

Sir Thomas had sympathy, "Come on, son. Let us return to the house. I happen to know that Mary's home is not more than five minutes from here. All will be well."

"Five minutes indeed, sir?" And with that, Mr. Mara's mind was made up on the matter.

She was too close to him.

William watched as Mr. George Young led his Louisa up the path leading to her mother's childhood home. He stayed as far back as possible to keep out of sight and yet still be able to see them. He told himself that he had to ensure her safety. It was highly improper that she be allowed to go anywhere with a man unescorted. How could Sir Thomas not see that? How could Louisa not see it?

He shifted away from the beaten path to follow closer alongside and through the bit of forest that curtained them. She was laughing. He was making her laugh. William stopped for a moment as the truth took hold: of late all he had done was cause her unhappiness. He exhaled sharply and let the notion leave with the breath. It was much too heavy on his heart to feel that right now.

They came around the bend and suddenly it was there. At that moment, the sun reappeared between two clouds and a beam shone down on the structure. It was the façade that met them first: crumbling stone with moss claiming the bottom half of the house. It was plain. The roof was steepled and completely sunken in. The front door had a board nailed across it, barring entry, and five murky windows adorned the front wall.

William tugged at his cravat as he watched Louisa separate herself from Mr. Young and walk slowly towards the cottage, as if magnetized to it. She held a gloved hand just slightly at her mouth, her manner one of wonder. He wished to go to her, but he swallowed hard and remained in his spot behind a tall pine tree. Mr. Young shuffled his feet and studied the ground. William silently willed the man to stay where he was.

Louisa went to a window and pressed her hand to the glass. He could not tell if she could see inside. Her chest rose and fell slowly; she was taking it all in. Was she crying? It was difficult to tell. In his mind's eye he pictured himself going to her, putting his arms around her and pulling her close as he whispered "All is well, my darling. I am here."

But he was not there. He was a coward behind a tree. And the woman he loved stood grieving a lost mother but twenty feet away from him.

Just then Louisa raised her head and looked in his general direction. He brought his head quickly back behind the trunk. She had not seen him.

She sat down on a large rock to the side of the house. She was closer now. Eyes closed, she brought her hands together in prayer. He allowed himself to soak up the picture she created. Her spencer was brown, but her gloves and dress were white. She wore tiny white flowers in her blazing red hair that resembled little bells. He had earlier resisted the urge to take in their scent mixed with hers. William observed as a calm appeared to wash over her and he could swear that a white light emanated from her head and shoulders, if only for a moment.

His breath caught and he sighed. An image of his mother was brought forth from the far reaches of his memory and for once, it was not unwelcome.

Louisa opened her eyes and again looked in the direction of where he stood. The smallest evidence of a smile appeared on her face, but it was enough to disarm him. How he wished he could be the source of her smiles...

Thankfully, he was completely hidden from view.

"Mr. Young," she called. "I am ready to go now."

Louisa

Louisa returned to Cliffside feeling a mixture of grief and harmony. The house had not been as derelict as she had previously feared. The most notable part about it had been how much moss covered the foundation of the structure... as if at least one aspect of nature had not forgotten. She had imagined that her mother's spirit would speak to her on the grounds there. It had not. She felt her mother always, but had hoped the feeling would intensify somehow by being close to where she had once lived. Louisa took a deep breath and smiled. It is possible she had put too much stock in a broken old house.

Walking in the front door, Louisa recalled the moment she had felt strong arms about her and a whisper in her ear. She closed her eyes once more to invite the feeling back. It had been exquisite; a lifting of fear and sorrow, but it lasted only an instant. And then later she had prayed. Sitting on a rock, she had called on Mother Mary for protection and to ease the pain in her heart. It was working, if only a little.

Removing her gloves and spencer, she felt someone watching her. Out of the corner of her eye she spotted Mr. Mara standing by the hearth, staring at her...looking at once heartbroken and relieved. They had rarely spoken since that last conversation in her bedchamber. He now rose earlier and returned to the house only after the rest of them had already dined.

For her own part, Louisa could not find the motivation to seek him out. Instinctively she knew he needed space and yet, she felt his presence every second of the day no matter where he was. It was as if she could sense him thinking of her, wondering where she was and what her thoughts were. It was both endearing and infuriating. She decided to settle on an emotion somewhere in the middle.

"Does something offend you, Mr. Mara?" she addressed him without looking up. "I do believe you are staring at me. You must at least give me leave to attend to my appearance before surveying my person so gravely!"

He laughed briefly, possibly in spite of himself but soon again turned serious. "It was not my intention to stare, madam."

His response was cryptic and Louisa was not about to let him off so easily. "What was your intention, sir?"

"I- That is, I had no intention other than to greet you." He was holding his hat in front of him and nervously running his fingers about the brim. "I uh...I hope that Mr. Young was a gentleman."

"You know that he was."

William reared his head, indignant. "I know no such thing and really Miss De vale, it is highly improper that he escorted you anywhere without a proper chaperone. I am not sure what Mrs. Young was thinking..."

Louisa brought her hand to her temple in exasperation. "This is Mull, Mr. Mara not London. And you are fooling no one. I know that you followed us."

She made her way past him and climbed the stairs to her room. She knew she must try to keep a cool head and to remember that, in the end, she still loved this man.

Following her and stopping in her doorway he declared, "I do not know what to say, other than that your safety was all I thought of."

"Really?" she asked dubiously as she unpinned her long red hair and let it fall upon her shoulders.

"I saw the way he looked at you, Louisa. You do not know men. I shall leave it at that."

She rounded on him, "You shall leave it at what, pray tell, some vague evaluation of the feelings of a stranger? Really,

William, I am surprised at you. You ignore me for days and then sulk like a child upon seeing me with a new friend."

"He has no wish to be your friend, depend upon it," said William, his voice now cold.

"You do not know him. George is kind, quiet and a perfect gentleman. He struggles to express himself, I think. He reminds me of you in many ways..." Louisa trailed off at the declaration. At this William's face looked pained. "William, stop. I can feel you telling yourself all manner of things untrue," she said, that familiar tone of compassion now returning to her voice.

He looked away from her and held his body tightly, as if trying to mentally build a wall around himself.

Louisa approached him and cautiously touched his arm. He flinched. "You did not like seeing me with Mr. Young."

He would not look at her. "I did not."

She inched closer to him and said in a voice that was little more a whisper, "I am sorry for it. I look upon him simply as a new acquaintance."

His eyes were red, his jaw clenched. Louisa observed his struggle with concern. She wondered: What is he not saying? Why does he torture himself so?

"What is this hold you have over me?" he asked his breathing heavy.

The flood gates were finally opening.

"My heart felt as though it had been ripped from my chest when I saw you with him. Suddenly the possibility of you being with another man, any man, dawned on me. I had to push it out of my mind for fear of going mad. And when you turned and walked away with him...Blast it, woman! You win," he yelled.

She startled slightly and he could see he had upset her. "I am sorry. I should not have raised my voice." He took her hand and led her to the bed so they could sit. With a sigh, William brought her hands to his lips pressing desperately as if letting go could mean she might disappear.

"I have realized I cannot follow my pride. It pains me and it makes me question my strength as a man to be sure, but it cannot be helped. I adore you." He looked up at her with a raw openness she had never before witnessed. "I had an epiphany while I watched you today. You teach me what my mother tried to when I was young, though I would not listen. You instruct me on how to remember my goodness. You do this effortlessly. I do not know how you do it, but I know it is in my best interest to remain with you and allow you to work your magic."

His words were answered prayers and she could feel tears in her eyes. "It is not magic, sir."

"I believe that it is. I also believe you to be beautiful, exceptionally so."

She shook her head briefly and moved slightly away from him. "No, not exceptionally," she said.

"How can you say such a thing? It is my belief."

"Sir, beauty has never been my burden. I do not believe a woman can be deemed exceptionally beautiful unless it has harmed or held her back in some way. This has not been the case with me."

William ran his thumbs across her cheeks and kissed her briefly. "I will not argue with you. I did want to say however, that I asked you to believe me and to trust me. That was unfair since I was apparently unwilling to do the same for you. You say you love me; I will believe you. You say we can be happy together and though I know not how that can come to pass, I am willing to let you teach me. Louisa, I will stay with you as long as you will have me. I am at your command."

She let his words wash over her like a fall of light. Bringing her hands to his face and gently massaged his temples. "You are safe with me, William. I promise you. Everything shall be fine."

William sighed and surrendered himself to her will. He was vulnerable, which he disliked greatly, but at least he was in her arms.

CHAPTER 33

Ellie

I had to work at the dive shop in an hour so I asked Mrs. Dawes if I could help her while she opened up the store. My real motive was guidance and comfort. It felt like I was a little girl again, helping in the shop and listening to my mentor explain the mysteries of the Universe.

She was the one who made me realize that wisdom is not boastful. True wisdom is gentle and relevant. It comes to us when we are ready to hear it through a conduit we perceive as safe and loving. How many times Mrs. Dawes has been that conduit for me, I think to myself.

I open a box of Vitamin C bottles and begin stocking a display with the caption "Protect Yourself this Cold Season". Smiling to myself I think about how protected I feel. Ever since I began to witness my lifetime as Louisa I have felt less and less afraid. It is as if there had always been a blanket of love surrounding me and I have just recently reached for it and pulled it tight around me. I had been afraid, but more than that... I didn't believe that I deserved such a thing. The disbelief kept me quiet, kept me small, kept me suffering.

I was grateful for new beliefs.

Mrs. Dawes is humming "The Rainbow Connection", the Kermit the Frog song. I smile. She used to sing that to me until one day, when I was twelve, I told her it was a baby song.

"You know, Mrs. Dawes, it's the funniest thing. I feel Louisa, like you said I would. It's as though I carry her with me," I look over at my older friend who is smiling thoughtfully as she crouches on an old milk crate and prices boxes of raisins. "And it's as though I have her knowledge with me too. She has this feeling about her... like she can see everything: past, present and future. And it's like I can tap into that. Does that make sense?"

"Of course it does, love. It's clear that Louisa was incredibly spiritually aware. She's helping you, Ellie, but don't forget, she is you. Declan was right. You have everything she had. And what you describe about perceiving the past, present and future all at once makes sense. Time is an illusion anyway. And when you know that, you experience time with its spiritual purpose, healing."

I consider that for a moment. "So by tapping into this wisdom of Louisa's I can see that everything is always ok, like everything is happening the way it should? Is that what you mean?"

Mrs. Dawes walks over to me and gently squeezes my shoulders. "You're getting it. Let Louisa show you. She's a symbol in your mind of pure, compassionate love. Remember the meditations we used to do when you were little? Try that tonight. Let her take over and help you. We think we have to save the world, Ellie, but really all we need to remember is that there is no world to save. Heaven, indeed love, is all there is. It's a state of mind... a shift in how we perceive every little thing."

I hugged her and thanked her. Though I did not yet know what she meant, I had a feeling I would.

Walking along Little Tub Harbour, I thought of Scotland. How alike were the two villages who became namesakes? Was it a random coincidence? A glance at an old map to inspire a name? Then, the cover of a book I had once seen flashes in my mind's eye. I remember seeing it at the little book store once near the dive shop.

I hear a whisper: *Go*, it says.

Having a little time before I had to be at work, I decide to stop into the store and check it out. There was a passage I recalled and wanted to read. There was something important in it. Something I needed to know.

Without thinking, I was guided to the shelf of local books and the book nearly fell into my hands: The Bruce Beckons by W.

Sherwood Fox. I opened the book, randomly, to page 19 and read:

"A glance at Tobermory itself will give us at least a partial understanding of its life and importance. Some people call the place a harbour, but they fall short of the truth. Tobermory is two harbours, or rather three. Together the three form two havens..."

I gasped looking up from the book. The three form two havens. Somehow I knew this was about Louisa (me), William (Declan) and Spirit. I then look further down the page and read on.

"Who among its many settlers of Scottish birth or descent gave it its name? Nobody now knows. But whoever he was he must have been a man of Mull... The manifest resemblance so warmed his heart that he could not resist changing its name to something that kept bright every day the memory of his Scottish island home."

Louisa was with me, guiding my every step. I felt my resistance melting away, and in its place, a peaceful calm rising to the surface. This feeling may not last forever, but at least now I would recognize it when it returned.

I knew I had to see Declan. There was so much to learn and there was also much to uncover. There was still something about that lifetime with Louisa and William. There were secrets there that needed to be brought to light.

I decide to go to Declan's tonight and ask him to meditate with me. He may not see what I see, but I want his presence, his love and understanding. I was mildly aware of trepidation at the idea of being alone with Spirit. Not wanting to look at it too deeply however, I brush the thought aside and take out my phone to text Declan.

My hands quiver as I type: *I need to see you.*

CHAPTER 34

Declan

The image of Louisa is still fresh in my mind as I leave the store. There is a purity of soul about her and yet a naivety that could be her downfall. I sense it. William's love for her is mine and yet there is a dread that creeps up my spine and implants itself in the back of my mind. It makes me want to protect Ellie.

And there is so much of Ellie in Louisa that it made me want to fade into the vision, rest somewhere in the middle, to experience both women in a dance outside of time.

And again, crazy comes calling.

I prop up the collar of my coat and bury my hands in my pockets. Turning around, I head back down Bay Street to walk along Highway Six. The lighthouse is beckoning. My feet are heavy with resistance, but I tread forth. Every few minutes a car passes, slows a bit, but I'm walking in the wrong direction for hitching a ride. The closer I get to Big Tub Road, the more anxious I feel.

I start to wish I smoked. My hands and mouth feel idle.

And then I think of Ellie and I want to run back to her, throw her up against a wall, devour her lips and neck, wrap her legs around me. I want to push into her, to see how close I can get. I want her breasts pressed against my chest, my hands on her hips and her fingers in my hair. I want to hear her gasping for breath, calling my name, whispering "Oh" and "God" and "Yes".

As if intent on cooling my desire, the wind picks up and I curse out loud at the chill.

Motherfucking Tobermory.

I turn back. Crazy may be calling, but I'm not answering today.

Ellie

The dive shop remains empty the entire day until ten minutes before closing, when I hear the door chime and someone entering. It's Tynan.

His eyes are heavy and his face looks sullen, as though he has not slept well. His hands wring the leather strap of his bag and he hangs his head low.

"Hey Ellie, is it ok that I'm here? Are you pissed at me?" he asks.

I want to hug his denim-clad body and kiss his pale cheeks. "No, Tynan, I'm not pissed at you. I could never really be upset with you. I know that you were looking out for me and I really do appreciate it. It was difficult to hear about what happened with Declan." I look down briefly, getting a flash of Declan falling into rocky water. I wince. "I never want to think about him feeling that sad and desperate again." I could feel my eyes filling with tears. I remind myself that he is fine. "I thank God you were there. Declan is grateful too, you know."

Tynan is quiet and keeps his attention on the anti-fatigue mat at his feet. There is something more he wants to say. I am silent, giving him room to consider his words.

Finally, he looks up: "There is something dangerous about him, Ell. It's like he seriously considers himself a victim. There's violence in that belief. Whether he takes that out on himself or on another person, it's still frightening." He waits for me to say something, but I keep quiet. "All I'm saying is: be careful. I know that you love him. We can all see it. But I meant what I said, Ellie, you can't save him. Remember that."

Though I don't like hearing it, I know Tynan is right. I can only give Declan so much; the rest will be up to him. It pains me to think that I can't rescue him like I want to, but then I considered how selfish that was. I want him to be well; I want him to be normal so that we can be together.

And then the words *Just let go* are whispered between my ears.

All of that desire for control has to be given away. In my mind I ask: how?

And then in that moment, I picture myself surrendering it all to Louisa. I ask her to take it and to help me trust her. I have an inkling that none of the pain is really real, that it cannot be.

There is a voice, the same voice that spoke to Louisa that says: *Where you cannot feel affection, give it. Where darkness appears, shine light. Where madness seems to reign, offer sweet, sane love.*

Recalling that Tynan is still standing in front of me I turn to him and say quietly: "I will. I will remember that." He looks relieved. I know it wasn't easy for him to come here. Full of gratitude, I walk out from behind the counter and hug him tight.

"You're a good friend Tynan. You always have been." I sigh, readying to broach the one thing we never discuss. "Tynan?"

"Ellie?" he says, mocking me.

I lean back to look up at him. "If you ever want to talk about Guy and what happened in Montreal, I'm here for you. You know that, right?"

He releases me and runs his hand through his hair. Without looking at me he replies, "Two years, Ell and it's still not long enough. I'm still raw. And that's all I can say. 'Time heals all wounds' is a crock of shit."

I smile at the sentiment and wince at his pain. "I love you, Tynan."

"I love you too, Ell. I want to see you safe and happy. That's all. I promise," he says genuinely.

I squeeze his hands gently and as I look up into his eyes I get a flash.

It's in South Africa during a war. It's the late 1800s. Tynan is a soldier; British I think, short with kind brown eyes and a scar on his cheek. Guy is a woman, a black woman, dressed in old, tattered clothes, but beautiful. They are lovers, but something is wrong. She's angry with him. Her brother has been killed. It's raining and she's screaming. Tynan, the soldier, is trying to console her but she is beside herself with grief and unforgiveness. He ends up walking away. The sadness is heavy and wide, cloaking all in its wake.

"Tell him you're sorry," I say.

Tynan looks confused. "Tell who that I'm sorry?"

"Guy."

He goes white and tears threaten to spill from his eyes. His voice is trapped beneath the fear of reliving a pain he'd rather forget.

"He feels betrayed and he thinks you don't understand. Tell him that you do and that you're sorry."

Tynan backs away from me in disbelief. I tell him what I saw and ask him if history is repeating itself in any way. He nods slowly.

I give him a sympathetic smile. "I don't quite know what this is or how it works, but it seems like we carry pain with us from one lifetime to the next. I don't know if the pain is really only from the things that seem to happen to us in life or if it goes deeper than that. I don't know... "

"You have a gift, Ellie. Man, you have to do something about this!" Tynan is smiling through the tears. Eyes red and shining, he is excited for me.

I release a long-held breath. "I think you're right."

I pass Alistair in the hallway as I walk towards Declan's door. His demeanour is strange, as if he is unhappy with me. I greet him, but he just grunts in reply. I ask him how the dives are going and he mumbles something about the water being too cold.

"Well, it is November. The charters usually stop in October, but Dave made an exception for you guys." I don't really want to have a conversation with him when he's being so odd, but he just keeps standing there.

Finally he speaks. "Listen Ellie, I don't like all this past-life regression stuff. I don't think it's good for Declan or for his state of mind."

I'm angry. I want to shout at Alistair. What the hell does he know? He wasn't there! He didn't see what we saw.

And then a whisper: *He's scared.*

Of course he is scared. He's worried that his son is going to get worse instead of better and that I might hurt him.

"Alistair, I understand. But I'm seeing a change in him. And I love him, you know. I know it hasn't been long and that we barely know each other, but it can't be helped." I take a step towards him and am struck again by how similar father is to son. "I will watch over him. I promise you, I'll make sure he's ok."

Alistair lets out a quiet, strangled cry. "He's my boy, you know? It's excruciating to see him in pain. I want to take it from him and bear it as my own." His eyes are wet now. "Christ, and now I'm crying." He wipes at his face with his palm. "Alright, Ellie, I'll trust you. Be good to him, eh? I need a drink."

I nod and take one step closer and kiss his cheek. "Go get that drink."

And as he walks away I see a vision of him twenty years ago with Declan on his shoulders. There was happiness there. There was so much love.

It never really left.

Declan opens the door and immediately pulls me to him. He holds me tight and whispers in my ear: "I almost forgot how pretty you are." He has a tone of playfulness I don't ever recall hearing from him before. It lights me up.

"Oh yeah?" I giggle, putting my cold hands beneath his sweater and laughing at his squeals of surprise.

As punishment, he pins me against the wall and kisses me fully, momentarily taking my breath away. I am overwhelmed at his strength and allow myself to succumb to it. There is a blur of touches, kisses and moans. We both drop to our knees and he gently guides me down to the floor. I toss a shoe that found itself beneath me towards the door and bring my hands to his waist. I arch my back to more fully feel his weight upon me. My mind is spinning trying to take in every sensation. His one hand is tangled in my hand as the other caresses my hip.

Kissing my neck softly, he speaks in a voice barely above a whisper: "I can't believe I found you again. You've been living in my mind for two hundred and twenty-two years... maybe longer. I've missed your body."

I want to lose myself in him. His hand moves up to my breast and I shiver. I want more of his mouth, more of his hands, more of him. But a voice keeps saying: *Later.*

I go still and bring my hands to his elbows to gently stop him. "Later," I whisper. He sighs loudly and deflates on top of me.

Half-jokingly he says, "Ellie, you're killing me."

Hugging my knees tightly to myself, I get comfortable on the sofa and accept a mug of tea from Declan. He winks at me and I can feel myself blushing.

"So how do we do this?" he asks innocently.

"We're going to sit up straight, but make sure that we're comfortable and then I'll lead us into a meditation. We'll just quiet our minds. I'm going to call in Louisa though. She will direct what we see and feel. Sound ok?"

Declan looks confused. "How are you going to call in Louisa? First of all, she's dead and second of all, she's you!"

I realize that I'm not sure how to explain this to him because I don't feel I fully comprehend it myself. "We're all energy, Declan. The memory of Louisa is enough. I call on the energy of who I remember myself to have been and that's all we need. It's hard to explain in words," I tell him gently.

"No, no. I think I get it. She exists even though we can't see her and she's a part of you but really, she is a part of us all. Is that close?" he asks hopefully.

In his questions and conclusions I get an image of Declan as a young boy and it warms my heart. I want to hug him. "You are adorable. That is definitely close."

Declan smiles at me, pleased with himself. "Sexy, Ellie...not adorable, sexy," he corrects me.

CHAPTER 35

Louisa

The sun peeked through the clouds for an exceptional appearance considering it was November in Mull. Louisa could scarcely contain her excitement as she buttoned her spencer and put on her gloves. William would speak to her father this morning and ask to court her.

It seemed almost silly to Louisa that he should go through this formality, but William would brook no opposition. She was a lady and would be treated as one. Louisa found the idea quite humorous. If she was indeed a lady she would not have allowed William to even cross the threshold of her bedchamber, never mind all the events that transpired within it.

Yes, it was scandalous, but no one in Tobermory would care. Everyone in the village adored William: the men for his good sense and ability to hold his drink, the women for his good manners and handsome appearance. They loved Louisa too and news of their attachment would travel fast.

Louisa was on her way to the market to purchase some eggs and post her letter. She had not forgotten her plan. On the contrary, she was more resolved than ever to take the next steps. William would know his worth and she would have the kind soul she knew he was.

Happiness overcame her as she walked. She felt as though she was floating! The way that he kissed her and held her close made her weak, but that was not all she thought of. His kindness to others, the way he looked when he wanted to tell her something, his manner of walking, and how respectful he was to her father. And though he would not count it as a virtue, Louisa adored how unsure of himself he could be at times. He, a man of twenty-five who had become so successful so quickly and of his own wits and talents would still occasion to doubt his actions. Louisa knew it was because he was humble. There was a little boy inside of him who still searched for approval and a loving voice that would tell him everything would be alright.

William

They sat opposite each other in front of the fire in the parlour. Sir Thomas observed William strangely, clearly puzzled at the young man's nervous demeanour. "Thank you for agreeing to see me, Sir Thomas," said William, running his hands down the arms of the chair.

Sir Thomas reached across to tap William's knee to reassure him. "Of course, lad! I am happy to hear anything you have to say."

"You are too kind, sir." William looked away a moment and then anxiously crossed and then uncrossed his legs. He had to force himself to stay seated in the chair, because all he really wanted to do was pace. "Sir Thomas, I have requested this interview so that I may confess to you that I uh...that is I have recently found that I am quite fond of your daughter...Louisa, sir."

Sir Thomas could not help but laugh. "Recently? Come, man. I have eyes! You have been hopelessly in love with my daughter since Oban, more likely London!" He paused, perhaps noting William's discomfort at the idea that his feelings were known to everyone. "But I am being unkind and interrupting you. Pray, continue," he said quickly.

"Yes, well I uh...I would like to have your permission, sir, to court your daughter." He was now thoroughly embarrassed by his anxiety, not to mention his blatant inability to hide his feelings.

Sir Thomas laughed and then shouted, "Court her? Mr. Mara, really, is that what you want? Is that what Louisa wants? Never mind, I already know the answer to both of those questions." He continued, ignoring William's look of horror. "The answer of course is no. Come now lad, you want to marry her do you not? And I know my Louisa, the girl who swore she would never marry! Ha! Well, I see the way she looks at you and I can hear the adoration in her voice when she says your name. You are both done for and the sooner you admit it the better!"

William was at a loss. How could he possibly respond to such a speech? After a moment he decided that full honesty was required. Indeed Sir Thomas seemed to expect nothing less.

"Sir, you are correct. I am utterly besotted with your daughter. Louisa is exceptional and I suppose the reason I asked you to court her instead of marry her was that I was seeking some time to endeavour to deserve her." William sighed and raked his hands through his hair. "I would marry her tomorrow, but to be frank, I did not think you would permit it. I am not a gentleman and as you are aware, the comparatively small fortune I have made has been in trade. In short, I did not think you would believe me suitable for Louisa."

Sir Thomas observed William for a moment with an expression of sympathy. "I understand your concerns, lad; I do. You need not worry, however. We are in a unique position here. She has no need for the good opinion of the *ton*, nor does she require a wealthy gentleman for protection. Not only that, I trust my daughter's judgment implicitly. If she has fallen in love with you, and I believe strongly that she has, then I want nothing more than to see her happy."

Sir Thomas sighed and leaned forward. "I will not pretend to be ignorant of other feelings you may have. I know it cannot be easy to be a man in love with a woman who does not need his protection. Such a thing can torture our pride. Can we both agree however, that she is not a common female?"

Mr. Mara smiled at the question. "We can, most heartily, sir."

"Indeed she is uncommon. And she has been transformed by this place. In London, she was always alone and with a book in her hands. She would attend balls of course, but she never seemed to be particularly interested in anyone she met there. I worried for her. But now she is outside so often, looking at the sea, gardening, talking to people in the village. It is clear to me that bringing her here was the right thing to do. And it warms my heart that she has found a partner with whom to share her life. I can leave this world a much happier man, Mr. Mara."

William could not find the words to respond to such a speech. He gave a tight smile and a nod to stave off the emotion that threatened to overwhelm him.

"You are a good man, Mr. Mara. Think what you will, but I must have it said: you do deserve my Louisa. Take that to heart, son. It is high praise indeed."

William extended his hand to Louisa's father and he shook it. He knew that Sir Thomas liked him, but never did he imagine that the gentleman would be so open and approving of their attachment. He was overcome.

"I do take that to heart and I thank you. And you are correct, sir. I most fervently wish to make Louisa my wife. If I have your permission, I will ask her this afternoon when she returns from the market."

Sir Thomas smiled widely. "Why wait until she returns? Run! Find her and ask her now. Ladies love that kind of devotion," he mused as if remembering something. "I ran after Louisa's mother you know. "

William remained seated unsure if Sir Thomas planned to finish his thought. His foot tapping the wood floor however broke the older man's reverie.

"What are you still doing here, Mr. Mara? She is waiting."

Sir Thomas stood up and grabbed William by the shoulders. Laughing, he bid him be gone.

And with that, William was off. The air was damp and chilled, but a ray of sunlight illuminated the path to the village. He was anxious, excited and tense. It also crossed his mind how changed his emotions were since he and Louisa first confessed their feelings to one another. There was less fear and more trust. It was not necessarily the most comfortable place for him to find himself, but he decided he had no choice but to let it be. William did not want to live without Louisa. He was meant to be with her, he knew this and he could wait no longer to be completely honest with her.

He ran. He ran so fast, he nearly passed her on the path. A flash of white, of brown and of red caught his eye.

"Louisa?" he called back. "Is that you?"

It was her. She was back a few feet and to his left behind a copse of trees. She was on the ground, tending to the wild dog from the day of her fall. There was blood all over her dress. William went white.

"Yes, William. It is me," she replied in a weak voice. He ran to her and tried to assess the damage. "The dog is injured, my dear. I am perfectly well."

He sighed loudly with relief. "Thank God for that! What is the matter?"

She pointed to the dog's paw, bleeding from a large thorn. The animal looked weak and beleaguered as did Louisa. She appeared to be touching the dog's foot, but barely. Her hands hovered just above its fur. Her eyes were closed and it seemed as though she was listening to something. William looked around briefly and tried to hear what she was hearing. The forest was silent. He looked at her confounded and a little afraid.

"Louisa, what are you doing with that dog? He is not well, my love; he could be ill beyond that wound to his foot. You should come away from him," said William, attempting to sound calm.

She remained still for another moment and then opened her eyes to him. He watched as she tore a piece of cloth from her skirts and tied it about the wound. William offered his hand to help her stand. She accepted and said as she stood, "I have done all I can. I must return to the cottage and clean up." Her voice was flat. He had never heard her speak thus.

"Of course, Louisa, but are you certain you are well? You did not answer me; why did you have your hands on him? It looked as if you did more than just remove the thorn." He halted her from walking away and gently demanded her attention.

Louisa let out a quick exhale and brought the back of her hand to her forehead. "I will tell you William, but I do not want to hear any scolding." He looked at her strangely but then nodded in agreement. "I was praying for the dog's healing and as I did I heard a voice."

"A voice?" he asked dubiously.

She shut her eyes in annoyance. "Please let me finish." He apologized and bowed his head, prompting her to continue. "I have told you before that I hear guidance from time to time. I heard Mother Mary. She was instructing me to hold my hands over the dog. As I did, something extraordinary happened. Heat came from my hands, William. I swear to you. And though my eyes were closed, I peeked and when I did I saw the most brilliant light coming from each hand. It was as though Mother Mary was healing the animal through me...using my body, my hands."

She was lit from within. He looked at her with all the love in his chest and though he did not know what to think about what she had said, he knew she believed. Louisa thought Mary, Mother of God was speaking to her and guiding her. And it occurred to William that perhaps she was. Perhaps we all have some divine guide who whispers, tries to get our attention and who loves us beyond what we know love to be.

He looked at Louisa and silently said in his mind I want you to be my guide. I want to see what you see, hear what you hear. He opened his arms to her, inviting her into his embrace.

"But I am soiled!" she cried.

"Nonsense," he said with a peaceful smile. "Come."

Louisa

Walking arm in arm, Louisa reluctantly left the dog behind. She knew he would heal, but she loathed leaving him alone. At that thought a voice said, "We, none of us, are ever alone," and she smiled. It was true. Looking up at William she noticed a look of serenity on his face she had not recalled seeing before. He was changed somehow. It was then that she remembered he was to speak with her father.

"Did you ask him then?" Louisa bounced up and down to her words.

"I did."

"And?" she prodded.

"And I will not be courting you, Louisa. That decision has been made." His expression was serious.

She looked at him confused and noticed the slightest upturning of his mouth. "Is that so?" He shook his head and grinned. "Really William, I am exhausted and covered in dog's blood! Are you going to tease me now? It is hardly fair."

He chuckled and then took pity. "You would like to talk about this now?" She nodded emphatically. "Very well then, I did ask your father for permission to court you and he laughed at me. He saw right through me, Louisa. I am certain that you knew this already. In any case, I have come to the conclusion that there is no one else for me. I want you to be my wife, if you will have me. Will you consent to it? Is this what you want as well?"

She turned to him and hugged him tightly. "You know that it is! I adore you, William. I do not want to be apart from you! Yes, I consent. I will marry you." She said the words into his chest, but he heard her loud and clear. They would be together. She lifted her head to look up at him and was rewarded with a stunning smile. That he was happy moved her to tears. This tender, handsome man who carried so much guilt was overflowing with joy. She would make it her mission to keep him so. "If I clean myself, will you kiss me?"

"I will kiss you now, if you will allow it." But he did not wait for her permission. He leaned in and took her mouth quickly. She tried to follow his lead. He parted her lips with his own and Louisa nearly forgot to breathe. With eyes closed and her mind light as a feather, all she could perceive was pure light and soft, warm mouths. Indeed her cousin was correct; kissing was divine.

CHAPTER 36

Louisa

"Mistress, what on earth happened?" Janey was the first to happen upon them as they walked in the door.

"I was helping an injured dog." Louisa's words came out dreamily and nearly incoherent as she stared at William.

"Is that so? Well, I can see that you are alright. Come with me to the kitchen, love; let's get you cleaned up," called Janey.

Louisa looked down at her dress, suddenly recalling she was still covered in blood. "Oh yes of course, Janey. But first, William and I have news!" She exclaimed, grasping William's hand.

Janey clapped her hands together and beamed, "You are to be married?" Louisa shook her head in assent and Janey squealed with excitement. "Oh happy day! I just knew you two were in love. I told Edward weeks ago that we would soon hear wedding bells."

Edward walked into the room at that moment and rolled his eyes mockingly. "You said it two days ago and I believe your words were: "Those two had better hurry up and get married because I don't want to pretend to not hear what goes on behind closed doors any longer."

William's jaw dropped, but Louisa just laughed. "I am sorry for it, Janey. We promise to practice more prudence. Edward, will you not wish us joy?"

Edward smiled widely and went to them. "Of course! Mr. Mara, you are a fortunate man, sir. I hope you will both live a long and happy life together."

William was still stunned at his earlier declaration, but managed to say, "I thank you, Edward."

Janey stepped to Louisa and grabbed her hand, leading her to the kitchen. "Come now."

She helped Louisa wash her hands, arms and hair at the basin and then led her upstairs to her chamber to undress. Janey informed her that all her clothes were soaked through with the blood and would have to be burnt. Louisa barely listened while she hummed an Irish love song.

"So when is the happy day, Miss De vale? Has it been decided?" asked Janey as she brushed out Louisa's hair.

"It has not. I hope it will be soon. It is my dearest wish to wed here in Scotland, but I do not yet know what William would like."

"Mistress, forgive me for speaking plainly, but if it is your wish to wed soon, then it is his as well. There are benefits to being married that men are always in a rush for," exclaimed Janey with a laugh. Louisa blushed. "I am sorry, miss; I did not mean to embarrass you. All I really meant was that it is clear Mr. Mara fancies you."

Louisa recovered herself. "I am not so embarrassed. The truth is I am excited. I never thought I would marry and now it seems I can think of nothing else but wanting to be so. William is more than I thought could exist together in one man. He enlivens me, challenges me. He cares about what I think. I would marry him tomorrow!"

Janey brought her hand to her heart. "I am so happy to hear it, miss." She helped Louisa put on a new dress and styled her hair.

Louisa's thoughts turned to what would be expected of her after the wedding. Would William want to return to London? How often would he travel? Would he consider staying here in Tobermory? What of her father? She breathed deep and let the questions go.

A moment later she heard: *Follow the wind.* The message may have seemed vague to others, but to Louisa it was clear: She could be happy anywhere if she allowed herself to be. Her job was to adhere to take each day as it came, nothing more.

"What think you of Scotland, Janey?"

Janey removed the hairpins in her mouth to reply. "I like it well enough, miss. It is perhaps a little gloomier than our beloved England, but it is wild in the most beautiful way. I also adore the sea. Why do you ask?"

Louisa lowered her head and took a deep breath. "I was only wondering. It feels right to stay here. Mull is mysterious and yet I find the unknown strangely comforting. My mother is from this place and I feel closer to her here, at least sometimes I do. I am changed since we have come, more my own self perhaps. I cannot explain it Janey, but I feel I will spend the rest of my life here. Do you suppose Mr. Mara feels the same?"

"It's best to ask the gentleman himself, miss. I am certain the two of you can work it out." Janey returned to styling Louisa's hair. "Do you really see yourself here at a cottage though? You are a lady accustomed to living in a grand home in London. Would it not pain you to give that up?"

Louisa turned. "Why should I have to Janey? Could I not keep the house in London and spend my springs and summers here?"

"Of course, child; I did not mean to imply that you would never go back to London. I suppose I was just surprised that you would want to stay in this cottage. It is very...um...snug," she replied gently.

Louisa was sad for a moment, finding it difficult to imagine herself happy anywhere but here. Was she failing Mother Mary by feeling this way? Was she wrong to want to stay? "If I am honest Janey, part of me is sensing that big changes are afoot and I want everything to stay the same. I want my father close, William happy and my spirit free. Tobermory has given me all of that and more. London could change everything. I am not certain that I am ready to face that."

Janey squeezed Louisa's arms gently. "Tobermory is merely where all of this was shown to you. It has always been so. You are free, my dear. You always were. Everything that you have here you can have anywhere, and that is the truth."

So now her Mother Mary was speaking through

people...perhaps she always had, thought Louisa.

That evening dinner was a light and celebratory affair. Louisa insisted that Janey and Edward dine with them. Sir Thomas carried most of the conversation, relating how he and Louisa's mother had courted and eventually came to be married. Louisa watched William as he listened to the tale and then saw his attention appear to wander. Something was amiss and she was determined to find out what it was.

Having gained her father's easy permission to speak to William alone after dessert, Louisa led him into Sir Thomas's tiny library. There was a wingback and an old wooden stool; William took the latter.

She took his hands in hers. He stroked her palms with his thumbs, but kept his head lowered. "I could not help but notice how troubled you looked during dinner, William. What is it?"

"It is nothing, my love. I am sorry if I have upset you unnecessarily. Truly, I am a very happy man."

Louisa was dubious, but decided to trust him for the moment. "There is something else I wished to speak to you about. I would like to set a date for our wedding if that suits you. Have you spoken yet to my father about this?"

William raised his head and tensed for a moment. "I have not. What is your feeling on the matter?"

"I was about to ask you the same, but I am willing to speak first. I wish to marry here. The parish will soon be finished and I would dearly love to exchange our vows there. Tobermory is you. This is where I fell in love with you. It would break my heart to leave this place without being able to call myself your wife," she declared.

She was finding it difficult to make this speech and maintain eye contact with him. She had not realized how nervous she was that he may not feel the same way as she. So when he stood and picked her up in his arms and twirled her about the room, she was nothing short of shocked.

"Louisa! You have no idea how pleased and relieved this makes me. It is exactly what I would wish. I received word today that I have business in Glasgow that must be attended to, but that shan't take long. We can be married within six weeks if you wish! Would that make you happy, my love?"

Louisa was still trying to recover from his grand and impulsive gesture. She laughed and declared, "Yes indeed! I confess I was afraid you would prefer to return to London. I am most pleased to be wrong again in my assumption."

Placing her feet back on the floor, William bent to kiss her. "I will make a confession of my own. You were correct when you thought I looked disturbed at dinner earlier. I was." His face was so close to hers. "It crossed my mind how accustomed you are to grand balls and assemblies. I knew it would be wrong of me to deny you the splendid wedding you deserve."

William released her and crossed the room to gaze out the window. He squared his shoulders and sighed. "I am aware of the differences in our stations...acutely so. You have been so kind as to try and abate my concerns in this matter, but I fear when we are married it shall all come to a head. You know how the *ton* will talk. Who am I to them but an imposter? And how shall I bear hearing them speak of you with such venom? It will drive me mad to know people are thinking ill of you." He pumped his fist as he spoke through gritted teeth. "You may say I am reacting excessively, but that is how I feel. I am a man, Louisa, and when you are my wife, my job is to protect you. How can I do this when I am the subject of your humiliation?"

Louisa walked up behind him and tentatively wrapped her arms around his waist. She wanted to comfort him, but also felt a tinge of guilt at allowing herself to indulge in touching him. She whispered into his back. "You could never humiliate me. I love you. All will be well William, I promise you."

He turned to look at her questioningly. "You speak as though you have done something...as if you know something. What is it Louisa? What have you done?"

Taken aback by his sudden questions, Louisa quickly lied. "Nothing, William! My goodness, I have done nothing. Is it not enough that I know all will be well? I feel it. Do you not trust my feelings?" It was unfair to hide from him what she had done to secure his introduction into society, but she told herself that she wanted it to be a surprise. Of course the other part of her had been afraid he would flatly refuse to engage in her plan.

She would not dwell on these thoughts however; they would lead her nowhere good.

He pulled her towards him bringing his hands to her waist. "I do trust you my darling. I do. I trust you more than anyone else. I apologize."

Placing her hands on his chest she said, "I accept your apology, sir." She looked into his eyes and was taken aback by what she saw there, a combination of fire and guilt. Louisa knew not what to say and so decided to change the subject altogether.

"So when will you venture to Glasgow and how long must I bear your absence?"

His gaze cooled. "I shall leave one week hence and will return in a fortnight or so." She allowed herself to pout for a moment. "It will go by quickly, Louisa. You will have to have a dress made and you will have many letters to write informing all of your acquaintances. I hope you shall write to me as well. My solicitor will forward all of my correspondence to Glasgow while I am there. I promise I will be no longer than three weeks. It is not easy for me to leave you. You do know that do you not?"

Louisa considered his words. If he took care of this business now, it would mean he would not have to do it after they were married. "I do, sir. And is it too impertinent to ask where you plan to take me on our honeymoon?"

William looked down. Clearly he had not made plans of any kind.

She spoke first, "For my part, I would dearly love to explore more of Scotland. It is in my blood after all. And nothing would please me more, dear William, than to return to Oban and the inn where we had our first real conversation. You were so handsome sitting there in the dining hall. I stood and watched you for a few moments, you know. It was as if I had been granted a glimpse into my future."

He said nothing and acted quickly. Placing a hand behind her head, and another at the small of her back he drew her to him and kissed her thoroughly. It seemed the only response within him. Louisa was startled and yet she felt no fear.

His hands moved to her hips and he shifted her closer. A growl, soft and low escaped his lips. He thrust her against the wall of the tiny room in one fluid movement, their mouths never parting. Louisa's mind raced as she struggled to keep up with him, trying to anticipate the strength of his feeling.

In surrender, she raised her arms above her head and he took his hand up to pin them in place. Her breathing was strangled and staccato beneath his hunger. Quietly, she called his name.

And as if she had just slapped him, he stopped suddenly. Wiping his mouth with the back of his hand, he withdrew from her.

"I am no gentleman," he uttered in disgust.

Louisa's heart still raced and she was already grieving the loss of his body. "Do not torture yourself, my darling. I did not want to stop. Please, look at me."

He raked his hand through his hair and deigned to meet her eyes.

"Your desire for me frightens me. It frightens me because it mirrors my own. We are the same. If we were alone in this house right now…"

"Cease!" he warned.

"…I would let you take me and I would feel no regrets."

William flashed a rakish smile, but instead of coming for her once more, he turned to quit the room. "Louisa, I know not what to do with you. But for now, I must seek water…very cold water."

She laughed as he left and brought her arms about herself and squeezed. She would not regret anything that happened between them. Not ever. Her faith and her safety were woven into something beyond this world and William was a part of that. This, she knew for certain.

CHAPTER 37

Louisa

The weeks of William's absence were busy and yet lonely. Louisa had found a local woman who could make her wedding gown. Because her taste was simple, it had not been difficult. The material was brought in from Oban and the dressmaker simply fashioned it after one of Louisa's gowns that she had brought with her from London. Everything was falling into place. The church was finished and the first service would take place this Sunday. William would return the following day.

Louisa sat in her room in quiet contemplation and called on the guidance of Mother Mary. She knew it was silly to feel so gutted by the absence of another person, even if he was her fiancé.

Mother Mary told her to let go. *You are loved completely child, you know this. All you need do is remember.*

Louisa felt better. It always felt better to quiet her mind. And yet she felt uneasy. A sense of foreboding crept into her mind. There was a knock at the door that stopped the sensation dead in its tracks...for now.

It was Janey. There was a letter from William.

November 8, 1790

My Dearest Louisa,

My journey has been long but thankfully the roads were clear.

I have been in Glasgow but a day and already I feel your absence greatly. It is warmer here than Tobermory and yet somehow it is colder. I miss the sea, the untamed wind and most of all, I miss you. Glasgow is very modern of course. My room is warm and I am quite comfortable and yet I find myself yearning for my draughty quarters at Cliffside. There I think of you at night and know you are a mere three doors down the hall. Here I think of you and know you are more than 100 miles away. I know not which the greater torture is.

Though business shall fill my days, my mind will always harbour space for you. I carry you with me, your love and your spirit. There is never a time when you are not bound to my being. Somehow this comforts me more than anything. I was content in the knowledge that your presence filled a room, made it better without effort. Now, however, I know you fill the world. You transcend it. Your kindness, intelligence and compassion are of heaven, surely. I know not how it is that you are mine. If it was not such a vain question, I would ask you why you chose me? I suppose the why is immaterial. My only alternative then is undying gratitude.

Tomorrow I will begin to wrap up my dealings here and will be able to think about the wedding, more specifically the wedding date. What think you of December 17th? I will admit it holds special meaning for me. It was my mother's birthday. Did I ever tell you her name was Olivia? I suppose I have not.

My shame over the low station my mother held before she married my father is deep. Conflictingly, so is my love for her. She was a remarkable woman who simply did what she had to do to survive. I cannot hate her, though I tried to for years. I blamed her for our poverty. My father did not speak often about his former life, but I gleaned bits and pieces throughout the years. Any intelligence I received only served to further my resentment. I can only look back on my behaviour now with guilt. My mother is never coming back and I know I can never make it up to her. She would forgive me, I think. As I said, she was a lot like you and I know you would forgive.

I hope my letter finds you well, my love. I know I am not as educated as the men that you are used to and that my writing may not be as legible, but I do hope it is clear how dear you are to me. I would and I will do anything for you.

Your face and form stalk me in dreams.

Such is my plight while separated from you.

I love you, Louisa.

Yours in every way,
William Matthew Mara

Louisa hugged the letter to her breast and proceeded to read it eight times over. She read it until she had memorized nearly every word and could hear his voice uttering each syllable.

Knowing there was work to be done; she eventually made her way to the kitchen and began peeling potatoes while Janey did the laundry. Without thought for who was within earshot, she sang aloud.

"I know where I'm going
And I know who's going with me
I know who I love
And the dear knows who I'll marry."

She did not hear her father approach and was startled when he entered and asked, "Wherever did you learn that song, my dear?"

"Hello Father, I did not see you standing there. Is anything amiss?"

"All is well. I was only wondering how you came to know the song you were singing just now," he asked again.

"Oh! I learned it from a few of the village girls. I overheard them singing it and asked them to teach it to me. It is beautiful is it not?" she exclaimed happily.

Sir Thomas wiped a tear from his eyes and smiled widely at his daughter. "It is indeed, Louisa. Your mother used to sing that song. She sang it most often in the days leading up to our wedding."

Louisa gasped. "Really father? How wonderful!" She went to him and hugged him tightly. "Perhaps she is singing it right now, right along with me?"

Her father released her and looked at her with complete adoration in his eyes. "Perhaps she is, my darling, perhaps she is." He wiped his eyes once more and clapped his hands in resolution. "Now, where is Janey? I wish to have a cup of tea!"

Louisa laughed and turned to grab the kettle and take it to the fire. It would be her pleasure to make her father some tea.

At long last Monday had come. Louisa had slept for only an hour and yet she was awake at dawn, fuelled by love. She implored Janey to help her select the perfect dress and to arrange her hair in a new and becoming way. She did not know why she was so nervous. Because of the uncertainty of when he would be crossing the sea, Louisa had no idea when to expect him and therefore resolved to be fully dressed and ready for him at eight in the morning.

At noon the residents of Cliffside cottage were disappointed though unsurprised to see the sky cloud over and rain begin to fall. Louisa tried to occupy herself in the cottage. She reached for a book, a favourite of hers. It was a collection of poems by Thomas Gray. Turning the page she read "Hymn to Adversity" and could hear the last three lines in her head as though William himself was reading them:

> *Teach me to love and to forgive,*
> *Exact my own defects to scan,*
> *What others are, to feel, and know myself a Man.*

He was a man beginning to know himself, Louisa was sure of it. And remembering this made her all the more impatient to see him and to feel his arms around her. She strode to the window in frustration, but looking out saw nothing but November rain, heavy and insistent. Where was he? She briefly wondered if the weather would keep William away.

Her thoughts only proved to drive herself mad and so she decided to see if Janey needed any help in the kitchen. Her father had been invited to dine with a family in the village so she could not share her anxiety with him. Before she went to see Janey, she could not resist looking through the large window at the front of the cottage. She was rewarded. There was a figure coming up the path to Cliffside. Having a thought for neither wind nor rain, she raced outside toward him. Finally, he was home!

William

Running through the driving rain, Louisa was a mixture of laughter and tears. She was still wearing her slippers. Their eyes met, but upon seeing William's face, Louisa's smile disappeared.

He didn't care.

Pulling a letter from his coat he screamed, "Louisa! How could you?"

"William, I..."

"Answer me woman! What were you thinking? What made you think it was acceptable to pry into *my* family affairs?" he shouted with fury.

"William, is it not best we discuss this indoors? I am drenched." She had to raise her voice to be heard above the pounding of the rain, but she appeared to tremble with fear as she did.

Without waiting for him to answer, Louisa fled to the house with William following close behind her. In his head he counted accusations, readying to be right. Reaching the front door, she entered quickly and flew past a concerned Janey to her bedchamber. He heard her crawl on to the bed, her cries coming in choking heaves.

He planted a hard knock at her door.

"If you are still angry with me, I shall not grant you entrance," she shouted.

William felt a knot of self-righteous indignation deep in his gut. He had not been so angry since the death of his parents. The feeling was overwhelming.

It seemed she would stow herself away lest she drown in his

rage.

William burst through the door in defiance. He stopped a moment seeing her crying on her bed, but with a grunt he walked toward her. He could not contain his ire any longer.

"I have had a letter from my paternal grandmother, Lady Mara, Louisa. She writes that she received a letter from you forwarded by your solicitor, Mr. Michaels. She goes on to say that you took it upon yourself to make her aware of my existence, that you acknowledged yourself and your father as close friends of mine and that you would implore her to introduce me into society as a recognized relation. Does this all sound familiar?" He was seething as he stood over her. Louisa would not look up from the bed.

"She goes on to inform me that she had heard of my existence some years ago after the death of my parents. Apparently she considered finding me at that time, but knew she could not be responsible for my upbringing and was fearful of witnessing the conditions in which I lived. Furthermore, she has heard I have made a living for myself representing the British Fisheries Association, but she again chose not to contact me. Knowing you and Sir Thomas to be a reputable and noble family, she writes that she will agree to meet with me at your father's home in London, but that she makes no promises of furthering our connection beyond the meeting." His tone was biting, his breathing ragged.

"Louisa, I demand that you look at me," William bellowed. "You are to be my wife. I cannot have such deceit! I will not have it!" He stepped forward and kicked the wooden chair in front of him.

Her sobs slowed and stretched. She was shivering. He resisted the impulse to warm her body with his own. A moment later her crying stopped, but her face remained turned toward the wall as she lay on her side. She said slowly, "I will not speak to you, sir, nor will I look at you until you cease your tirade. If my father were here he would have you thrown from the house."

William took a long, deep breath and finally sat on the chair. He felt as though he were ready to burst. How could she not see how wrong she was? His emotions since leaving Glasgow had been tumultuous to say the least. He was angry indeed, but he was also hurt. Why had she done this? Over and over again she had told him that his past and his current situation in life made no difference to her. And yet now, here she was applying to a wealthy grandmother he did not even know to introduce him into society. It seemed to William this was only to make him acceptable to her friends in the *ton*. She had lied to him. She had made him feel an equal and all the while secretly looked down upon him.

William cradled his head in his hands and drew a deep, strangled breath. He could hear Louisa shift in the bed and then he felt her reach for him. He pulled away quickly and looked at her face. She looked as though he had slapped her.

"I, I do not know what to say. You are so cross with me. I was only trying to help you," she whispered.

William heard her. "I only want the truth, Louisa." He bore his eyes into her, to hold her there in place, to answer him.

"It was all for you. I wrote to Mr. Michaels and asked him to find your grandmother and give her my letter, this is true, my intention in doing so was only to secure your comfort. I did not think you would ever be easy in accepting help from me...in introducing you into society. And yet it was clear you felt it necessary to do so. I suppose I was worried you would wish to wait ten years until you were able to do so of your own accord. The thought of having to wait so long to be with you was unbearable. It also seemed entirely unnecessary to me since you are in fact the son of a gentleman."

She searched his face for sympathy. He offered none.

At length he decided to reply, "You do not understand. I have felt rejected by my father's family my entire life. This was a confirmation of all I have felt. My grandmother is mildly interested in who I am now because of my connection to you and your father. Do you not see how offensive that is?" He spat the words. "Can you not comprehend how that makes me feel? And more than that Louisa, this whole ordeal has made me feel rejected by *you*, the one person in my life whom I have ever trusted. I feel betrayed, saddened and unworthy. *You* have made me feel this way. You who I love beyond all reason; you have brought me to my knees! I know not what to do." William turned away for fear of seeing something that would break his will and his will was that she should suffer.

"My intentions mean nothing to you? I wanted only for you to feel as though you belonged. I tried to do that with my words, even with my body and it was all for naught. You refused to believe me. I did not think Mrs. Mara would speak of my letter to you. In truth I asked her not to. I am sorry William. I never meant to harm you. I do see you as my equal. If I had not, would I have agreed to marry you?" She lowered her head and grew grave as she appeared to consider her next words. "If you wish to cancel our engagement, I will understand. I will not force you to stay with me. You are free to go if you wish."

William sat still for fear that any movement would lead her to assume what his answer would be. He did want her to feel badly for what she had done. He wanted to feel right while she begged his forgiveness, but it appeared that this was not to happen. She had leapt straight to cutting him loose.

Louisa sat up and studied him for a moment. "I know what you are thinking and it drives me mad!" She pounded the bed with her fist. "You think I am perfectly well without you. That is true William. I do not need you in my life." At her words he drew a breath in sharply and turned away. "Listen to me, please! I do not need you, my love, but I want you. You are more than this guilt, suspicion and anger! You are kindness at your core; I know it. I would share this life with you, but I will not ever let you berate me like this again. You have jumped to cruel assumptions. I am sorry that your grandmother is such a small and unfeeling woman, but you choose to be affronted by her!"

At this William seethed, "I choose no such thing, madam! She hates me and I have done nothing and it is most unfair." He looked at her, disgusted. "What would you have me do, Louisa? Shall I rejoice at her letter, at the news of her apathy towards me?"

She softened her tone and said, "Perhaps I should not have gone behind your back to contact your father's mother, but I confess I felt it the right thing to do at the time. Can you not see that it is possible you were meant to face this? You have been harbouring such resentment. Would you really carry that into our marriage? Would it not be best to heal it, William? Your grandmother can only harm you to the degree that you allow it. I offer you my support, my love and my embrace." Louisa looked down at her hands as she nervously wrung them together. "Should you find yourself still hating me however, I will release you. You need only say the word."

William hung his head and raked his fingers through his hair. "It is all too painful." His once forceful voice was now hushed and frail.

She attempted to reach out to him. "My darling...William? Will you not look at me? It pains me to see you so tortured. You will not allow me to comfort you and I understand. If you are determined to push me away, I will not fight you. My love for you will never change. You can come to me in a year; in ten years or in ten lifetimes and I will welcome you. I will still love you as I do now." She paused a moment. William kept his head down. "It would appear to be the best if we do not marry. Would you agree?"

He exhaled a stifled cry, but then nodded his head weakly in assent. Everything was happening so fast. For days he had been planning what to say to her and now it was all falling apart.

He heard Louisa take a deep breath and looked up to see her wipe her eyes and leave the room.

Where was she going?

He rose to follow her.

Coming down the stairs he saw her head to the kitchen. As he rounded the corner, he could see she intended to go outside. She was no longer crying. She was calm, eerily so. It was almost as though she was sleepwalking. He wanted to stop her. He opened his mouth to call her name, but no sound escaped his lips.

Edward and Janey were not about...probably taking cover in their bedchambers.

William watched as Louisa pulled on Edward's slicker and her mud boots and opened the door. The wind nearly knocked her over, but she went forth, her hair flailing wildly in the violent breeze. William scrambled to follow her.

He saw her wrapping her arms tightly about her body. The rain blurred his vision although he was able to spy her climbing the hill to the cliff. William continued to watch her as he walked on, but was slowed by the mud claiming his boots. With every step he took he sunk further. He called her name but she did not turn. She scaled the incline in a few short moments, seemingly without effort.

"Louisa!" he called again. She was out of sight now. With every last bit of determination, he finally made it to the top of the hill. His heart beat fast. He bent over briefly to catch his breath.

There she was at the edge. Her form lit by moonlight.

A great gust of wind roared loudly in his ears and nearly knocked him to the ground as thunder rolled. William blinked and opened his eyes once more to a sight distorted by rain and confusion.

Her hair swept northward, horizontally. Her arms outstretched.

She flew.

And in a flash of bright, white light she was gone.

Ellie and Louisa

With eyes closed Mother Mary was heard clear and strong: *Be still child. The wind shall carry you and you will not be harmed. All is well.*

A breath and a scream. A strong current of wind. A crash and a flash.

There was wet, there was darkness, and then there was light.

CHAPTER 38

Ellie

The fire long since burnt out meant the room was cold. I shivered. My eyes were slowly adjusting to the room and I was gradually remembering where my body had been all this time. I looked over at Declan. His eyes appeared heavy and were still closed. He gave the impression of being agitated, making low, frightened noises.

If he was seeing what I had just seen then his reaction is more than understandable.

I cannot stop shaking. Somehow I rise to make tea and wait for him to come back in his own time.

I feel a million emotions at once and I witness myself trying to wade through them all, as if I were still drowning in the sea.

I try to concentrate on the water tap, the kettle. I am gasping for air. My head aches. My bones are cracking, crushed.

Just turn on the water, Ellie.

I left them. What was I doing up there? I had no business being up there.

The water, Ellie, just turn it on.

Father, William, Janey, Edward...I left them. I did not listen. Mary said *"Let go."* I did not listen.

Put your hand on the faucet and turn.

My hands shake as I turn the cold water on. I straddle two worlds, not trusting what I am seeing.

I had experienced her death and yet there seemed to be nothing final about it. In that last vision, I became her. I felt her faith and yet her hopelessness. I felt her serenity and her sadness.

How long will I carry the pain of this? When may I lay this burden down? Do you hear me?

I do. And you can let this go.

My nose is running and I realize that I have been crying. I

wipe my face with the back of my arm.

I pour the boiled water into a teapot and bring it with two mugs to where Declan is seated. Pouring my own cup, I hear him sigh. He opens his eyes and looks at me with a secret sadness only I am privy to.

"I drove you to your death," he says quietly. He takes his mug and warms his hands with it. He stares into the hot liquid as if recalling the drop, as if replaying the sight of a love lost to jagged rocks and saltwater.

I shake my head slowly. My voice is thick from silent cries. "No, you didn't. She walked up to the cliff to clear her mind, to just get out. The wind took her." I think about moving closer to him to give him comfort, but I am too exhausted.

Declan takes a sharp breath. "I saw you fall. Jesus Christ, Ellie, you look so much like her!" He stands up and starts to pace the room. "I feel like I have carried the guilt of this for two hundred years. Watching you fall off that cliff was like having my guts ripped out of me! I ran to the edge. I don't know what I was hoping to find. Looking down, I saw you face down in the water, your coat on the rocky shore and that dog...That goddamn dog was there! He got to you before I could." The tone of his voice is icy. The vision is fresh. "That pissed me off. So you know what I did? I shot him. I went back to the house, grabbed Edward's rifle, climbed down the side of the cliff and I shot him."

My eyes are laden with hurts ready to be let go. I yawn, allowing fatigue to rule despite the drama. Declan looks jarringly different and yet familiar, as if some ghostly aspect of William has invaded him...taken over. Even his voice has changed slightly.

For a moment, I do not know what to say.

"I'm sorry you had to relive that."

He stops pacing to look me straight in the eye. "I have to make amends to you and I have no clue how to do that. How the hell am I supposed to make up for all I've done to you when I can barely think straight most days?"

Working through my weariness, I go to him. At first he will not let me near, but he relents when he sees the look in my eyes. "Do you love me?" I ask.

He shakes his head and throws up his hands as if my question was ridiculous. "You know that I do. You are my *anam cara*. But my mind, Ellie! My fucked-up mind makes me half a man. I can't expect you to take care of me. I am supposed to take care of you, protect you!"

I smile at him, not having the strength to fight him. "You do all of that Declan. You do. You are not responsible for Louisa's death. William wasn't either." I stroke his temples and kiss his chin gently.

He looks down briefly and then catches my eyes. "You say that, but I can feel the guilt in me as if it were a part of me. I can't just shut my eyes and pretend it isn't there. The truth is that I've felt it all along. Now it has a name and a reason."

"But, Declan, you were there; you saw how guilty William was his entire life. Louisa's death just added fuel to the fire. It's as if our lives are a product of all the guilt we've carried and we just keep playing it out in different bodies with different problems." Now this did not even feel like me speaking. Ellie was half-asleep. Something else had taken over.

Declan looks at me, confused. "I don't know what you're talking about. I did things. I was cruel to you in that lifetime and in this one. There were hurtful things that occurred. That is why I feel guilty."

I sigh. All I could do was assure him that I did not resent him in any way, not as Louisa and not as Ellie. "It's all forgiven, Declan." I hug him close and wish I could fall asleep on his chest, but I want my own bed. I make small circles on his back with my fingertips and ask him to take me home.

He agrees.

The door is thankfully unlocked, another reason I love living in a small town. The house is dark and I wonder where Frances is. I check my phone and notice I have a text from her: *Staying at Jack's tonight.*

Right. I can't think about this now.

I feel numb and yet strangely alive. It's as if I have new eyes with which to look upon the world. I hear Louisa's voice tell me that an awakening is taking place and that it will be gentle.

All is well, she says. I feel it is true.

I take off my coat and Declan takes it from me, hanging it on the coat rack. I had almost forgotten he was here. Walking into the kitchen I go straight to the window to look out onto the bay. The sun has been set for hours now, but there are specks of light littering the harbour.

It calms me further.

I focus on one particular light directly in front of me and I close my eyes. In my mind's eye I picture my body dropping away and my luminous, love-filled essence floating into the light...becoming the light. I feel at peace. My being expands and I see only shimmering oneness.

It's unclear how much time has passed, but I begin to return to my body again and feel Declan coming up behind me. He sweeps my hair to one side and bends down to softly kiss my neck and nuzzle my ear. Immediately I am back in my mother's kitchen with him, my senses at attention.

I am tired no longer.

He gently grips my rib cage bringing his hands up to my breasts.

I breathe in.

The difference in feeling between this world and the one I have just left becoming obvious: one utterly physical, the other transcendent. I decide to let go and give my body to this man who so desperately needs it. I need him too.

"Where is your room?" he asks, his breath heavy with

meaning.

"Upstairs."

My eyes are closed savouring the feel of his hands on me and so I am shocked briefly as Declan pulls away and picks me up in one quick move. Carrying me up the stairs he says not a word. He is silent need.

Setting me down on my feet he bows his forehead to mine. He is finding it difficult to look me in the eye and I don't press him. He hugs me closer and kisses my neck, at first softly and then hungrily. He's craving connection and release. Putting my hands at his waist I arch into him. Leading him to the bed, I lay back and look up at him, biting my lip. He holds my neck gently and pulls my face to his with ease.

His body speaks desire: pure and simple. I surrender to it. I surrender to him.

He slowly strips me bare from my waist up. My arms move to cover my chest. He gently removes them, places them intertwined above my head. My eyes close. I remind myself to breathe.

My black mini-skirt and tights are next. He sweeps a gaze over me. I feel exposed and completely self-conscious until I catch his eye and see the longing there. He removes the last shred of clothing. And it's just me. Struggling for a full breath. Waiting.

Declan kneels over me, his palm flat on my stomach. "It feels as though I have waited forever to see you like this."

I swallow hard and shiver as he sheds his own clothes. I don't know where to look so I stare bravely, eyes wide. I take him all in.

He captures my mouth with a fervour I've never met with before and I forget where I am. My only thought, my only sense is that I want to melt into this man and be consumed by feeling. Shifting from my lips to my neck he starts a dizzying descent...down, down, down. His hands are anchored at my hips. Instinctively I run my fingers through his hair, grasping his head, guiding him.

"How is it possible that your skin is this soft?" His words drip with honey, hands reaching up to my breasts. It's been so long...

"*Ádhraím thú.*" His voice is like gravel, gritty and deep.

His mouth is at my navel. I writhe. He is making my mind spin with want. I am growing impatient, but he insists on going slow. Painfully slow.

Moving his hands to my waist, he gently parts my legs with his elbows and his mouth is at my thigh tasting one and then the other.

"Ellie..."

Feeling his breath upon my skin, I succumb to a home I've never known, safe and warm. I let myself fade into it, falling slowly until beckoned back by delicious freedom, released. Gently, I tug at his hair, urging him up. I want him, all of him. He slowly crawls along my body, resting himself atop me, lips gracing my neck and biting gently at my ear. I raise my hips in question and in one swift move he answers.

He stirs within me slowly at first until it seems he is finally as lost as I. Giving and taking in a delicious rhythm, he is bringing me to the brink...brings me as far as we can possibly go. All the while he whispers: "*Ádhraím thú*" over and over until we cry out in a language all can understand.

I reach for him, pulling his forehead to mine. Breathless, we entwine our bodies. No words are spoken. We drift to sleep.

CHAPTER 39

Ellie

The sunlight makes its presence known through the slats of my blinds. Declan is sleeping soundly as ribbons of light beams stream across his naked skin. I reluctantly decide to leave him be. The light is so bright that my skin glows pink and I can barely see around my room. I pull on my favourite grey Nordic sweater and a pair of yoga pants and quickly pin my hair into a messy bun. I am trying my best not to awaken him. He looks so serene, so untouched by worry.

I hear Louisa whisper: *That is who we really are.*

Finally finding clean socks, I tiptoe to his side and place a kiss on his warm forehead. He stirs slightly. I see his chest rise and fall and I think of what he would have looked like as a sleeping baby, how his mother must have loved to watch him slumber. I want to fade into a moment of beauty like that.

Silently blessing him, I turn to go.

Coming down the stairs I hear my mother singing in the kitchen. I stand down the hall a bit just to watch her for a moment. Dressed in a long white T-shirt, she moves with the song, slow and easy. Her blonde waves fly gracefully as she spins, spatula in hand. I'm her child again; I run to her.

Laughing in surprise she says, "Ellie! I thought you were still asleep, baby. How are you? It seems so long since I've seen you." She looks concerned but trusting and I want to burst out saying that I need her help, that I will always need her help. But I don't.

"I know," I reply instead.

She pours me a cup of coffee and we sit at the kitchen table. We share a comfortable silence while she rubs my back. I close my eyes briefly and see a flash of Janey in my mind's eye. It washes over me. Of course...Frances was Janey.

"Is Declan here? I saw men's shoes by the door."

I nod and tell her he's upstairs sleeping. I ask her why Jack's not with her.

"He's busy with Declan's portrait. It is stunning Ellie, truly stunning. You'll have to go see it," she says, bringing her bare legs up and crossing them beneath her.

"I will," I say. "Are you guys back together?"

Her cheeks flush and she smiles slightly. "That's not an easy question to answer... " I rush to tell her she doesn't owe me an explanation.

She shakes her head, "No it's fine. I ran into him buying a bottle of wine yesterday and we got to talking. He's...different. I mean, he's the same, but I guess I'm different. I like who I am and no one can change that. I know that now. And I suppose it's just become obvious to me that I want to spend time with people who make me laugh and lift me up." She twists her mug round and round on the wooden table, studies it with a smile. "He does that."

"If you're happy mom, then I'm happy." And I mean it. For so long I thought Frances existed solely for me: to get me things, make me food, listen to me. I'm only now beginning to see the bigger picture of her life, her purpose. I see how we help one another, how we learn from each other.

She has pride in her eyes as she looks at me. "Let's talk about you! What did you and Mrs. Dawes uncover?"

I tell her everything. Every word gently rushes out of me into her patient and open ears. I tell her about William and Louisa. I tell her about Declan and how he tried to take his life before we met. I tell her about the guilt that he has carried. All mom does is nod, brush her hair from her eyes and offer silent reassurance. I finish the whole story by relating my light experience in the kitchen. I have no wisdom or brilliant insight to offer, I simply give her what I know.

"My goodness, Ellie, you had a spiritual experience."

I laugh out loud, "That's definitely what it felt like!"

Frances narrows her eyes at me. "Don't pretend to fully comprehend what happened to you. You need help...divine help in order to understand all of this."

"I have Louisa," I say, wondering if that's divine enough.

"Perfect! She's your guide through all of this then."

"The visions were always this thing that made me different. I get it now though, or at least I think I'm getting it. It seems I'm supposed to help people remember things. I think I'm supposed to help them look at all their deep seated stuff...guilt, shame, grief..."

Frances reaches over and gently parts a lock of hair from my face and I wonder if motherly love ever really stops. "I am so happy for you."

"I do feel leftover guilt from Louisa dying that night, and I can see how it's possible that my soul has carried that all this time." Frances is looking at me like she wants to say something. "What is it?" I ask.

She bites her lip. "It's just...I'm just happy we can talk about this now. For so long I felt like you were only comfortable with Mrs. Dawes and then for years you didn't want to talk about it at all. This is nice."

"I think I'm meant to do something with these visions. I think I'm supposed to start helping others...like soon," I confide.

Frances reaches a hand to my chin. "As long as it's helpful; why not, right?"

If she's right, if this is helping me and helping others, then I'm happy with that.

I am happier.

I let her words hang in the quiet morning lull.

Leaving the kitchen, I decide to see if Declan is up. Just as I begin to round the staircase, there is a knock at the door.

I see a mass of red curls through the slit of the curtain beside the door. It's Mrs. Dawes.

"This is a nice surprise," I tell her as I take her purple coat and orange scarf.

"Well, love, I just couldn't wait to see you and ask you how the meditation went last night." She bobs her shoulders up and down in excitement. I just love when she pretends like she doesn't know exactly what happened. She's not fooling this girl.

"I'm sure you could tell the story just as well as I could!" I exclaim and she gives me a cryptic look.

The wood floors above are creaking. Declan is awake.

Calling his name I ask him to meet us in the kitchen as I lead Mrs. Dawes to the kitchen table. Frances stands to hug her and it feels as if worlds are colliding for me. It's been fourteen years since the two women have come together for me. It makes me nervous, as if I'm not worthy of all the fuss. The thought comes and goes. My doubts and fears don't seem to have the weight they once did.

We all sit down and wait for Declan. We don't have to wait long.

He's gorgeously dishevelled and glowing. "Good morning, ladies." He stretches his arms above his head with a yawn.

Mrs. Dawes pipes up, "Ellie was just about to tell us about what happened last night."

Declan coughs nervously, waiting for her to clarify as he pours himself a coffee.

"About what you saw with Louisa..." she's smirking as she registers the relief on his face.

I relate the whole story again adding the experience I had while making the tea and Mrs. Dawes gives a knowing nod. She tells us that it's possible after a lengthy regression to be between two lives. She also says that Louisa's voice was trying to slowly guide me back to the present moment.

I'm confused. "But how can Louisa's voice be guiding me back when I felt stuck between being me and Louisa?"

Frances pipes up, "It's all symbolic, Ellie. When you receive guidance from Louisa, it's not her, the woman. It's what she represents. All that matters is that it's helpful for you."

"Your mother is right, love. Louisa had Mother Mary. Think about that. Her mother, Mary, died when she was twelve. It was the perfect symbol of divine love for her when, perhaps, thinking of her own mother may have been too upsetting. Speaking of which..."

"What?" I panic for a moment, but don't exactly know why.

Mrs. Dawes looks from me to Frances and back to me again. "I wasn't sure if I should tell you this or not, but well...I was your mother in that lifetime."

My heart leaps to my throat and a thousand thoughts rush through my mind. In less than a few seconds I know that what she says is true, and yet I wonder why she never told me.

"But..." I start.

"I know, Ellie. You feel like I should have told you before. I'm sorry that I didn't. All I can say is that it would not have been helpful for you to know."

I trust her even though I feel dismissed. Sometimes the hardest thing to know is that you just don't know.

Declan is fascinated. He leans closer as he asks, "Who else was back there with us?"

Mrs. Dawes chuckles at him. "Well, let's see. Tynan was there. He was Sir Thomas."

"Shut the fuck up!" I say without thinking. Frances looks at me sideways and I mouth an apology.

"And Alistair... He was Edward. Oh and Janey..."

"...Is Frances!" I declare proudly and look over at her. She's beaming. It's sinking in further now. I have been avoiding the pain of these past few days for so long and yet, it was not that bad. Of course, it all happened exactly as it should have, but my avoidance of it was so much worse and way more agonizing than the experience itself.

"One more thing I wanted to share with you, Ellie, and you too, Declan...and sure, Frances...you too." She laughs to herself.

"Remember that I said time is an illusion. Even Einstein knew that for crying out loud! Technically you are living both these lives simultaneously as well as many others. My point is: the healing you do now helps that lifetime too. Suffering is lessened. Hearts are mended."

Declan wears a stunned expression. "Are you serious? Like, Ellie and I talking about all of this past life stuff and working through it...that helps us back then?"

"Yes, that's right." Her expression is that of a proud teacher amused at her bright student.

"Holy shit," shouts Declan as he stands from the table and rakes a hand through his hair. "That's what I dreamt last night."

CHAPTER 40

William

William sat in front of the roaring fire clutching a bottle of whiskey. It was Christmas Day, one month exactly since she left, since she fell. The pain had not abated with time. The idea that it could seemed cruelly absurd.

The wind outside the house carried a voice of vengeance high-pitched and bent on driving its witnesses mad. It was coming for him. He drove an angel to her death and he would have to pay the price in one way or another. Let it be the wind that would usher him to hell or the sea that would swallow him up. He would stay here until it happened.

It would surely happen.

Sir Thomas had left a week ago, taking Janey with him but Edward refused to abandon him. William was too tired to convince him otherwise. The past few weeks he felt as if he barely existed, as if the real version of him hovered above and watched the whole sad scene play out below.

Louisa's father had been achingly silent after her death. He did not seem angry with William, but he would barely say a word to him and this made everything worse somehow. When he did speak, it was only to convince himself that she had not committed suicide.

"I know my daughter, Mr. Mara," he had said with tear-swelled eyes. "She would not take her own life. She would not do it!"

All William wanted was for Sir Thomas to shake him, punch him and then have him thrown into the ocean. But that was selfish was it not? He wanted physical pain to replace the spiritual pain he now felt, the pain that rocked his soul beyond reason. He wanted a bodily death to escape the torture of his mind. Alas, he deserved all of it.

In the week since the departure of Sir Thomas and Janey, William thought of little else but Louisa. There was not an inch in this house, it seemed, that did not contain something of her. But he liked it that way. To him, she was this house and he could not leave it, not yet.

When Janey had been packing up Louisa's clothes, she had taken pity on him and left him one dress. It was the one she had worn that evening in Oban. It seemed a lifetime ago that he saw her there, coming toward him; the lightness of her preceding her actual presence. He hung the gown in the window and left it slightly ajar allowing the wind to blow through it, sending her scent everywhere. He let it overwhelm him until he dropped to his knees in a cry so maddened by grief he did not recognize it as his own.

Edward had found him thus. That was one hour ago.

Having sent the older man back to bed, William relaxed into his sullen solitude. He was drunk and so when an apparition of the most beautiful auburn-haired woman appeared before him, he had to blink and shake himself.

"Louisa?"

"Hello, William." Her presence was bright, but real. She looked vibrant, flushed but cool. She was seated across from him in the chair she had taken so many times before.

"It cannot be." he whispered in shock sitting straight up, nearly dropping his bottle.

"Shh... I am not here to haunt you, my love, or to frighten Edward. You need me and so I am here. It is that simple."

William dropped to his knees before her and she bent to meet him. "Louisa! It cannot be! I saw you fall..."

She cocked her head to the side and drew him closer with the kindness in her eyes. "I know you have been drinking, but you still have sense. I am here to help you, not to stay. I cannot stay. You know that, my love."

Her words left him blurred and confused. Was it the drink

233

that would make him see such things? Was he finally going insane? Tears were in his eyes, distorting his view of her. His breath held. He reached out a hand to touch her and held it an inch from her cheek, trembling.

Her voice was like smoke floating thickly about his ears, "You may touch me. I do feel real. I feel just as I did before."

He touched her hair first and felt the shock of the strands silky and real beneath his fingers. Looking up she nodded her acquiescence for him to proceed. He ran his hands along her eyes and down the bridge of her nose. She drew in a breath and her cheeks coloured at his touch. William closed his eyes and swallowed hard bringing his fingertips to her lips. Two perfect pink crescents parting, breathing and waiting. His mouth closed the distance and he marvelled at her warmth, her softness. He wanted to explore her body further but there was so much to ask her, tell her. He wanted so desperately to hear her voice again.

William gently grasped her neck and rested his forehead on hers, closing his eyes in agony. "Why did you leave me?"

Louisa stroked his hair and simply whispered "Shh... All is well."

His words were husky and loaded with hurt, "I deserve nothing like this." And with an eagerness one could only call grief-stricken he picked her up and carried her to his room.

It was dark, but by now he knew this cottage like the back of his hand. William clutched Louisa to him painfully. He would not lose her. If this were a dream, he would not wake up.

Placing her on the bed he absorbed the sight of her. Her green eyes seemed larger, clearer than before. She seemed so full of health and peace. He wanted to drink in her essence, but he needed an answer first.

Supporting himself as he lay over her he asked again, "Why, Louisa?"

She kissed the palm of her hand and then brought it to his cheek. "It was written, my love. My choice was merely to let go with love, or to fall in fear."

"Louisa, please! I cannot take your philosophical musings right now. You know what I am asking."

She bowed her head. "Yes, I know," she whispered. "The truth is that I could not bear to see you hating me and in that moment William, you hated me." He started to protest but she stopped him. "People are quite capable of hate, my love. We build lives around it. Nevertheless, I saw it in you and I ran. I know now that what we see in others exists in us, that there was hate in my heart too. I panicked. My intention was not to jump, but the wind was strong and my mind was a mess. I was carried away… swept up and dropped. I felt nothing though, this you should know. My body felt no pain and my soul never stopped."

"I drove you to it then. I drove you to the cliff's edge with my anger."

Louisa breathed slowly, an air of calm floating lightly about her and within her. "It was my choice to run. You did not drive me to anything. It is done. I am happy where I am and I am with you…always. I will not abandon you, my darling."

He fought tears as she spoke. He clung to her. "And yet you are still dead are you not? I do not understand Louisa! You are still gone from me. It is true, is it not?" he cried desperately.

She pulled him down and he lay hard and heaving on top of her. "My body is dead. I am here now like this because it is helpful for you. That is all you need to know. Can you accept that?"

William laid his head on her chest refusing to weep. He would allow her to comfort him. "I can." He heard her sigh and wrapped his arms tightly around her. "I love you, Louisa. This past month has been my own version of hell. I have shed more tears for you than…"

Louisa kissed the top of his head. "I know."

"Do you miss me where you are?" he asked shyly, as a child would.

She laughed lightly, "I don't have to miss you where I am William, for you are there too. Everyone we love is there."

"I am there? But I am here! How can that be?"

"Do not distress yourself, my love. You do not have to believe anything I have said, but I will ask you to try and remember that I have said it." She stroked his back with her fingertips.

"I can do that."

"Thank you, William. Hush now. Close your eyes. Know that I am with you."

He panicked and raised his head to look at her. "You are not leaving me again?"

Louisa smiled and brought her lips to his. He was lost to her then. Opening his mouth to deepen the kiss he felt his body relax for the first time in weeks. His hands grasped hers and their arms fanned out like wings.

The wind blew light through the partially opened window, but neither felt the chill. They had ventured to a haven in between where only lovers go.

There was nowhere else in the world but where they were.

There was no one else.

And finally William slept.

CHAPTER 41

Ellie

Jack and I are sitting in the living room. Mom is getting ready to teach her Nia class in Lion's Head and Declan is upstairs in the shower. Jack just dropped in…unexpectedly. Apparently he's going to do that now.

Larger than life is Jack.

He's studying me. He looks so amused that it makes me nervous. The thought occurs to me that he's mentally holding something over me. I can feel it dangling heavy above me.

He doesn't blink. "I've been meaning to ask you, Ellie. Does Declan know about that painting?"

I clear my throat, cross and uncross my legs. "Which painting?"

Jack grinned wide, "You know which painting, Ellie Stewart. Don't pull that crap. Little Miss "I'm my own woman" showing up at my apartment naked as the day God made you under the pink North Face coat your mother bought you."

"Keep your voice down!" My tone is a loud whisper, but I really want to scream at him. I knew the bastard would bring this up…my little act of teenage rebellion. Damn.

"Ellie, it's not a big deal. Teenage girls are so not my thing. It was like painting a shoe." He was laughing, having a great time. I was seething. I didn't want Declan to hear him.

"Jack, for the love of God! Please, stop talking about this!"

"I'm teasing you, Ellie. A little parental defiance never hurt anyone. And you were perfect, by the way."

Now I was interested. "Perfect? How?"

His smile warms. "You don't need me to tell you that, surely. You are beautiful and you've got the soul to match. I've always thought so."

Just then I hear someone coming down the stairs. I turn just in time to see Declan bolt past us.

Oh crap.

He heard everything.

Declan

November slaps me in the face as I break free of the house. I need to get high somehow. I need to have one last time at the top.

I itch at my side and bring a hand through my hair.

My heart beats in a rhythm I wish I could change. It's out of sync with my resolve. Each step I take distances me from insanity. I know where I'm going.

Coming around Bay Street, I spot my father. He sits on the bench between the inn and the liquor store. The same bench I found Ellie sitting on only a few days before.

He spots me and raises his hand and waves me over. The worry on his face hits me first.

"Declan, I'm so glad you're here. I was just going to try calling you."

I put my hands in my pockets to warm them. "What is it?"

He motions for me to sit beside him and I do. He sighs heavily and I feel as though he is in need of unloading a weight...like he's worked up a bunch of courage to get to this moment. "Declan, did I neglect you?"

Really? This is the question? I answer quickly, "Not at all, Dad. I've spent a lot of time with Ellie. You know that."

He smiles weakly. "I didn't mean this past week, lad. I was referring to your childhood... your whole life really."

Now I want to groan, but the look in his eye makes me stop. He's asked me this question before and the answer is still the same. "No," I tell him. "You and Mom were always great. You need to let go of this guilt, Dad. You're too old for this shit." I put my hand on his shoulder and he looks up at me. "I know you really want to move on and travel and stuff like that, so just do it.

It's ok, really. I'm ok."

He mulls over my words with a faraway look. The clouds are low above us, blanketing us in silence. "I hope you don't hate me for this, but I think I'm afraid of your happiness." I give him a questioning look. "You've always been sad, Declan. It was your normal. The prospect of you being happy...scares me a little. I won't begrudge you joy, of course. I just wanted to be honest with you. You're a man; you have been for some time now. You deserve honesty from me."

I know what he's saying because it's how I feel too. I'm afraid of my own happiness. In fact, the idea kind of scares the shit out of me because where do you go from there? What if it's not what you thought or it doesn't last? At least my depression was predictable. I confide all of this in my father. The words pour out quickly, as if I am emptying pebbles from my hand. I am letting go of things I had no clue I had been holding onto.

He reaches out to hug me and for the first time since I was a child it registers with me that he is expressing love and not pity. He needs my love as much as I need his. We are equals.

I'm at the top of the lighthouse. Looking out across the water, I hear shoes crunching in the gravel and I turn to see a streak of blonde and black racing towards me.

She's running. Why is she running? She's crying. Shit, why is she crying? She disappears beneath the deck and I can hear scratching on the metal shell of the structure.

"Ellie?" I call. "Ellie! What the hell are you doing?"

More scratching, more sobbing.

"Are you trying to climb? Jesus Christ, Ellie! There's a fucking door!" I stop myself, realizing I'm yelling. "I'm coming down," I say, more calmly now.

When my feet hit the ground, I run towards her and scoop her up in my arms, wrapping her legs around my waist. She's heaving and emotional.

I kiss her temple. "What is it, Ellie? What's wrong?"

Through her sobs she attempts, "What the hell were you doing up there?"

I set her down to look in her face. "What?"

"You totally freaked me out! I ran into Alistair and he said you walked in this direction. I was so... I was so afraid you were going to..." And then she starts laughing, a deep and ridiculous belly laugh. "I am such an idiot! How could I jump to such a crazy conclusion?"

I'm laughing too. It's all just so absurd. And in that moment of uncontrollable laughter, I realize how seriously I take my sadness, how I let it draw me in and pull me under, and for what?

This is a release. All we've been through, all we've seen, it's caught up with us. We're letting it all out.

"Thanks for being worried, I guess," I tell her, the chuckles now subsiding. My stomach hurts.

She shakes her head. "Don't thank me. I promise to be a little less reactive."

Ellie's eyes are full of humour. I just have to tease her. "So, tell me about this painting."

A veil of confusion is drawn over her face. "The painting?" she asks quietly.

"Come on, Ellie...the painting that Jack did? I overheard the whole thing. After I was done here I was going to the bank machine to take out some money. I'm going to buy it from him."

She shakes her head in disbelief. "You're not mad? You want to buy it?"

"You're goddamned right I want to buy it. No one else is going to have that. Besides, I am going to paint you and I'm going to do it a hell of a lot better than Jack Bailey ever could. And do you know why?" I pull her close and catch the scent of her hair: vanilla and lavender.

She shakes her head, bites her lip.

"Because I know what your body can do. And I know the